"Knit together an interesting older protagonist, an astute knitting group, a friend accused of murder, [and] a daughter with secrets, and you have a purl of a mystery."

—Sherry Harris, Agatha Award–nominated author of the Sarah Winston Garage Sale mysteries and the Chloe Jackson Seaglass Saloon mysteries

"Such a cozy combination—knitting and murder. A delightful, well-crafted mystery!"

—Essie Lang, author of the Castle Bookshop mysteries

"This heartwarming mystery knits together family and friends in pursuit of a cunning killer."

—Maya Corrigan, author of the Five-Ingredient Mystery series

"Charming, crafty, and so very cozy! Emmie Caldwell has stitched together an entertaining, well-plotted mystery that's as cozy as a favorite sweater. The clues are artfully woven into the story, and Lia and her daughter, Hayley, are a dynamic sleuthing duo. *A Wicked Yarn* is bound to delight fans of crafting cozies!"

—Sarah Fox, author of *Much Ado About Nutmeg*

Stitched

in

Crime

A CRAFT FAIR KNITTERS MYSTERY

EMMIE CALDWELL

BERKLEY PRIME CRIME
New York

BERKLEY PRIME CRIME
Published by Berkley
An imprint of Penguin Random House LLC
penguinrandomhouse.com

ISBN: 9780593101704

First Edition: December 2021

Printed in the United States of America
1 3 5 7 9 10 8 6 4 2

Book design by George Towne

*For Suzanne, with love and gratitude for so
many things, but mostly for just being you*

Chapter 1

It was the dream again. Cori could only watch as Jessica walked away. She wanted to call out, *No! Stay here!* But she couldn't. She could only follow. As she did every time.

Jessica had always been her favorite babysitter. She made her laugh and played games with her. And she read to her better than anyone. She'd do funny voices and make up things that Cori knew weren't really in the story. They made the story so much better!

But Jessica didn't come to babysit anymore. She told Cori she was getting too busy. She was in college now, and she had a boyfriend. Was that where she was going? To see her boyfriend? That was why Cori followed. She was curious.

At first, Jessica caught her following and told her to go home. "You can't come with me, Cori," she said, her hands sternly on her hips.

"Why not!"

"Because you can't. Now, go back!"

But Cori didn't want to go back. She started to cry.

Jessica hesitated, and Cori thought she might relent and let her come with her, until Jessica said, "I'll come see you another time."

"When?" Cori asked.

Jessica looked impatient, but she said, "Tomorrow. Okay?"

Cori sniffed hard. "Promise."

"I promise. Now, go home."

Cori turned around, but after a few steps she stopped and looked back. She saw Jessica walking again, and she hid behind a tree until Jessica got far ahead. Then Cori followed.

She wasn't supposed to go there, she knew that. There were lots of trees that made it dark and places where you could fall down real far. Her mother told Cori not to ever go there unless she or someone big was with her. But Jessica was a big person, wasn't she? She didn't know Cori was there, but that didn't matter, did it? It only meant she wouldn't tell Cori's mom, but that made it even better.

It was a long walk, a lot of it was uphill, and Cori got tired. She had to sit down. Jessica kept walking, but she wasn't going very fast and there was the path to stay on. Cori could catch up. When she felt better, Cori ran up the path but stopped when she heard voices. She hid behind a clump of bushes and crouched way down. She recognized Jessica's voice, but she didn't know the other one. Jessica was talking the most, so Cori listened to her. She liked listening to Jessica, and after a while Cori decided to come out. Maybe Jessica would tell her a story—like the ones she used to read aloud to Cori. Jessica would be so surprised to see her, but she wouldn't mind. It would be such a good joke!

The sun blinded Cori when she came out from her hiding place, shining right into her eyes. She put her hands up to shade them, but it didn't help. She was standing still and blinking from the sun when she heard Jessica scream.

"Jessica!" Cori cried, and she ran blindly toward the scream—until she saw the big, dark figure. It wasn't Jessica. It was the other voice. It started to come toward her, and Cori screamed, and screamed, and screamed.

Until she woke up.

Chapter 2

L ia heard the shout and looked up from her booth.

"Everyone! Your attention, please." Belinda, the Crandalsburg Craft Fair's manager, stood in the center of the fair barn, a folded newspaper held high. "Our craft fair got some great publicity today!" she announced as she turned toward the vendor next to Lia. "Thanks to our new member, Cori Littlefield. It's a full-page story loaded with color photos of Cori's creations!"

The vendors clapped and cheered as Belinda handed out extra copies of the paper to pass around.

"Cori, that's wonderful!" Lia cried from her knitting booth.

Lia had been delighted to hear about their new vendor, especially when she learned that the stall would be filled with crocheted items. Not your usual shawls and throws, though. Cori Littlefield crocheted artistic and wonderfully realistic vegetables, flowers, whimsical animals, and just about anything that happened to come into her creative mind and through her nimble fingers.

Other vendors came over to congratulate the crochet artist. Cori certainly deserved the praise, and she looked genuinely pleased. But when, after a few minutes, Lia saw the young woman's smiles along with her posture stiffen, she stepped in.

"Cori needs a little time to get ready, guys. Let's save the rest of this for later, okay?"

Lia had recently given up her end-of-the-row spot to Cori, after Belinda, her longtime friend as well as the craft fair manager, approached her about it. Lia had at first hesitated. She'd grown accustomed to her spot. But after learning that Cori needed to be near an exit to avoid feeling closed in, she'd readily agreed.

"The easiest for everyone, of course, would be to just put her in the empty booth farther up the row," Belinda had said. "Everyone *else*, that is, not Cori. But besides the advantage of the side exit, I think you're the perfect person to be next to her. She's, well, just a little different; anxious, you might say. She'll be fine, really, but she might need to leave the barn once in a while to be alone for a few minutes. I fell in love with her work and felt any inconvenience that might cause would be well worth it. She'll be a great addition to the craft fair."

Belinda hadn't added what Lia knew must be going through her mind: that the craft fair needed a boost after what it had gone through only a few weeks earlier. The discovery of Belinda's murdered ex-husband in the middle of the empty craft fair barn had not been good for the fair's business, to say the least, and Belinda had been in grave danger, financially and otherwise, when suspicion was cast her way. Attendance numbers had dropped drastically, only slowly recovering after the actual murderer had been arrested and the news media turned to other stories. An exciting new vendor for the fair, therefore, was a definite plus.

"Need some fresh air?" Lia asked Cori after the other vendors left to go back to their stations.

Cori shook her head. "I'm okay. Thanks." She brushed back the bangs of her short brown hair. "It was nice of them."

"We're all really happy for you, Cori. This'll be so great for your booth. You just might sell out this weekend!"

"Then I'll have to get busy working on more things!" Cori said it with a laugh, which Lia was glad to hear. The first weekend that this young woman—thirty-two in Lia's book was still young—had joined the fair, she had struggled as a salesperson, an important skill that all the vendors had to learn. Lia had given her tips about dealing with customers, but because of her intense shyness, Lia was sure it had required much concentration and effort. She could only imagine the exhaustion it brought on and understood the need for occasional recharging breaks.

"Yes, crochet lots of your beautiful art," Lia encouraged her. "The world will be eager for it."

Cori laughed again, and Lia decided her neighbor was fine. Once the craft fair barn doors were opened and shoppers rushed to Cori's booth, she would be ready to deal with them. And with a little luck, Lia's booth would catch a bit of spillover, not that her Ninth Street Knits needed much help. Over the months, its sales had been steady, both from returning customers and from newcomers drawn by word of mouth—the best kind of publicity.

Lia's late husband, Tom, would have been proud of how she'd turned her knitting skills into a new career, with the help, of course, of her wonderful knitting friends. Losing him just as they'd decided to take an early retirement had been a blow, but she'd managed to struggle through the terrible twist life had thrown her and come to a pretty good place. Surrounded now with new friends and with a new purpose, Lia was more content than she'd ever expected to be.

She had been seeing positive changes in Belinda, too, the latest being Belinda's cheery, rallying announcement that morning. The old Belinda had tended toward impatient faultfinding, a product of her personal struggles and insecurities. But she'd been working on being a more engaging manager, which had the effect of easing her own problems. Funny how that worked.

"Here we go, guys!" Bill Landry, the craft fair's security officer, called out, giving everyone a heads-up that he was about to open the doors.

Lia saw vendors turn as a group toward the main entrance, faces bright and hopeful. A new day at the Crandalsburg Craft Fair was about to begin, and who knew what it would bring on that August Sunday morning?

As Bill slid the large barn doors apart, Lia was happy to see a healthy number of eager shoppers waiting on the other side. It wasn't the huge crowd it had once been, but it looked a little larger than last week's, which was encouraging.

The usual pattern for new arrivals was to work their way gradually down the line of booths. That meant stopping first at Gilbert Bowen's candles to the immediate left or Lou Krause's metal sculptures on the right. The exception to that was Carolyn Hanson's marvelous baked goods, which pulled many regulars directly across the barn to her centrally located booth.

Lia was used to waiting for shoppers to eventually make

their way to her far-corner spot and had a folding chair to sit on and knit until that happened. But that morning she saw several people bustling in her direction, though they passed her by in favor of Cori. Lia wasn't the least bit surprised.

"Here they are!" one woman called to her lagging friend. "Those crocheted things we saw in the paper!"

Another two had quick-stepped around her to reach Cori's counter first. "Oh, look at those!" one said to her companion. "Crocheted hyacinths in little pots. How clever."

"And these teddy bears!" another cried. "Have you ever seen anything so sweet?"

The crowd continued to grow, a few possibly drawn by curiosity over what the fuss was about but staying to browse and many to buy. Lia did get an overflow customer from the group, but only because the woman couldn't reach Cori's counter yet. She bought two pairs of Lia's cozy knit bed socks.

"Future Christmas presents," the woman explained. Lia complimented her on her foresight and planning, then watched her customer rejoin the others clustered around Cori's booth. Lia glanced to her right at Olivia, who'd been watching from behind her stacks of handmade soaps and essential oils. Olivia grinned and shrugged, knowing, as all vendors did, that business ebbed and flowed and usually evened out in the long run. Their time, she seemed to say, would come.

As the crowd in front of Creative Crochets began to show signs of impatience with the slow service, Lia asked Olivia to keep an eye on her booth and slipped over to give Cori a hand.

"The turquoise wall hanging?" Lia asked the woman

who pointed over the counter, the noise level making it difficult to communicate. Getting head bobs in response, Lia detached the piece from its hook and showed the woman its price tag. She took the cash payment and quickly made change from the stash Cori slid toward her.

Lia next handled the sale of three mini teddy bears, and after that a life-sized crocheted parakeet, one of Lia's favorites, which she was almost sad to see go. Between the two of them, the crowd of customers gradually thinned to a manageable size, and Lia noticed someone looking at the knit place mats on her own counter.

"I think you're in good shape, Cori," she said. "I've got to go."

"Thanks, Lia!" Cori said as she bagged her own customer's purchase.

Lia gave her a congratulatory shoulder squeeze and hurried back to her booth, arriving just as the shopper there had lined up four multistriped mats to buy. Whew!

With that kind of busyness, Lia wasn't surprised when an hour or so later Cori, looking pale, said she needed a break. A scene like what she'd just gone through would have been stressful for anyone and might have been multiplied by ten for her. Things had slowed for the moment, and Lia nodded and waved her off, watching sympathetically as her craft booth neighbor trudged out.

When Cori returned several minutes later, she had more color in her cheeks. Lia leaned over to say, "I sold two of your bananas and a bunch of grapes! From the way that customer was eyeing your other ones, I think she'll be back for more fruit." Cori smiled and sank onto her own folding chair. "Still tired?" Lia asked.

Cori nodded. "But not so much from the sales. I didn't sleep so well last night."

"That's a shame. Just when you could use some extra energy." The look that crossed Cori's face made Lia ask, "Do you often have trouble sleeping?"

Cori shook her head, but the shadows under her eyes seemed to darken. "Only when the nightmare comes back," she said.

Just then a customer asked Lia if she could see a particular sweater hanging at the back of the booth. Lia left Cori with some reluctance but felt better later when she glanced back and saw Cori chatting easily with a customer of her own.

A few minutes before closing time, Lia wasn't surprised to see Cori beginning to pack up and looking eager to take off. Though she was more than two decades younger and in apparent good health, the emotional strain clearly took a greater toll on the crochet artist than hours of standing took on Lia.

"Go ahead," Lia urged, sure that Belinda wouldn't mind her leaving a bit early. "The fair is emptying out. No need to wait." Unfortunately, only minutes after Cori left, a man dashed into the barn and headed straight for the crochet booth.

"Where is she?" he asked Lia, his eyes scouring the empty station as though expecting to find Cori tucked in a shadowy corner. "Is she still here?"

"I'm so sorry," Lia said. "She's not. But she'll be back Saturday when the craft fair reopens. We're only here on weekends."

"Shoot!" The thirty-something man dressed in a gray tee and jeans slapped his side and looked so crestfallen that Lia asked if she could help.

He pulled a photo out of his back pocket. "I wanted to ask if she could stitch up something to look like this." The photo was of a small black-and-white dog. "It's my daughter's. We saw those pictures of the crocheted animals in the paper, and my wife thought Sophia would really like one of Maxie for her birthday. She loves things like that. But her birthday's in three weeks. I don't know how fast this lady can do it."

"I don't know, either. But I'd be happy to get the photo and your contact information to Cori so she can call and discuss it."

His face lit up. "That'd be great!" He snatched the pen Lia offered him and scribbled his name and phone number on the back of the photo, explaining at the same time how he'd been held up by heavy traffic coming away from a baseball game. "I promised my wife I'd stop here right after the game, but I didn't exactly time it right." He handed her the photo. "I really appreciate this."

"I hope it'll all work out," Lia said.

He left, along with the last of the shoppers, and as Bill closed the large doors, Lia felt, rather than heard, a collective sigh from her fellow vendors. After a long day, there was always some degree of fatigue and a readiness to head home and put one's feet up. But from the satisfied faces she saw around her, Lia was sure there were sighs of contentment, too. The craft fair had seen a good crowd that day, with much credit due to Cori's excellent publicity. When fairgoers were drawn by a particular vendor, they seldom stopped with one but checked out the rest, turning it into a win-win for everyone.

Lia finished securing her own booth, then headed down the side hallway to Belinda's office. She was glad to see the door halfway open, a more welcoming sign than had usually faced craft fair members in the past. She also heard voices and recognized the deeper one as belonging to Mark Simmons, the fair's scenic photographer. Lia paused, and within moments Mark, thanking Belinda, stepped out. He and Lia wished each other a cheery good week as he passed, and Lia went in to see her friend.

"Can I get Cori's phone number?" Lia explained about the last-minute customer request for the crochet artist.

"Sure." Belinda rustled through her disordered desk, from which she somehow managed to handle, and handle well, the craft fair and all the midweek events for the barn. She came up with the contact number and wrote it down for Lia. "So Cori's doing okay, huh?"

"Her business was spectacular today," Lia said. "And I think she's getting more comfortable each week dealing with her customers."

"Great. I hoped she would."

"Cori's obviously very skilled at crochet artistry. Does she do it full-time and sell them elsewhere?"

Belinda scrunched her face. "I don't believe so. As you know, many of our vendors make crafts as a side gig or turn a hobby into a second career after retiring."

"Like me," Lia said with a grin, thinking how different her years as a surgical nurse were from what she did now, managing and knitting for the Ninth Street Knits booth. Both were fulfilling, but they were poles apart in skills.

"Exactly. But I didn't get the impression that Cori had much of a first career." Belinda tented her hands thoughtfully under her chin. "I don't require résumés, of course. I only care about what a prospective vendor can offer our craft fair. A single young woman like Cori might need more than a weekend's worth of work to support herself."

Lia glanced at the number Belinda had written down for her. "Is she on her own?"

Belinda shrugged. "I guess you'll find out tomorrow." She picked up a file and stood to slide it into a cabinet drawer. "Speaking of living arrangements, how's it working out with Hayley?"

Lia smiled. "As you know, I love my daughter dearly, and I was more than delighted to have her move in with me after she took the job at the alpaca farm."

"But?"

Lia laughed. "The problem is my little house! When I bought it after Tom died, Hayley was living in Philadelphia, and I thought I only needed a place big enough for one. One, that is, and an occasional guest. That worked fine when Hayley came for short visits. Now that she's been here for over two months with all her things, it's feeling a bit . . . tight."

Belinda locked up her desk drawer and pulled a large tote out from under the desk. "It was meant to be temporary, right? Has she been looking for a place of her own?"

"When she's had time. But her new job has been taking up a lot of it. Since the Webers never had a marketing person before, she—and they—have pretty much had to figure out exactly what her job entails, day by day."

"Sounds like fun!" Belinda said as she rolled her eyes. She gestured toward the door and picked up her keys, ready to lock up her office for the day.

"It is, most of the time," Lia said as she led the way into the hall. "And Hayley's texted that she'll have dinner ready when I get home tonight, which will be great." She looked over to Belinda. "Would you like to join us?"

"Thanks, but believe it or not I have plans."

"You do? I mean, how nice!"

"We'll see." Belinda locked her door and joined Lia to walk toward the side exit. "I joined a book club last week," she said. "Everyone brings something for a potluck dinner before we discuss."

"Sounds great. And you're bringing . . . ?" Lia asked, aware of Belinda's total disinterest in cooking.

Belinda grinned. "Whatever I can pick up at TopValU Food on the way home."

They bid good night to Bill, who locked up the barn behind them. As she continued to her car, Lia smiled to herself, pleased to learn that Belinda was making an effort to socialize more. She only hoped her new group was more particular about books than they were about food. On a Sunday evening and shortly before closing time, who knew what TopValU, Crandalsburg's main supermarket, would have available. Or even edible.

On that thought, Lia climbed into her Camry and headed toward home, curious to see what Hayley had cooked up for her there.

Chapter 3

Lia turned onto her quiet, tree-shaded street and parked behind Hayley's Nissan. As usual, the sight of her pre–Civil War house made her feel happy, especially on a sunny Sunday evening after a good craft fair day. As she headed up the short walk, she picked up the sweet smell of freshly cut grass. Hayley must have run the mower that afternoon. How nice! Lia stepped onto her porch, just big enough for two welcoming rocking chairs, and into her house, unsurprised to find the path from the living room to the kitchen had been turned into an obstacle course with packing boxes.

Lia sidestepped partway through, pausing when her tan-and-white ragdoll cat jumped down from her spot on the sofa to hurry over and gaze pleadingly up at Lia.

"Why, hello, Daphne," Lia said, returning the look. "How are you? Was there something you wanted?" she teased.

Daphne wiggled her backside and mewed in answer, which Lia took to mean, *Why are you dawdling so?* She scooped up the fluffy feline and was rewarded with purrs and kitty kisses, which went on until Lia's arms began to tire. Daphne was not a lightweight. She carried the cat back to the sofa and gently deposited her there, picking up a tantalizing aroma in the air as she did so.

"Baked ham?" she called out.

"Not *just* ham," Hayley called out from the kitchen. "Ham basted with brown sugar, mustard, and vinegar."

"Wow!" Lia headed over to the kitchen. "A new recipe you found online?" she asked from the doorway.

"Yup." Hayley glanced up from the stove, where she stirred at a small pot. "The mashed potatoes are from a box, though."

"My usual choice, too. Anything I can do?"

"Nope. Everything's just about ready."

"Great. I'll do a quick washup and be right down."

Lia trotted up the narrow stairs, once again wondering how the house's original inhabitants had managed it with their superwide skirts, and hurried through a quick change into at-home comfort clothes. Once back downstairs, she helped get dinner on the table. Within minutes Lia was heaping praise on Hayley for her accomplishment.

"You're becoming a gourmet cook," Lia said. "I remember not too long ago when you'd choose to go hungry rather than boil an egg."

"Yeah," Hayley agreed, spearing one of her tender-crisp green beans. "I'm kind of surprised myself. Not that I think a lot about it. But when I have the time, it's fun to try things. By the way, I should be able to get a few of those boxes out of here tomorrow and take them to the farm."

"Ah."

"They're for this fundraising event I'm putting together: Food, Fun, and Alpacas!"

Lia grinned. "Catchy title."

Hayley laughed. "It was the best we could come up with. Eats, Amusements, and Alpacas just didn't do it."

"No, not much of a ring to that. But it sounds like a terrific event. And maybe a big undertaking?" Lia asked. She cut a piece from her ham slice.

"Well, there'll be tents and games to arrange, and alpaca pettings to get ready for, of course, along with a lot of logistics to figure out. But it won't be all on me. I'll be coordinating with the people from the Crandalsburg Parks Booster Club, the group that's fundraising."

Hayley's grimace prompted Lia to ask, "Is that a good thing?"

Hayley laughed. "I guess I'll find out!" She gulped down some water, then added, "The problem comes mostly from the woman who heads that group. She's, um, on the pushy side. And she's older, maybe mid-sixties or so. But I get the feeling she considers me an inexperienced kid who needs to be supervised and directed every step of the way. And some of her ideas are just plain awful."

"Show her that you're in charge," Lia advised.

"It's just . . . well, I have to work out a balance between running a successful event, which could draw more of the same in the future, and satisfying our current client." She grinned. "I can't let the two things be mutually exclusive."

"You'll manage it," Lia said. She wished she could offer more concrete advice, but that might put her in the same position as Hayley's overbearing client. It was probably better to let Hayley work it out on her own, and for Lia to be the sounding board. From her time as a surgical nurse, with the occasional need to pour out the day's frustrations to

Tom, she knew how comforting a pair of listening ears could be.

The thought of those days brought the usual ache, but it was getting better. Slowly, but definitely better.

T he next morning, Lia called Cori about her new customer's request and arranged to drop off the photo he'd left with her. Hayley, true to her promise, had cleared several of her boxes from the downstairs area, giving a little more breathing space to the living room. Once the fundraising event Hayley was working on was over, Lia's house would hopefully look much less like a storage locker, though Lia knew many of Hayley's personal boxed-up things would remain. But at least the area around Lia's knitting chair had remained clear. Hayley understood that space was sacrosanct and had so far avoided piling anything near it. So far.

Maybe Lia could pitch in on the search for an apartment?

With that thought, she gathered up her keys, the dog photo, and the paper with Cori's address and headed out her door, smiling over the fresh tidiness of her lawn as she did so. There were definite advantages to having a housemate. That and the occasional gourmet dinner like the one Lia had come home to the previous night. Maybe she shouldn't press too much on that apartment search. Her little house wasn't actually bursting . . . yet.

Lia soon discovered that the house Cori Littlefield lived in was surprisingly large. Large, that is, for a single woman whose means of income, as far as Lia knew, was fairly modest. She double-checked the address Cori gave her to be sure she hadn't misread it, but it was correct. Spotting the beautiful crocheted wreath on the door also convinced her, its multiple crocheted flowers picking up the bright blue color of the well-kept, century-old house's siding. Lia climbed the three steps to the wraparound porch and knocked on the door. Soon she heard locks turning, and the door opened a crack on its chain as Cori peered out.

"It's you!" Cori closed the door in order to slip the chain, then opened it wider to silently face Lia.

"Good morning," Lia said. "I hope I didn't disturb you." She started to reach into her purse for the photo, ready to hand it over and leave, but Cori unexpectedly stepped back.

"No, it's fine. I was waiting." She smiled shyly. "Want to come in?"

"Thank you, I'd love to. Just for a minute." Lia stepped into the small foyer and followed Cori's gesture toward the living room on the right. It held an interesting mix of decorating styles, hinting at having been furnished over several years. A sprinkling of antiques mingled with maple tables, and Lia wondered if the wall-to-wall carpeting hid a hardwood floor. As she sank onto the flower-printed sofa, she recognized the stained-glass Tiffany-style lamp beside it as similar to one she had coveted when she and Tom were first married.

"I have lemonade," Cori said, indicating a tray with glasses and a pitcher. "Would you like some?"

"How nice," Lia said, genuinely pleased. "What a lovely place you have," she added as Cori poured out two glasses. "I love houses with lots of character."

Cori handed Lia her lemonade, then sat on one of the side chairs. "It's my mom's," she said.

Lia nodded, wondering if Cori's mother would soon appear.

"I moved back about a month ago," Cori said. "I used to live in York."

"Did you? I lived in York for many years." Lia talked

about the knitting group that she drove back to meet with once a week. "We started getting together years ago at one woman's home."

Cori seemed to be waiting for more, so Lia went on. "We all love to knit, but over time we began running out of people to knit *for*. So when the opportunity to run a booth at the craft fair came up, we jumped at it. Now we can knit to our heart's content. The house we meet at, Jen Beasley's, is on Ninth Street in York. That's how my craft booth got its name: Ninth Street Knits."

Cori nodded. "I wondered about that." She smiled, but when she didn't offer anything about herself, Lia decided to ask.

"Did you sell your crocheted art when you were in York?"

"A little. There was a craft store that took things on consignment. At first, people that came there mostly wanted to try making their own versions." She grinned. "They found out it wasn't so easy."

"I'm sure they did!" Lia grinned back. "Oh, before I forget, let me give you the photo of the dog that this man hopes you can duplicate in yarn. His contact information is on the back." Lia got it out of her purse and held it out.

"Cute dog," Cori said, taking it. She studied it several moments, then nodded. "I think I can do that."

"Great. You'll make his daughter very happy, I'm sure."

"Would you like to see some of the things I've been working on?" Cori asked.

"I'd love to." Lia set down her lemonade and followed Cori to the back of the house, where Cori said her workroom was located. They passed through the kitchen, but no mom was there, nor did Lia hear sounds of another person in the house.

Cori showed her around the workroom, which contained a dizzying array of crocheted angels, flowers, animals, and birds lined up on several tables.

"My goodness!" Lia exclaimed. "I guess you're ready for the next rush. These are wonderful!" She picked up one of the angels. "Do you follow patterns?" she asked.

"Sometimes," Cori said, clearly pleased to talk about her craft. "But I can figure out a lot of these on my own. After a while, you learn."

"How long have you done this?" Lia set down the angel and picked up one of the birds, a red cardinal.

"Oh gosh! I started way back. My mom taught me how to crochet when I was little, and I liked it. It was relaxing."

The phone in the kitchen rang. Cori jumped. "Once I learned, I couldn't stop!" she said, glancing nervously back at the kitchen as the phone continued to ring. By the fourth ring she gave in. "I'd better get it. It might be important."

Lia smiled and nodded. While Cori dealt with the phone, Lia examined several crocheted carrots, peppers, and lettuce arranged prettily in a small basket. Behind that was a folded afghan. Lia lingered over the afghan, fingering it and admiring the color pattern, until something on the corner of the table caught her eye. It was a diorama of some sort in a three-sided shadow box, tucked at the back.

Lia reached over to carefully lift the box and bring it closer for examination. There was a sloping green crocheted hill and two crocheted figures, along with a scattering of flowers and a small bush. Studying it closely, Lia realized it depicted a nursery rhyme: "Jack and Jill went up the hill to fetch a pail of water. Jack fell down and broke his crown, and Jill came tumbling after."

Except . . . something was wrong. Instead of Jack at the bottom of the hill, a female figure lay there, a small red bucket tipped on its side beside her. The male figure stood at the top, looking down at Jill. Though Lia told herself she was being silly, that a crocheted figure couldn't really show what he was thinking, his crocheted eyebrows looked menacing.

"That shouldn't be out!" Cori had returned. She rushed over and snatched it from Lia.

"I'm so sorry," Lia said. "I wanted to see it better. I was very careful." She paused. "Is it supposed to be Jack and Jill?"

"Jessica! Not Jill, Jess— No! It's nothing! Just something I made up. It's stupid." She hurried the shadow box out of the room, and Lia heard her running up the stairs.

When Cori came back down, Lia had returned to the living room, and she apologized once more. Cori waved it away, though she still seemed flustered. "I have to go out," she said. "My phone call . . . ," she added, vaguely implying something important about it.

"Of course," Lia said. "I didn't mean to stay this long. Thank you so much for the lemonade! I hope your special order works out."

"My . . . ? Oh, the dog. Yes. Thank you for bringing me the photo."

Cori walked Lia to the door, where she politely but briskly said good-bye, and Lia left with a highly unsettled feeling. Something was wrong, but she had no idea what it was. Her protective impulses kicked in, wanting to help. But with what? Lia couldn't just bumble into Cori's life. She'd have to wait until she understood more.

Chapter 4

After returning home, Lia wandered restlessly through the house, finding it difficult to settle down. Her visit with Cori continued to disturb her, in particular the young woman's reaction to Lia's discovery of the shadow box. Why did she whisk it out of sight? Lia suspected she had bumbled into something that was very private to Cori. But what? An inverted nursery rhyme? It was all so puzzling.

Lia tried knitting, her go-to activity whenever she needed calming—or any other time, actually—and it did help. Seeing the Fair Isle pattern grow on the cowl scarf as she worked was wonderfully satisfying, and Daphne was as usual the perfect companion, lying cozily beside her and never tempted to bat at the yarn.

To keep her thoughts from endlessly rerunning her morning scene, Lia listened first to music, then to an audio book—a Dorothy Sayers mystery—but eventually it had to end. If she had her druthers, she'd happily knit most of the day, but her fingers begged for a break. Unfortunately, doing so opened the floodgates for all the concerns she'd so efficiently held back.

Should she call Cori? she wondered as she packed away her knitting. Would her young friend want to be called? Lia stared down at her phone. Cori didn't know Lia that well. That morning's visit had been a first, and their conversations before that had been mainly craft fair related. It was probably best to hold off, Lia decided, and give their friendship time to develop. When and if Cori felt like talking about what troubled her, she would let Lia know.

That decision made, Lia got busy with housework, though with a house that size, it was quickly cleaned and tidied—as tidy as any place could be with random boxes and stacks of papers spread over half of it. Still, she dusted the tops of the boxes and lined up and anchored Hayley's papers, which gave her some satisfaction.

Hayley texted that she'd be late and would grab a bite for herself when she got home, so Lia went ahead with her own dinner, warming up a serving of Hayley's delicious leftover ham and vegetables. As she ate, she found that, though she'd grown used to dining alone before Hayley moved back, it now felt oddly solitary, so after finishing dinner she gave Belinda a call.

"How did your book club go?" she asked, leaning back on the sofa, a newly made mug of coffee steaming on the table at her side.

"Okay, I guess." Belinda's lack of enthusiasm flowed through the phone.

"What did the group read?" Lia tested her coffee but found it still too hot and set it back down.

"Oh, something about a guy who lives in the mountains somewhere."

"Something? Somewhere? Did you read it?" Lia asked. Daphne, realizing that Lia's lap was free of knitting paraphernalia, hurried over to jump up, her bushy ragdoll tail tickling Lia's face until she settled down.

"Yeah, I read it," Belinda said. "All the way to the bitter end. The guy was a loser, leaving everything behind like he did to play monk or something, and then wondering why he wasn't happy. Like, duh!"

"Maybe he left in the first place because he wasn't happy," Lia offered. "Maybe he found some clarity through roughing it on his own, or whatever?"

"That's what a couple of the members said. I didn't see it."

Lia heard clinking noises in the background and guessed her friend was in her kitchen. "Did you enjoy the potluck at least? What did you find at the store to take along?" Lia ran her hand over Daphne's furry back and felt the soft vibrations of her purrs.

"It was my lucky night. I snagged their last veggie platter with dip. The others brought homemade things like meatballs in sauce or whatever, and it was all pretty good! The food definitely made slogging through that book worth it. The members aren't too bad, either."

Coming from Belinda, Lia thought, that was high praise. "Sounds like a pretty good time."

"Yeah. But I'll try to steer them to books I'd rather read when I've been in the group a little longer. One good thing, it's getting me back into reading. I'll look into what's out there. Gotta be something better than mountain man. Did you get to Cori's place today?"

"I did." Lia considered mentioning the shadow box matter and decided against it. "Cori seemed confident she could do a yarn version of the dog in the photo."

"Good. So, is she independently wealthy or what?"

Lia laughed. "She seems to be happily working on her crochet art in a lovely house that belongs to her mother, a mother who I did not see during my visit."

"Okay. So Cori's in a stable enough situation to carry on with the craft fair. That's all that concerns me for the time being."

"Cori has plenty of stock ready to go," Lia said. "All of it amazing."

"Even better. That newspaper story ramped up our attendance and was a plus for all the vendors."

"It certainly was. It was good to see smiles back on faces."

Lia reached for her coffee, which had cooled enough by then, and enjoyed a first sip. Daphne snuggled a little closer and let out a contented sigh.

"I'm going out tomorrow night," Belinda said.

"Oh? Something special?" Lia asked idly while scratching lightly at Daphne's ears.

"Not special, just out." Belinda paused. "For dinner. A guy from the book club."

Lia picked up with some astonishment what her friend was really saying. "You mean a date?"

"Not a date. Just . . . dinner. Chad and I were the only ones with the same reaction to the 'mountain' book. It's probably better to talk about it away from the others, who were so head over heels in love with the whole story. We can trash it privately to our heart's content."

"Chad?"

"Yes, Chad. And that's all I'm going to say for now, so don't bother trying."

"I wasn't . . . ," Lia began, but she grinned. "Okay, I was. And I won't anymore, I promise. Have a good time." Hayley walked through the door at that point and, seeing Lia on the phone, waved and continued on to the kitchen.

"Thanks. It's just good to get out of the house once in a while." There was a pause, after which Belinda said, "Hey, I've got a call waiting that I think I'd better take. Do you mind?"

"Go right ahead. Hayley just came home. Talk to you later." Lia set down her phone and thought about Belinda's surprising news. Then she called out, "Glad you didn't have to stay too late. Busy day?" She heard a groan from Hayley in response.

"You could say that. Tell you about it in a minute."

Lia waited as Hayley finished putting her dinner together. When she brought it out to the dining table, Lia grabbed her coffee mug and joined her. Watching Hayley jab her fork into the food told Lia volumes about her daughter's mood.

"That woman!" Hayley finally said.

"The head of the fundraiser group?"

Hayley bobbed her head, having just shoveled in a forkful of mashed potatoes. Eventually she said, "It's an all-volunteer group, maybe about thirty people all told, but you'd think it was her personal, for-profit outfit. Last week she explicitly told me to hire musicians, so I spent hours looking into that. Lucky for me that I didn't actually hire the ones I was going to because today she lets me know *she* got some. Oh, and the bounce house we discussed *thoroughly* before she gave me the go-ahead on it? Now she doesn't want it anymore."

"Oh dear."

"Now, I know I should have got everything down in writing from the start. But at the time I couldn't even pin her down enough for that, and Mr. Weber didn't back me up when I pressed it. I think she managed to convince him that she had it all perfectly planned in her head and it was just a matter of delegating to me."

"This is a first for the Webers," Lia said. "That makes it much harder for you. Can I get you something to drink?" she offered.

"Whiskey on the rocks?" Hayley said with a lopsided grin. "The woman is leading me to that."

"Would an iced tea do instead?" Lia asked with a smile, and getting a nod from Hayley, she went into the kitchen. "What's new with Brady?" she asked as she poured out the tea.

Hayley perked up at the question. "He's been working hard with the physical therapist and doing great! She claimed she never saw anyone so motivated."

"Brady loves his police work," Lia said, setting the iced tea glass at Hayley's place.

Hayley nodded. "He would have been devastated if that injury had forced him out," she said. Lia caught Hayley's use of the word *injury* rather than *bullet wound* and guessed that it made it a little less scary for her. The night that Brady took a bullet to the shoulder while bravely stopping a murderer had made the danger he faced in his job much more real for her daughter.

"Brady's not crazy about the desk work he's been assigned to," Hayley went on, "but that'll only last until he gets an all clear from the doctor."

"Sounds like they're looking after him well." Lia saw that the change of subject had lifted Hayley's mood, which was what she'd aimed for, and they moved on to other soothing subjects until Hayley finished her dinner and took her dishes to the kitchen.

Lia clicked on the TV for a little more distraction. As

she flipped through the local channels, a breaking news announcement caught her attention.

"A Crandalsburg rescue team has recovered the body of a woman at the base of Long Run Falls. It's presumed she fell somehow . . ."

The report continued with talk of further investigation, a call for any possible witnesses, and the information that the identity of the woman was being withheld until family notification. But Lia had frozen at "body of a woman" and "fallen." Visions of Cori's strange tableau swam before her. It was only Daphne's nudge at her knee that dismissed them. She lifted the large cat to her lap and hugged her closely.

Chapter 5

The next morning, Lia had just finished straightening up her kitchen when the call she'd been fearing deep down came.

"No! Not Cori!" Lia sank into her chair after Belinda told her the news.

"I'm afraid so," Belinda said with a slight catch in her voice. "They released her name a little while ago. Still no information on how it happened."

"I just saw her yesterday," Lia breathed.

"I know. It's an awful shock," Belinda said. "And so young."

"Oh gosh, her poor mother!" Lia said. "How terrible for her."

"A sister was mentioned," Belinda said. "So there's that. I mean, for some kind of support."

"Good." Lia could clearly imagine the horror and pain of losing a daughter. Cori's mother would need all the support she could get. "I don't suppose any arrangements have been made yet?" Lia asked.

"No. I'll let you know if I hear," Belinda said.

Lia thanked her and promised to help spread the word. Funerals were not anything she looked forward to, as they inevitably brought up memories of Tom's. But she had drawn so much comfort from the many friends who came to his service that she would never hesitate to do the same for others whenever she could.

Belinda called back later that day. "The wake is Thursday, seven to nine, at the Shubert Funeral Home."

"So soon," Lia commented as she made a note of it. "And the funeral?" she asked.

"Private."

That made Lia blink, but she nodded. That decision was up to the family. She wrote down the vendors' names that Belinda gave her and began making calls to pass the information on. When she'd finished that sad task, she called Jen Beasley about needing to miss the Ninth Street Knitters meeting at her house Thursday evening.

"How about we postpone to Friday?" Jen asked. "If that works for you, it's fine with me. I can check with the others."

"I hate to put you to the trouble, Jen, but that would be lovely. I made a slew of calls myself, and I'm just about talked out."

"Go have a cup of tea," Jen said. "I'll let you know when it's set."

Lia did as she was told but added two chocolate cookies to the mix. Small comforts, but they sometimes meant a lot.

Hayley offered to accompany her to the wake, but Lia assured her it wasn't necessary. "You never met Cori. After the long hours you've been putting in, you need a different kind of break," she said. "There'll be plenty of craft fair folks for me to mingle with."

When she walked into the funeral home, Lia saw that was true. Though their somber faces and attire were jarringly different from what she was used to seeing each weekend, soft smiles and hand squeezes came as she wove her way through to the head of the room, where she assumed Cori's family would be. The coffin, she found, was thankfully closed. Lia saw no apparent receiving line, so she hesitated, unsure of whom to approach. Maggie Wood, whose quilt booth stood directly across the craft fair barn from Lia's, came to her aid, the large woman engulfing her first in a hug.

"Sad time," she said as she stepped back. Maggie's usually colorful apparel had been muted that evening to a pale blue, a shade Lia was surprised her ebullient friend even owned. Maggie's mass of red hair had been tamed into a tight bun, exposing the gray roots edging her face and adding a serious note. Nothing, however, could be done about the naturally high color of Maggie's face or the bright blue of her eyes.

"Very sad," Lia agreed. "Have you spoken to the family yet?"

"That's Cori's sister over there." Maggie indicated a tall woman of about forty wearing a dark suit, who stood speaking with an older couple. Lia didn't detect any resemblance to Cori. The woman's in-charge bearing, in fact, might have said "funeral director" to Lia more than "family member," but she took Maggie's word for it.

The older couple moved on, and Lia said, "I'll go say a word." She walked over and introduced herself, which produced a smile of recognition from the woman.

"Yes, Cori mentioned you. I'm Cori's half sister, Robin Wendt. Thank you so much for coming."

Half sister. That could explain the lack of resemblance. They spoke briefly of the tragic loss, Lia aware that Robin must have had to repeat the same words often enough by then to make them almost automatic.

"Is your mother here?" Lia asked, not spotting anyone in their vicinity who might fit the role.

"I'm afraid not," Robin said. "My mother was in a terrible car accident a few weeks ago. She's recovering, but she couldn't possibly leave the nursing facility to be here."

"How awful. Cori did say it was her mother's house when I dropped something off to her there the other day. But she didn't mention the accident."

Robin nodded as though that was to be expected. "It was my mother's request that I bring Cori back to Crandalsburg to live in her house. Cori was, well, struggling on her own in York. Our mother thought it would help her out."

"It apparently did. Cori's crochet booth was becoming very successful at the craft fair," Lia said.

"Yes. She was so happy about that. So excited. And then *this* happened." Robin glanced ruefully toward the coffin, then dabbed at her eyes with a handkerchief she'd been holding. "On top of losing my sister," she said after drawing a deep breath, "I feel so terribly guilty. Along with bringing Cori back home, I had promised my mother to look after her."

Lia had no answer for that other than, "I'm sorry." Another couple approached, whom Robin apparently knew, and Lia withdrew.

A dark-suited gentleman, apparently an actual funeral home employee, politely pointed out a table with light refreshments in an outer room. Lia went over, more as a courtesy than from any thirst or hunger. She'd offered her condolences to the only family member of Cori's she knew to be there, but it was only appropriate to linger awhile. She picked up a glass of some sort of punch and sipped it as she glanced around. At such gatherings, there was often a table covered with remembrances of the deceased— photos, various memorabilia—but she didn't see one. A single framed photo of Cori had been placed on the closed lid of the casket, that of a much younger Cori, which led Lia to suspect it was a high school graduation photo. Lia thought a piece of Cori's crochet art would have been a nice touch, perhaps an angel, but there were none of Cori's creations to be seen. Cori's sister certainly must have had her hands full with her mother's severe injury followed by Cori's sudden tragic death. Lia wished, now, that she'd offered to help with the arrangements—if she'd only known whom to extend her offer to.

There were several lovely baskets of flowers flanking the casket. The craft fair vendors had pooled their resources and sent a large wreath, and a few bouquets dotted the area. Cori would have appreciated that.

Lia spotted Belinda. She apparently hadn't spoken to Robin yet and was heading her way, so Lia took her glass with her to join a group of other craft fair people. Zach Goodwin, who sold honey from his apiary, was with his wife, Florrie, who added her preserved jams and jellies to his booth. Olivia stood alongside them, as did the fair's popular baker, Carolyn Hanson.

They had all arrived some time before Lia, and after welcoming Lia and chatting for a while, each found a reason to leave, Zach and Florrie pleading fatigue, Olivia wanting to catch the end of her seven-year-old's first soccer practice, and Carolyn simply bidding Lia a pleasant good night before taking off.

A second wave of mourners began filling the room.

When she recognized none of them, Lia decided to head back to the refreshments table, thinking she might find Belinda there. Instead, she encountered a young woman, apparently in some distress over a spilled drink. Lia grabbed a handful of paper napkins to help.

"Thanks," the woman said, as they dropped their soggy napkins into a nearby trash can. "That was so clumsy of me. Amanda Briggs," she said, holding out her hand.

"Lia Geiger," Lia said, shaking the petite brunette's hand. She judged her to be in her early thirties and asked, "Were you a friend of Cori's?"

Amanda blinked her large brown eyes rapidly as she nodded. "We were friends in school. I didn't know she was back in Crandalsburg. I feel so bad that I didn't get to see her before, before . . ." She swallowed hard.

"I worked next to Cori at the craft fair," Lia said. "I got the impression she wasn't one to socialize much."

That made Amanda smile. "You're right. Neither of us were, at least back then. Which is why we became friends, I suppose. Birds of a feather and all that. So I shouldn't be surprised that she didn't get in touch with me. She probably intended to, like in six months or so. Maybe."

Amanda grinned over that, and Lia smiled back. "I'm sure she would have. Joining the craft fair seemed to be a pretty overwhelming endeavor for her. I had the feeling it sapped most of her time and energy."

"I'm amazed she did that. The Cori I knew in school always sat at the back of the room and generally avoided people."

"But you became her friend. That must have been good for her."

Amanda smiled shyly. "I'd like to think so. Everyone needs at least one person to talk to, to confide in." She grimaced. "But looking back, I wish she had someone who could have helped her more, a counselor, maybe. Cori had emotional problems that I had no clue what to do about."

"Emotional problems?" Lia thought about Cori's explanation for her trouble sleeping. "Did they give her nightmares?"

"Yes. The same one, over and over." Amanda frowned. She took a fresh drink from the table and looked down at it for several moments. "Cori's sister, Robin?" she said, looking up. "She told me tonight that Cori was still having that nightmare. She said Cori's fall might not have been an accident. She thinks Cori might have jumped."

"Oh! What a horrible idea! Why would she think that?"

"Because Cori's nightmare was about exactly what killed her. It was about falling from the top of Long Run Falls. Except . . ." Amanda struggled to compose herself. "Except," she said. "When Cori told me about the nightmare, she never said *she* had fallen. It was about seeing someone *else* fall. And she said it wasn't just a dream. It was a memory. Cori said she'd actually seen that happen, when she was six or seven."

Lia's mind flashed to Cori's shadow box. "Did that someone who fell have a name?" she asked softly.

Amanda nodded. "Jessica."

Amanda shared several more details of what Cori had told her concerning the fall. Then she excused herself, leaving a stunned Lia by herself at the refreshments table. *Jessica. The name Cori gave to the Jill figure in her shadow box.* An older woman, whom Lia had noticed working her phone nearby, tucked it into her purse and walked over to the table with the aid of her cane. Lia shook herself out of her thoughts and nodded to her.

"Just texted my granddaughter that she could pick me up

now," the woman said to Lia, then laughed at herself. "I text maybe twice a year and have to relearn it every time."

"It's handy when you need it," Lia said, smiling politely.

"It is." The woman picked up a cup of punch and took a sip. "Shirley Dunn," she said. "I'm a longtime friend of Cori's mother, Judith."

Lia introduced herself, adding how she knew Cori. "I heard about her mother's accident. How very unfortunate."

Shirley nodded. "Terribly," she agreed. "Especially since it wasn't her fault at all. Her lawyer's already set up a lawsuit, which is only right. But it won't make up for all the pain and suffering." She followed that with a long sigh. "To lose Cori was a dreadful blow, but doubly so when Judith was the least able to protect her. In her grief, my poor friend kept saying, 'If only I had been home. If only I could have stopped her!'"

"Stopped Cori from going to the falls?" Lia asked.

"Yes." Shirley turned rheumy eyes on Lia. "But that's what's so puzzling to me. Why would Cori suddenly want to go there? She was afraid of that spot ever since she was a little girl!" She shook her head sadly. "The whole thing doesn't make any sense to me. Not at all." She dropped her paper cup into the trash and walked off, Lia watching as the older woman leaned heavily on her cane.

Chapter 6

As the Ninth Street Knitters gathered at Jen Beasley's home in York, Lia settled into her favorite chair, thinking about how Daphne had always curled up on the floor beside her. Bob Beasley's allergy spike had called for Daphne's move to Lia's home some weeks ago, a change that made Lia and Daphne happy and Bob's breathing much better. Though a sacrifice for both Bob and Jen, it was made easier by seeing their sweet cat go to a loving home.

Lia pulled out the scarf she'd been working on and glanced around at the others. Maureen and Diana, as usual, chatted rapidly with each other as they took adjoining seats on the sofa, and Tracy, the youngest of the group, smiled at Lia as she cast on yarn for the start of a new baby sweater, her favorite item to knit. Jen came in from the kitchen after organizing all the snacks and drinks brought for the knitting session.

As Jen took her seat, she asked Lia about the wake. "Was there a large turnout? There usually is for someone so young."

"Everyone from the craft fair showed up," Lia said. "And there were quite a few others." Lia didn't add that she suspected most of those were friends of Cori's sister, not Cori.

"So this was for a vendor?" Tracy asked. "What was the craft?"

Lia set down the coffee mug. "Cori did crochet art, wonderfully creative pieces."

"Oh!" Tracy stopped her casting. "Was that Cori Littlefield? I saw the photos and article about her. My neighbor gets the Crandalsburg paper."

"It was," Lia said. "Cori's booth did fantastic business on Sunday because of that story. Sadly, it was her last day there."

"Wait!" Maureen broke away from her conversation with Diana. "Did you say Cori Littlefield? I knew her! She worked as a temp in our office last summer. She's dead? How terrible! What happened, Lia?"

Lia told what she knew and saw reactions from Maureen and the others similar to what her own had been.

"A waterfall?" Diana asked. Her knuckles whitened as she clutched the lush blue stitches on her circular needle, reminding Lia that Diana had once admitted to a fear of heights. "What was she doing there? Did they say?"

Lia shook her head. "I've told you all I know." She paused. What Amanda had told her the previous night weighed on Lia enough to want to know more. It was time to get input on that from the others. "At least about the circumstances of her death. But at the wake last night, I spoke with a woman who had been Cori's school friend."

All knitting needles stopped moving as Lia explained about Cori's recurring nightmare and her long-ago claim to Amanda that the dream came from something she'd actually witnessed.

"Could that be true?" Diana asked.

"When did Cori say she'd witnessed it?" Tracy asked. "As a child?"

"Amanda said she would have been six or seven," Lia said.

"That's young!" Tracy said. "She might have imagined it or seen something on TV that became real to her."

"I agree," Lia said. "Which is why I wanted to verify it. I spent some time online today."

"And . . . ?" Jen asked.

"I found something that Cori might have witnessed. Twenty-six years ago, when Cori would have been six years old, a woman named Jessica Ackerman fell to her death from the top of Long Run Falls. It was ruled accidental."

"Wow!" Diana said. "The same place."

"Did Cori tell anyone else?" Jen asked.

"Amanda thinks not. When Cori confided in her, she swore Amanda to secrecy. They were both only twelve at the time, and Amanda didn't think to question that then. She only knew that Cori was frightened."

"Of what?" Maureen asked.

Lia paused, remembering Amanda's words to her at the wake, spoken before others came to the refreshments table. "Cori said there was a second person on the cliff when Jessica fell. Someone who Cori believed pushed Jessica off the rocks."

"Oh my gosh," Tracy said. "That's a whole different kettle of fish. That's murder."

"Yes," Lia agreed. Her gaze flitted around the room. "If it's true."

"Right," Diana said. "If it's true. Can you trust the memory of a six-year-old?"

"That's something I can't answer," Lia said. "But there's something else." She described Cori's Jack and Jill shadow box. "Cori blurted out that the figure at the bottom of the hill wasn't Jill, but Jessica. It clearly upset Cori, but she didn't want to talk about it."

"That poor thing," Jen said. "Having something like that haunting her all her life. I hate to ask it, but could she have been so overwhelmed by it that she took her own life?"

The others winced, and Lia said, "It's possible. But I have another question." She cleared her throat. "Could Cori have been murdered?"

"Why would you think that?" Jen asked.

"Because," Lia said, "Cori's life was on an upswing as her crochet art had started to take off, thanks to the newspaper publicity. She was excited and happy, not, as far as I could tell, suicidal. But that same publicity might have reminded the wrong person of her existence. What if Cori actually did see someone push Jessica off the rocks near the waterfall, someone who then spotted six-year-old Cori before she presumably ran off. Wouldn't that person feel threatened to know that the child, now grown up, might be ready to speak up?"

"I think that's a good possibility," Maureen said. "It fits everything we know much better than accident or suicide. But . . ." Maureen looked pointedly at Lia. "It would also mean there's a murderer out there who needs to be caught."

Lia knew where Maureen was going.

"You already came up with the information about Jessica," Maureen continued. "You might be able to prove that

Cori was murdered by looking into it further. If it's true, that poor girl deserves justice, don't you think?"

"She does, of course," Lia agreed, and she didn't admit that she was already leaning in that direction. But after what happened the last time . . .

"You wouldn't be on your own," Maureen said. "I'll pitch in, too. Maybe between the two of us we can come up with enough information to get the police interested."

"The *two* of us?" Diana asked. "Um, I believe there's five people here." Her gaze swept the room.

Tracy nodded. "I have no idea what I can contribute, but count me in."

"And me," Jen said. "Mostly to make sure Lia doesn't get herself in trouble."

Trouble? What*ever* could go wrong when you're sniffing around a possible murder? Of course Lia had a pretty good idea, but she felt Cori deserved to have answers. With everyone having written off her young friend's death as an accident or suicide, Lia might be Cori's only chance at revealing the truth. While she understood the potential danger, Lia told herself she would absolutely not get herself in too deep. Only enough, as Maureen said, to get the police interested and then leave it up to them.

With that promise to herself, Lia loosened up a bit of yarn and got busy knitting, a skill she felt much more confident about and whose endpoint she could predict much more safely.

Chapter 7

When she got home from the knitters' meeting, Lia logged onto her laptop, wanting to reread what she'd already found about Jessica before continuing her research. Her little house was quiet, since Hayley had gone with Brady to a cookout given by friends of his. Lia was happy to see Hayley make more friends in Crandalsburg as well as get a pleasant break from the stress of planning her first Weber Farm event.

The first thing Lia pulled up was Jessica's obituary, which stated that the nineteen-year-old had graduated from Crandalsburg High School—no surprise there—and that she'd been active in the school's drama club, starring in more than one performance. At the time of her death, she had been attending nearby Aymesburg College, pursuing double degrees in theater art and education. Lia thought the education degree was probably Jessica's parents' idea, a practical backup to the riskier goal of an acting career.

Lia made a few notes and, after a further search produced nothing more, logged off. She faced long hours at the craft fair the next day, and she had to get her rest. Hayley hadn't mentioned when she'd be home, nor had Lia asked. Her daughter was an adult. Besides, Hayley was out with a young man who, along with having impressed Lia personally, also happened to be a police officer.

But Lia's thoughts flew back to Jessica, whose mother must also have assumed that her young adult daughter would be safe on that dreadful day. A chilling concept and one that Lia did not want seeping into her dreams that night. So instead of climbing into bed, she went to find a book that would fill her mind with pleasanter thoughts. She found a history of Fair Isle knitting on her bedroom shelf, next to a bevy of other knitting books, which would definitely work. Lia carried it into her bed and plumped up her pillows to read as Daphne jumped up to join her, curling cozily at Lia's feet.

S aturday morning the craft fair vendors arrived in a more somber mood than on the previous Sunday. They had lost one of their own, and quiet smiles and nods replaced the usual cheery greetings. A sign stood at the front of Cori's booth to explain her absence to any shoppers who might not have heard the news, along with a small bouquet. Lia noticed that all of Cori's crocheted items were gone.

"Her sister came yesterday and loaded everything up," Belinda explained when Lia asked. "I'd hoped she'd agree to keep running the booth a little longer. I could easily find someone to handle it, and it would continue to be a draw for the craft fair. But she declined. Said something like Cori's handiwork was all they had left of her now."

Lia nodded as she slipped a cardigan sweater onto a hanger, though she remembered how the room she had seen at the house was stacked high with more of Cori's crocheted art. "Did she tell you about their mother being in a nursing facility?"

"Uh-huh." Belinda fingered a lacey knit scarf, folded on Lia's counter. "Pretty sad."

"Robin also told someone she thought Cori's death might have been a suicide instead of an accident." Lia related her conversation with Amanda, including Cori's nightmares and her claim that they came from an actual memory.

Belinda frowned. "That's serious stuff. What do you make of it?"

Before Lia could answer, Mark Simmons walked in from the parking lot, his arms wrapped around a box of his scenic photos, and stopped to read the sign at Cori's booth. "Such a shame," he said, shaking his head sadly, not the first vendor to do so. Lia expected to see similar reactions from others throughout the day as well as be drawn into difficult conversations about Cori's death, each shopper not realizing they weren't the first to bring it up.

"Mark," Belinda said, "about that question you asked me the other day . . ." She turned to walk along with the photographer toward his own booth, putting off discussion about Cori's nightmares to another time.

Lia hung her sweater next to a line of others, spacing them neatly, then tidied the knit pieces on her front counter, musing as she worked over Jessica and what little she knew about her. Lia had already calculated that if she had lived, Jessica would be about forty-five. As Lia's gaze roamed over the craft fair vendors readying their own booths, it paused at Nicole Griffin, the craft fair's basket weaver.

Situated at opposite corners of the barn, Lia and Nicole had had only minimal interaction so far, but as she watched the fair-haired woman organizing her many unique baskets, it occurred to Lia that she could be in her early forties. If Nicole had grown up in Crandalsburg, she might have known Jessica.

Bill Landry called out that he was about to open the entrance doors, so Lia returned to the business at hand, which would be to greet the craft fair shoppers and hopefully interest a few in her collection of knits. That took up most of the morning, and as she'd expected, Lia dealt with many questions about Cori. But to balance those somber discussions, a shopper bought a lovely vest that Jen had finished some months ago but which had lingered unappreciated at the booth.

"This will be perfect for in between seasons," the woman said happily as she handed over her credit card.

Lia agreed. "This neutral color will go with almost everything," she said, adding that the beige complimented the woman's auburn hair nicely, a comment that brought a dimpled smile to her shopper.

Lia also sold the sweater she'd watched Diana work on for many weeks, a lush raspberry-colored pullover. A comment during that sale about future chilly weather hinted that Lia's customer had grown weary of the August heat. So had she, as a matter of fact, and she was grateful for the overhead fans and any breeze that made its way through the open doors.

Belinda had brought in a couple of food vendors as soon as the weather warmed. Set up outside the barn, they offered, among other things, cool drinks and ice cream. When foot traffic slowed, Lia noticed a few craftspeople heading outside for a break and probably a cool treat. One of those was Nicole.

"Mind watching my booth for a minute?" Lia asked Olivia, who'd just closed on a nice sale of several handmade soaps. Olivia nodded agreeably, and Lia followed the others, glad to see Nicole veering toward the ice cream stand. Lia got in line behind her.

"Perfect day for double-dip chocolate chip," Lia commented to the basket weaver.

"I'm going for the peanut butter swirl," Nicole answered. "I've been hooked on it since the stand first set up."

They chatted about how business had been for each of them that morning, and as Lia saw Nicole's turn coming up, she asked, "Mind waiting a bit for me? There's something I'd like to talk to you about."

"Sure," Nicole said, looking mildly curious, and once she got her cone, she moved off to the side to wait and lick slowly at her ice cream.

"Thanks," Lia said as she joined her. With food not allowed inside the barn, she was sure Nicole had planned for a few minutes' break. "How about we grab that," Lia suggested, pointing to an empty picnic table.

Nicole led the way, her long summery skirt swishing above her sandals. As she nimbly swung her legs over the table's attached bench, Lia pictured the basket weaver sitting comfortably cross-legged on a floor as she worked at her craft, all joints and muscles kept stretched and agile. Lia couldn't see herself knitting that way, but as she took her own seat a lot less gracefully, she vowed to try something—maybe yoga?—to keep in better shape.

"What's up?" Nicole asked genially before taking a small bite of her cone.

"Did you happen to go to Crandalsburg High?" Lia asked, getting right down to business.

"Sure did. Class of 'ninety-four."

Ah. The year behind Jessica's class. Lia had checked on the size of the school, which seemed modest enough for students in different grades to interact with one another. "Did you happen to know Jessica Ackerman?"

Nicole lowered her ice cream cone and stared silently for a moment. "You know, I thought about her just recently. She died in an accident at Long Run Falls, just like Cori did."

"That's what I understand," Lia said.

"It was years before I went to the falls again," Nicole said. "Having something like that happen to a girl you knew really shakes you up at that age."

"I can imagine," Lia said. "Or at any age," she added, to which Nicole nodded in agreement. "Did you know Jessica well?" Lia asked.

"Not too well. She was a year ahead of me." Nicole quickly licked at a precarious ice cream drip. "She was pretty and popular and acted in a lot of the school plays. Starred in most of them, it seemed. I expected to see her on TV before too long." She fingered the flower pendant that dangled from a chain over her white tee. "Such a shame."

"What about her close friends?" Lia asked. "Are any of them still in the area? I'd love to talk with them."

Nicole threw Lia a puzzled look. "You would? Why?

Lia paused. How to explain? She gazed briefly at groups of shoppers wandering in the distance. "Cori was having nightmares," she said. "About Jessica's death. Now that Cori died in exactly the same way, I'd like an explanation."

Nicole pondered that. "I can't imagine what that could be. But maybe Jessica's old friends will have some idea." She frowned in concentration. "Shelly Higgins and Jessica were good buddies, but I think Shelly moved away. Ah! Crystal Potter is still around. She has a hair salon, Crystal's

Cuts and Curls, over on Elm Grove." Nicole shook her head. "That's all I can come up with right now." Her phone buzzed, and she checked it. "Sorry, I've got a customer waiting," she said. "I'd better go. But if I think of any others, I'll let you know."

Nicole swung her legs free, then paused before getting up. "Let me know what you find, okay? Cori's death was a shock, as bad as Jessica's."

"I will," Lia promised. She watched as Nicole dropped the last of her cone into the trash basket, then turned to deal with her own neglected one. But she licked at it automatically, her thoughts far beyond double-dip chocolate chip.

Chapter 8

Hayley returned from her jog that evening, blond hair tied back and face flushed. She went straight to the kitchen for a chilled bottle of water before flopping on the sofa with an "Oof!" She held the cold bottle to her face for several moments, then twisted off the cap and guzzled about a quarter of the contents.

"I thought it would be a little cooler by this time," she said to Lia, who watched from her chair, knitting needles in hand. "But even sticking to the shade didn't help much."

"It got toasty inside the craft fair barn by late afternoon, too," Lia said. She'd been home for an hour and had her dinner—a tasty chilled shrimp and pasta salad. But Hayley had put off eating until after her run. "Ready for some food?" Lia asked.

"In a minute," Hayley said, reaching over to pet Daphne, who was keeping her distance from Hayley's radiating heat for the moment. "I'll help myself."

Brady was on duty that night, which explained Hayley's presence on a Saturday night. Not, as she continued to claim, that they had a serious relationship. They simply happened to enjoy a lot of the same things, she'd explained often, to which Lia always solemnly nodded.

"How was the cookout last night?" Lia asked.

"Fun!" Hayley said. "They set up a badminton net, and we all played before Mike got the grill going."

From Hayley's chatter the day before as she got ready to go out, Lia knew that the grill master and host, Mike Wagner, was married to Brooke, who was one of Brady's fellow police officers. "Was it a large group?" Lia asked. She stretched out the scarf she was working on and saw it was growing nicely.

"About ten of us, I guess. A couple of other police friends of Brooke's, and some of Mike's teacher friends. Oh, and Brooke's sister, Erin."

Hayley's tone had taken on a slight edge when mentioning Erin, and Lia glanced up from her knitting. But Hayley was downing more water. After she'd finished, she jumped up. "I think I'll have some of that shrimp stuff. Okay if I bring it in here?"

Lia smiled. "Fine with me. Though you might get more attention than you want from Daphne."

"You'll be good, won't you, Daph?" Hayley asked, leaning over to the cat, who blinked back innocently. Hayley grinned and went off to fetch her dinner, returning soon with a tall glass of iced tea and a plate piled high with pasta salad.

"So," she said, as she settled back down on the sofa. "How was your Ninth Street Knitters meeting the other night? Everyone okay?"

"They're all fine." Lia unrolled a length of yarn from the

ball next to her. "They want me to look into Cori's death."
Lia bit her tongue. She hadn't intended to talk about that,
but the words just spilled out.

"Her death?" Hayley asked. "It was an accident, right?"

"That's what it's been called, but some questions have
come up." Now that she'd started, she might as well get it
all out. Lia described Cori's shadow box and told Hayley
about the recurring nightmares. "Cori claimed they were
not just dreams but memories."

"Wow!" Hayley had lowered her plate to her lap as she
listened, which prompted Daphne to inch a little closer.
"Could that be true? How old would Cori have been when
Jessica died?"

"Six," Lia said. "Which I realize is a bit young to expect
credibility. In addition to that, her school friend Amanda
felt Cori struggled with emotional problems. I admit I saw
some signs of that myself. But still, I feel uneasy about the
whole thing. I've decided to look into it. I already came up
with the name of one of Jessica's high school friends."

"Who's that?" Hayley stabbed a fork into a shrimp.

"A woman who runs the hair salon, Crystal's Cuts and
Curls."

"I've heard of that place." Hayley picked up her iced tea
glass. "I could use a trim. Want me to check her out?"

"No!" The word came out more forcefully than Lia had
intended. She smiled apologetically. "I mean . . . you have
enough to deal with right now, what with the fundraising
event coming up. I have plenty more free time."

Hayley grinned. "I know what you're really thinking,
Mom. That I'll get myself in another jam. I could warn you
off, too, you know, from dipping into this." She scooped up
some pasta. "But it's just a haircut."

Lia smiled back. "Of course. But humor me, okay? And

I really don't want to distract you from your work right now." Her smile broadened. "The better that goes, the sooner these boxes and papers of yours might disappear."

"Hah! There's that. But promise to keep me in the loop at least?"

"I promise." To change the subject, Lia asked about progress on the fundraising event.

"It's coming together," Hayley said. She scraped up the last of her dinner, then set the plate on the end table.

The flat tone Hayley used prompted Lia to ask. "Problems?"

Hayley shrugged. "Not really. Well, yeah, really. That woman is driving me nuts."

"The booster club head?" Lia said. "Does she have a name?"

Hayley's lips twisted. "King. Mrs. King. Fitting. She thinks she is one. Or a queen, I suppose. Every time her name pops up on my phone lately, I want to scream."

"She calls a lot?"

Hayley groaned. "Like, every five minutes—or it seems like it. And if I don't answer, she'll text until I respond. Things like, 'Did you remember to . . . ' something or other, or 'I just had a wonderful idea,' which it usually isn't. Her latest thing? She wants me to offer alpaca rides, you know, like pony rides. No way the Webers would go for something like that. Alpacas' backs aren't designed for carrying anything heavy. It could really hurt them. But Bethanne King won't let it go."

"Can you bring in a pony instead?" Lia asked, unrolling a length of yarn. "That might satisfy her."

"Maybe. For about a minute. Then she'll come up with something else." Hayley grinned ruefully. "But it'll end. I keep reminding myself that. And it'll be the best darned

fundraising event ever, at least in these parts. And we'll get
so many other requests that we'll be turning people away,
and I'll never have to see Bethanne King ever, ever again."

Sunday morning, the craft fair began a little less som-
berly than it had the day before. The sign explaining
Cori's absence remained at the front of her booth, along
with the flower bouquet. But as they'd seen both the day
before, the sight wasn't as jarring to the vendors as they
passed by on the way to their own booths.

Lia noticed that the water in the flower vase had been
freshened by an early arrival, and a second smaller arrangement added. Belinda? Or Bill, who also had keys to
the craft fair barn? Whoever had done so, it was thoughtful,
and Lia vowed to bring a fresh bouquet the following weekend. The emptiness of the booth saddened her, and she
wished Cori's sister, Robin, had allowed Belinda to continue selling Cori's creations. To comfort herself, Lia pictured the beautiful crocheted pieces decorating their
mother's room at the nursing facility. She had no idea if that
was truly the case, but if Cori's work wasn't at the craft fair,
Lia couldn't think of a better place for it to be.

Olivia looked particularly upbeat as she lined up her
sweet-smelling soaps, potpourri, and lip balms, and Lia
leaned over their adjoining space to comment.

Olivia beamed. "I got a special order by email last night.
A basketful of almost every one of my products for a going-
away present. They'll be picking it up today."

"Wonderful!" Olivia's sales had been slow lately, and
considering her tendency toward worry and to instantly
fear that any downturn signaled doom to her business, this
was a welcome pick-me-up. Seeing a bright smile on her

neighbor was a lift for Lia as well, and she readied herself with a lighter heart for the new day.

Lia continued to field questions from shoppers about Cori for most of the day, but they had begun to dwindle, which was a relief. Not that Lia wanted to be reminded less about what had happened to her friend. But she had begun to view Cori's death as possibly more than the "unfortunate accident" phrase most shoppers used to describe it, and she disliked the feeling of pretense her neutral responses provoked.

Between those occasional discussions, Lia did make actual sales of her knits, which pleased her, especially the enthusiasm that came along with them from her customers. All the sweaters, shawls, or knit place mats had been made lovingly—by her or by her Ninth Street Knitting friends— and getting admiring feedback from buyers was almost as delightful as hearing praise of one's children. Jen, Tracy, and the others often referred to the time Lia spent at the craft fair on their behalf as a chore. But Lia never thought of it that way and in fact regretted that they missed out on the joy she got out of it.

By late afternoon things had slowed, and Lia was happy to settle onto her folding chair and knit for a while. She'd only worked a few rows when she spotted Nicole approaching with another woman about her age, dark-haired and a few inches shorter. Lia rolled up her knitting and stepped over to her counter.

"Lia, this is Lauren Schneider," Nicole said as they came up.

"Lauren Wolfe now," her companion said with a smile.

"Wolfe, right, sorry," Nicole said. "Lia, remember how I promised to think about Jessica's friends? Well, there I was last night, having dinner at Hoffman's with my husband, when I recognized Lauren sitting at another table! You hardly changed," she said to Lauren, who quickly laughed.

"Except for these gray hairs, you mean?" she said, pointing to the silvery strands highlighting her bangs. "My kids are aging me. Anyway," Lauren said, "Nicole asked if I'd come by and talk to you about Jessica, and I said sure! I've been meaning to stop in at the craft fair, but beyond that, Jessica and I were pretty close, back in high school. I haven't thought about her for a long time, I'm sorry to admit. This gives me the chance to make up for that."

Lia glanced at the overhead clock behind them. The craft fair would be closing in forty minutes. Not a good time to take a break, and she didn't want to rush through their conversation.

"I'd love to talk with you, Lauren, and I so appreciate your coming," Lia said. "How would you feel about browsing through the fair first, and maybe meeting for a drink somewhere after we close up?"

"Sure, that'd work for me," Lauren said. "My husband and the kids are at his mom's. They won't be home for a while." She turned to Nicole. "What about you? We could catch up a little more, too."

"That sounds like fun. How about that new restaurant on South Street? What's it called—1860 Ale House? I heard they have great appetizers."

The three agreed to meet there shortly after Lia and Nicole closed up their booths. Lia watched the two younger women head off in different directions—Nicole returning to her baskets booth and Lauren making a beeline for Tricia Newman's eye-catching handcrafted jewelry.

Chapter 9

As the last of the shoppers left the craft barn, Bill closed the large front doors behind them. Nicole must have been ready and waiting because she waved to Lia on her way to the side exit, calling out, "See you soon!"

Lia had been held up by a last-minute customer, so she quickly began packing. She saw Olivia looking pleased as she packed up her own merchandise and knew it was because of Olivia's significant order that day. Lia had hoped that the customer wouldn't be a no-show and was as elated as Olivia when she saw her booth neighbor handing the large filled basket over in the midafternoon.

"Have a good week!" Olivia called cheerily as she joined the line of exiting vendors.

"You, too," Lia called back, starting to scramble as she pictured Nicole and Lauren waiting for her. Finally she made it to her car and drove as speedily as allowed toward Crandalsburg.

Lia had never been to the Ale House and originally passed it by, missing what would have been a great parking space directly across from the place on South Street. She found another spot on the next block and quick-stepped back to the pub. When she pulled open the heavy door, it was to enter a dim enclosure of dark wood paneling and stained-glass windows. As Lia gave her eyes time to adjust from the brighter light outside, aromas of craft beers and fried onions drifted her way. Then she spotted Nicole waving from a table.

"Sorry to take so long," Lia said as she joined them, taking the chair next to Nicole and across from Lauren. The two had foam-topped glasses before them, and a waiter appeared with a platter of assorted appetizers to center on the table.

"We went ahead and ordered," Lauren said. "I hope you don't mind. We were hot and thirsty," she added, lifting her half-downed frosty glass of craft beer. "They have other cold drinks, too."

The waiter handed Lia a menu, but when she saw the long, detailed list she simply pointed to Nicole's amber brew. "The same as hers," she said.

"Good choice," he assured her, and Lia smiled at what was probably his standard response. Quick and easy was all that mattered to her at the moment.

"Help yourself," Lauren said, handing Lia a small plate. She transferred a fried mozzarella cheese stick to her own.

"Thanks," Lia said, and she chose a crispy chip to dip into one of the sauces.

"I have to show you what I found at the craft fair!" Lauren said. With a pleased smile, she reached down to the bag at her feet to pull out a beaded necklace. Lia recognized Tricia Newman's work. "And," Lauren said, lifting out her next item, "a lovely basket handwoven by the talented person sitting next to you." She held up a multicolored bread basket lined in red cotton.

"You managed to do some pretty good shopping in a short time!" Lia said.

"And I've just begun. I'm definitely going back, now that I've seen what great things are there." Lauren dropped the necklace into her new basket and bagged both just as Lia was served her ale.

After taking a cool sip, Lia asked Lauren about the family she'd mentioned earlier.

"Sophie and Lucas," Lauren said. "Twelve and ten and both into soccer big-time." She smiled fondly before biting into her cheese stick. "Matt's a great dad. I have an older son, Ben, from my first marriage, and he and Matt get along great. Better than with his own father," she added with a twist of her lips. "Turned out that marrying my high school sweetheart wasn't the greatest idea." She lifted her glass for a sip. "But we make mistakes when we're young, don't we? When we think we know everything."

"Amen," Nicole said, nodding. She plucked an onion ring from the platter.

"What about Jessica?" Lia asked, getting to their reason for being there. "Did she date anyone special?"

"During high school?" Lauren asked. "She dated, but no one for very long. But she was seeing someone when she was at Aymesburg."

Nicole piped in. "At Crandalsburg, Jessica seemed to be super-busy and into lots of different things, but mostly drama club. She really found her niche there."

"She did!" Lauren agreed. "I joined, too, but only because Jessica talked me into it. The first play I think I had one line, and I got stage fright so bad I totally blew it!" She laughed at the memory. "But Jessica was a natural. Miss Schiller picked up on that right away. Pretty soon she was giving Jessica big parts."

"I remember her being the lead in several productions," Nicole said. "My favorite was *Little Shop of Horrors*."

Lauren nodded. "She got the leads because she was so good! But some kids didn't like that and groused about it."

"You mean Tiffany?" Nicole said with a grin.

Lauren rolled her eyes. "Oh yes! Tiffany!"

"Were there problems between her and Jessica?" Lia asked, wondering who that was.

"The problems were mostly on Tiffany's side," Lauren said. "And her mother's. Tiffany probably couldn't say too much to Miss Schiller, but her mother would raise a big stink every time Tiffany wasn't given a good enough role. Funny thing was, both Jessica and Tiffany went on to Aymesburg to major in drama, and the *drama*"—Lauren emphasized the word—"continued as they competed for roles there, too. From what I remember, Jessica usually won out, which must have driven Tiffany and her mom bonkers all over again."

"What was Tiffany's last name?" Lia asked. She pulled a small notebook from her purse and flipped to the page where she'd already written the name of Jessica's hair stylist friend, Crystal Potter.

"Hurst," Lauren and Nicole said in unison.

"And did that change to a married name?" Lia asked

Nicole looked blank, but Lauren said, "She never married." When that drew a surprised look from Nicole, Lauren said, "I guess you haven't been keeping up with Crandalsburg High news. After Miss Schiller retired, Tiffany took her place. I'm sure she—and her mother—planned on bigger things than ending up back at Crandalsburg, like, maybe heading to Hollywood? But, as they say, life happens."

Indeed it does, Lia thought. While one is making other plans, as she knew only too well.

"You said Jessica was dating someone while she was in college," Lia said. "Was it serious?"

"That would be Kevin Shaw," Lauren said. "Actually, I think he was a lot more into her than she was with him. Jessica had her goals, and they didn't include settling down in Crandalsburg with a dentist."

"That's what Kevin went on to do?" Lia asked.

"Yup. He was in predental at Aymesburg. Now he has his practice here in town. Dr. Shaw."

Lia scribbled that down. "So, would you say Jessica was clear with Kevin that her plans for the future didn't include him?"

Lauren frowned as she stared down at her glass, running her finger along the condensation. "I don't think she was." She picked up the glass and took a quick swallow. "Jessica, well, she could be a little self-centered. She was lots of fun, of course, and when you're that age, sometimes that's all that matters. But if she'd lived, and I hate to say this, I don't think we would be such good friends today. She didn't treat some people very well."

"And that included Kevin?" Lia asked.

Lauren nodded. "I think he was starting to realize she was stringing him along, maybe even cheating on him. We were all at a party one time, Jessica and Kevin, my old boyfriend and me, and they had a fight. Kevin ended up storming out, and Rick and I had to give Jessica a ride home. She wasn't upset or worried, though. I remember she said—kinda snarkily—that he'd be back. Even back then I thought that was pretty cold."

Up until then, Nicole hadn't said anything negative about Jessica, but Lauren's comments seemed to have opened a door. "There were rumors, back in high school, about Jessica and Mr. Bernard," she said quietly.

Lauren winced at that but nodded. "Yeah."

"Who was Mr. Bernard?" Lia asked. She was picking up a new vibe from the two at the mention of the name.

"The French teacher," Nicole explained. "He was new to the school, young, and, well, kinda hot. A lot of us thought he was a little too flirty with the girls."

"Flirty?" Lia asked. "Lauren, you were close to Jessica. Did it go beyond flirty with her?"

"I really don't know," Lauren said. "Looking back I can see how bad that would have been. At the time it seemed exciting, I guess. But Jessica played it cool. She hinted but never said for sure. Maybe she was just teasing us all? I don't know. The funny thing, though . . ."

Lauren paused, staring down into her glass until Nicole prodded, "What?"

The other woman looked up. "A year after Jessica went off to Aymesburg, Mr. Bernard got a job offer to teach there. A definite step up for him, I'm sure. Jessica was the one who told me about it. He hadn't started there yet, so I don't know how she knew."

"How did she seem to feel about it?" Lia asked.

Lauren shifted in her chair. "I remember that she laughed. She said something like maybe she'd sign up for one of his classes, that she could use an easy A." Lauren looked at Lia unhappily. "Jessica wasn't very good in French."

The three of them were quiet for several moments, until the waiter came to ask if they needed anything. Lauren noticed the time. "Oh! I'd better go."

"I should, too," Nicole said.

"Thank you both for talking with me," Lia said. The

waiter produced the check and Lia quickly took it over the others' protests. As they got up to leave she said, "I just have one more question. My main reason for looking into Jessica's death is the similarity it had to Cori Littlefield's. Is there any other connection between the two that either of you are aware of?"

"Oh!" Lauren said. "I thought you knew."

"Knew what?" Lia asked.

"Jessica used to babysit for Cori. A lot." Lauren reached down for her craft fair bag. "The two of them got along really well. In fact, Jessica used to call Cori her little shadow."

Chapter 10

Monday morning, after Hayley had left for work, Lia pondered her next move. Lauren and Nicole had given her plenty of information about Jessica, including the link between Jessica and Cori. But which of those facts were important?

Cori's shadow box loomed in Lia's mind—that strange Jack and Jill tableau that put Jill at the bottom of the hill, a figure that Cori had called Jessica. And only hours after Cori had whisked it out of Lia's sight, she was lying at the bottom of Long Run Falls herself. Something was terribly wrong. But where should Lia start to uncover that?

Lia got up from her knitting chair to look into the mirror that hung on the wall next to her coat closet. Could her hair use a trim? Since she couldn't remember the last time she'd had one, the answer was *most likely*. Lia had never been overly concerned with her hair. Working as a surgical nurse had meant covering it most of the time, and she'd never fussed much with it otherwise. *Tidy* had been her main goal. But perhaps she'd slipped into frumpy? She was meeting the public now at the craft fair. It couldn't hurt to spruce up a bit. Aware that she was about to do exactly what she'd asked Hayley not to, Lia called for an appointment and hoped, while getting her hair done, that she'd learn a few things from Jessica's past friend Crystal Potter.

It turned out Mondays were slow at the hair salon. Lia was delighted to snag an appointment for eleven thirty that morning. On her way out, she saw her neighbor Sharon leaving the car she'd parked in front of her house. The silky tops of fresh corn peeked out of one of her bags.

"Looks like corn on the cob tonight," Lia called. "Farmers' market?"

"Yes!" Sharon grinned. "And fresh tomato and cucumber salad." She held up her second bag.

"Maybe I'll stop there on my way home. I'm off to get a haircut." Lia lifted a straggly end of her brown hair. "Any suggestions?"

Sharon laughed and ran her fingers through her no-nonsense cropped hair. "I'm the last person to ask about that. Something coming up?"

"No." Lia smiled. "It's more that I'm up to something." She explained her concerns about Jessica's and Cori's deaths. "On top of both being ruled accidental, Cori's sister has even suggested suicide. That just doesn't sit right with me." Sharon frowned, but as she opened her mouth to comment, Lia said, "I know what you're going to say, but this won't be anything like the last time. There'll be no risk taking, except"—Lia pointed to her hair with a grin—"maybe with how I end up looking today. But I can live with that. Hair grows."

Sharon rocked her head. "Just be careful, okay? And keep me updated. I felt bad about that poor woman, too. I mean Cori. I didn't know the other one."

"Maybe it will come to nothing," Lia said, though she didn't totally believe that. A secret had been buried in Crandalsburg for twenty-six years, she was sure. A secret that Cori had also kept but which might have led to her death. If that was true, Lia wanted justice to be done.

She was still thinking about that when Crystal Potter came up behind her chair at the salon.

"So, what are we doing today?" Crystal asked. Full-figured and with spiked, multicolored hair that looked both startling and professionally done, she gazed speculatively at Lia's own drab mop.

"Something simple," Lia said quickly. "Maybe just some shaping?"

Crystal shifted Lia's shoulder-length hair in different directions with splayed fingers and nodded. "Yeah, it needs that. How about a lot shorter? Maybe some highlights?"

"Maybe just an inch. I'll let those gray hairs sprinkled through be my highlights for now."

"Okay," Crystal said agreeably. "But think about it. You'd be surprised what a lift a mix of the right colors can give you. Let's get you shampooed."

Lia followed Crystal's lead through the modestly sized salon of four stations as she picked up the usual scents of hair spray and other products, noticing that only one other client occupied a chair that morning. Once she was installed in Crystal's chair, she chatted casually with the hair stylist as her scissors began to snip. Moving to Lia's subject of interest was easier than she'd expected, as Crystal soon asked what Lia did.

"I knit, and I manage the Ninth Street Knits booth at the Crandalsburg Craft Fair."

Crystal's face lit up. "I knit, too!" Then she wrinkled her nose. "Or I used to. I had to stop. Cutting hair all day, you know." She flexed her fingers. "Beginnings of arthritis. Doc said I shouldn't overdo." She ran a comb through Lia's damp locks, raised a section, and snipped at the ends. Her expression grew solemn. "A shame about that girl who did all the crochet stuff at the craft fair." She snipped some more. "I used to know her."

"You did?"

"Yeah, way back. I babysat for her sometimes, but I haven't seen her in years."

"Cori had the booth next to mine at the fair," Lia said.

"Oh yeah? What was she like all grown up? I sat for her when she was like three. After that I hardly ever saw her except in passing." Crystal switched to the other side of Lia's head.

"Cori was very sweet," Lia said. "Shy, but starting to come out of her shell, I thought. She'd become a real expert at crochet art, and she was excited at the response she was getting at the craft fair. I had the feeling it was the first time she had so much positive attention, and it was a little over-whelming."

Crystal nodded. "Yeah, that sounds like Cori. She was a good kid but pretty shy. I mean, hiding-under-the-bed shy. Funny how her older sister was the complete opposite."

"Robin?"

"Yeah, that was her name. She was a lot older than Cori. When I sat for them, Robin was around eleven. That's kind of an in-between age. You know, not old enough to be left alone but old enough to not like being babysat."

"That must have been a challenge for you," Lia said, "trying to find things to entertain both."

"Oh, Robin mostly sulked in her room," Crystal said, laughing. "Which was fine with me. The few times I tried to get her to join Cori and me, she ended up getting Cori upset. Robin could be pretty bossy. Typical, I guess, of older sisters," Crystal said with a grin. "Mine liked to tell me what to do until I got big enough to stand up for myself. I remember one time—" Crystal had to stop as she turned away to sneeze.

When she turned back, Lia quickly asked, "What was their mother like? Robin and Cori's."

"Mrs. Littlefield? She was nice. More like Cori than Robin, I'd say, meaning kind of quiet. Her second husband, Cori's father, died, you know. Some kind of accident."

"How sad," Lia said. "And Robin's father?"

"No idea," Crystal said. "But Mrs. Littlefield seemed to be okay, financially, I mean. She worked part-time, but they had a nice house and all. So that was good."

"You said you babysat Cori when she was three," Lia said. "Not after that?"

"Uh-uh. I got an after-school job working at a bakery. It paid better. One of my friends took over the babysitting."

"Was that Jessica Ackerman?"

Crystal's busy hands stopped as she looked at Lia's mirrored reflection in surprise. "It was! How did you know?"

"Nicole Griffin works at the craft fair, too. We talked about Jessica and how she had died in the same manner as Cori."

"Nicole? Yeah, I remember her from Crandalsburg High. Gosh, that's right about Jessica. I was at beauty school when I heard what happened to her. It was a real shock. But I didn't connect that with Cori until just now when you said that. But you know, how Jessica died always seemed strange to me."

"It did?"

"Uh-huh. I mean, why was Jessica up there at the falls? I could never understand that."

"She wasn't into hiking?"

"No, but it's not that so much. Getting to the falls wasn't a major hike, really. But there were other hiking trails, better ones, and much better views of the falls. The spot Jessica fell from was more neglected, and people mostly went there when they wanted privacy. You know, like kids who wanted to make out." Crystal ran her comb through Lia's hair before continuing, "But Jessica went there alone. That didn't make sense to me."

"How do you know that's the spot she fell from?" Lia asked.

"Because they found something of hers there. Her scarf. It wasn't in the papers, but Jessica's mom told me that at the funeral."

"I see." Lia tucked that interesting bit of information away. "So," she asked, "did Jessica babysit for Cori longer than you did?"

"Yeah, she liked babysitting. And it didn't tie her down as much as other jobs, I guess."

"I've heard how active Jessica was with the drama club."

Crystal nodded. "Oh yeah, she was a great actress."

Lia saw that her trim was nearing its finish. A blow-dry would come soon, making conversation difficult. Lia couldn't dawdle. "How about French?" she asked.

"French?" Crystal looked puzzled.

Thankfully, the stylist at another station turned on her

hair dryer, giving Lia's discussion more privacy. Lia still cautiously lowered her voice to avoid being overheard. "I understand there were rumors about the French teacher, Mr. Bernard, and Jessica." She gazed steadily at Crystal's reflection and added, "I'm not just being gossipy, Crystal. I have a very good reason, which has to do with both Jessica's and Cori's deaths."

"You don't think . . . ?" Crystal began.

"I don't think anything at this point. But learning as much as I can about both of them will help." Lia watched as Crystal appeared to mull that over.

"Jessica was a good friend to me back then," the hairdresser said slowly. "And she didn't do stupid things. But, yeah, there were rumors. I asked her right out one time. I said, 'Jess, what's going on? People are saying they saw you with Mr. B. out behind the bleachers. Alone!' She just laughed it off, but . . ." Crystal looked worriedly at Lia's reflection. "She never said it wasn't true.

"But," she continued, brightening a bit, "if there was something going on, at least it didn't last long. We graduated, and Jess went on to college. We kinda lost touch then, but I heard she had a boyfriend there. A regular one. Someone her age."

Yes, Lia thought to herself. *But then Mr. B. followed her to Aymesburg.*

At that point Crystal grabbed a brush and turned on the hair dryer, effectively putting an end to the discussion. Lia watched as her hairdo took shape—a very nice shape, it turned out, as it curled gently over her ears with bangs swept to one side—despite the distractions Lia had thrown Crystal's way.

By the time it was done, Crystal's next client had arrived. As Lia was settling her bill at the front counter, Crystal leaned closer to say, "Let me know what you come up with, I mean about Jessica and Cori, okay?"

"I will," Lia promised. "And thank you for your help. Would you keep this to yourself for now, please? As I said, I don't know if anything will come of my poking around."

Crystal nodded. "I hope it'll be nothing, actually. *Accident* sits with me much better than anything else. But if not, their families deserve the truth."

Lia couldn't agree more. She stepped aside to make way for the waiting client, then smiled as she caught sight of her stylish new do in the mirror. Sometimes, she thought to herself, risks paid off and snooping came with side benefits.

Chapter 11

After leaving Crystal's Cuts and Curls, Lia drove to the farmers' market on the outskirts of Crandalsburg, having been inspired by Sharon's bounty. As she browsed through the bins of peaches, green beans, and tomatoes, she caught a startling sight: Belinda, filling her own bags with vegetables! Belinda, whose idea of cooking was transferring a prepackaged dinner from her freezer to the microwave!

Lia sidled up to Belinda and asked, "What do you intend to do with those?" She nodded toward Belinda's bag of yellow squash.

Belinda caught her breath, then grinned. "Cook them, of course. Where did you come from?"

"From the tomato bin," Lia said. "Next to, not in. You'll be cooking yellow squash?"

"Why is that so surprising? I do cook once in a while," Belinda said defensively. For a day off and for shopping at

a farmers' market she was dressed rather nicely, Lia noticed, in a navy linen tunic over white capris, an outfit that
flattered her sturdy frame.

"Oh, you do, do you?" Lia teased. "Let me see, what was
the date of that dinner at your place? Two thousand fifteen?
Or was it sixteen?"

"Ha-ha," Belinda said dryly. "It so happens that someone at the book club last night brought a very tasty squash
casserole. She had printed up copies of the recipe to pass
around, and I thought I'd try it."

"Good for you," Lia said.

"What's good? The squash or my cooking it?"

"Both," Lia said, smiling.

"Hey," Belinda said suddenly. "Do you want to go somewhere for lunch when we're finished here? I have a cooler
in the car. We can leave all our stuff in it while we eat."

"You do?"

"Yeah, I was going to grab lunch and make a few other
stops. The car gets too hot for things like this."

"That sounds perfect, then." They agreed on Marie's,
the diner Brady had once taken Lia to for an impromptu
dinner, which she'd revisited several times since. She enjoyed the food and its quick, friendly service. Belinda, having several errands on her schedule, didn't have time to
linger, so quick worked for her.

Lia finished her shopping, then filled most of the space
in Belinda's cooler as Belinda added only her yellow squash
and two peaches. They then took off to meet up at Marie's,
snagging a table at the popular eatery.

Once they'd ordered, Lia asked, "Does this book club of
yours meet every week? If so, that's a pretty short time to
read a book."

"No, it's usually once a month. But we discussed a short-

story anthology this time—we could pick our own story—
so last night was a special meeting."

"I see." Lia took a sip of her ice water. "And did they
pick a book more to your taste for next month?"

Belinda laughed. "It was Chad's turn to pick, and he ran
it by me first, so yes, I think I'll like it."

"Ah, he ran it by you," Lia said, her eyes dancing.

"Don't go reading anything into that, Lia. We just happen to be on the same, uh, page as far as our reading goes.
No pun intended."

"Uh-huh." Lia reached for a packet of crackers and
ripped it open. "Are you planning to eat that squash casserole all on your own?"

"Well, no. Chad's going to grill some chicken breasts,
and I'm bringing the side dish."

"He said he liked it, didn't he?" Lia tried to keep from
grinning.

"Oh, stop it, Lia!" Belinda laughed. "We seem to get
along, and that's all I care about for now. With my history
of picking terrible matches, I'm not looking any further
ahead than being with someone I can get along with reasonably well, at least for this week."

"That's probably wise, though your history, as you call
it, concerns only one man: Darren," Lia said, referring to
Belinda's late ex-husband.

"Yeah, but that was a doozy, wouldn't you agree?"

The waitress brought their food, and Lia waited until all
the plates and bowls had been set down. "I have to admit he
was." She was thinking about all the lies and double dealing Darren had gotten away with before Belinda eventually
caught on. "But it's over, and you're much wiser now,
right?"

Belinda snorted softly but didn't argue. They both

turned to their food for a couple of minutes, then Belinda said, "Your hair looks nice, by the way. What did you do?"

"Got it trimmed. It needed it, but I also wanted to talk to the woman who runs the shop." Lia explained about Jessica, her connection to Cori, and what she'd found out so far, including from her hairdresser.

"You're getting involved in another murder case? After what happened with Darren's death?"

"I'm not getting involved," Lia protested. "And it's not clear if there's even been a murder. I'm simply not satisfied with how things stand right now." She smiled a little, adding, "It's kind of like spotting one stitch in a knit scarf that's out of sync. Any good knitter would want to unravel the few rows above to go down there and fix it. But if I find anything about Jessica's or Cori's death that is out of sync with the official call of accidental, I'll turn it over to the police and let them deal with it."

"Okay, then," Belinda said, though she looked skeptical. "I lost two of my vendors in the past few weeks, which was bad enough. I wouldn't like it if another vendor, who happens to be my best friend, put herself in any kind of jeopardy."

Lia was touched. Belinda so rarely expressed such feelings that Lia reached out for her hand. "Thank you," she said. "But I promise to keep well away from any hint of danger." As she released her friend's hand and returned to her lunch, Lia mused that Belinda's softer side seemed to be coming out more lately. Was it possibly Chad's influence? If so, Lia rooted for the success of that relationship one hundred percent.

When Hayley returned home that evening, the aroma of Lia's freshly baked peach cobbler welcomed her. "Oh wow!" she said, sniffing the air.

"And that's not all," Lia said, pleased with what she'd accomplished that day. "We'll have an herb-and-onion to-mato salad to go with our meat loaf and picked-this-morning corn on the cob. That is, as soon as you help me shuck them," Lia said.

"Yum." Hayley picked up Daphne and carried her into the kitchen. Several bagged ears of corn sat on the counter. She shifted Daphne to her hip in order to lean over and take a peek at the meat loaf baking in the oven. "Looks like there's plenty for one more. What would you think of me inviting Brady to join us?"

"Go right ahead! I'd enjoy seeing him."

Hayley carried Daphne back to the couch and got busy texting, but after a few minutes she reported that Brady would come later for dessert. "He already grabbed a burger with some friends but says the peach cobbler sounds great." Hayley grinned. "Along with seeing us, of course."

"Of course," Lia agreed with a smile. She put a large pot of water on the stove to start heating as Hayley took the corn and a paper bag for the shucked bits to the back-yard.

Before long they were savoring their meal, one of the treats summer bestowed that balanced the negatives of high heat and humidity. By the time they had readied the table for dessert, they heard friendly knocks on the door.

"Perfect timing," Hayley said, welcoming Brady with a hug.

"Coffee, iced coffee, iced tea, or other?" Lia called from the dining area.

"Iced tea, please, Mrs. Geiger." Brady stepped in, look-ing as tanned as his fair redhead's complexion allowed. His arm had long been out of a sling, and he'd regained much of the weight he'd lost while in the hospital. The tee shirt he wore tucked into his jeans outlined muscles that he'd been working hard to get back into shape.

Lia handled the drinks, while Hayley cut into the peach cobbler, whose cinnamony scent had spread throughout the house. Daphne, as usual, circled and bumped against Brady's ankles, a sign of the major effect he'd had on her from the start, much to the amusement of both Hayley and Lia. It had disconcerted Brady at first, but he'd become used to it since then.

He crouched down to pet Daphne, chuckling lightly at her apparent excitement. But when Hayley called him to the table, Brady said, "Sink first," and held up his hands to show the cat hair Daphne had gifted him with.

The three dug into their dessert, chatting casually. Lia asked Brady about his job, and he groaned over the boredom of the desk work he was still stuck with. "But it might be only a couple more weeks. By the way," he said, glancing at Hayley, "Brooke's sister came by today."

"Erin?" Hayley asked.

Lia heard a tightness in her voice, but Brady only said, "Uh-huh," his attention on his plate.

"Why was Erin there?" Hayley asked.

"Hmm? Oh, she brought in some gadget Brooke is borrowing. And a box of chocolate chip cookies she'd made herself. She passed them around."

With Hayley maintaining a silence, Lia said, "That was nice of her."

"Yeah, they were good!" Brady scooped up another forkful of his cobbler.

"So, are you still going to physical therapy?" Lia asked, glancing at Hayley's stiff frown.

"No, I can do the exercises at home now." Brady described a couple of them. He then asked politely about the craft fair. When Lia said her own booth was doing well but mentioned the death of one of the vendors recently, he said, "I heard about that. Was she someone you knew well?"

"I was just beginning to get to know her," Lia said. "Her death was a shock to us all."

Hayley jumped in to say, "Mom doesn't think it was accidental."

When Brady looked at Lia questioningly, she said, "What Hayley means is that I'm not *convinced* it was accidental."

"Why not?" he asked.

Lia paused. She didn't feel that what little she knew at that point warranted a report to the police, but discussing it with Brady could be helpful. Yes, he was relatively new to the force, but he was bright and had specialized training she didn't. Lia laid out the information she'd gathered about Cori and Jessica, then asked, "What do you think? Am I mistaken?"

Brady let his fork droop, apparently mulling over what she'd said, finally saying, "I don't really know. Everything you tell me is intriguing. But an awful lot of it depends on the accuracy of people's memories, as well as their truthfulness."

"I realize that," Lia admitted. "It's also early days, since I've just begun to poke around."

"Right," Brady said. "But the two deaths happening in the same way is odd." He paused. "I could run it by my supervisors if you like. Get their thoughts on it."

"That'd be great," Hayley said. "Don't you think, Mom?"

"I do, and I'd appreciate that, Brady," Lia said. "I'm sure an official investigation could do much better than I can."

"If they decide to launch one," Brady cautioned.

Lia heard the doubt in Brady's voice but decided to be hopeful. Surely the police had looked into cases with less evidence than what Lia had to give them. And if they didn't, well . . . she'd think about that when she had to.

Chapter 12

Having put her investigation into Brady's hands for the time being, Lia turned her thoughts to everyday things. It helped that she got a call the next morning from one of her craft fair regulars with a knitting request.

"Remember we talked about that cardigan sweater?" Helen Chandler asked.

Lia didn't have to think hard to remember the discussion. Helen had spent at least an hour with Lia, asking questions about alpaca yarn and poring over several of the pattern books Lia kept on hand at her booth. Helen thought she'd found what she wanted but had told Lia she'd like to sleep on it, just to be sure.

"Have you decided?" Lia asked.

"I have. Let's go with that cardigan with the chevron pattern."

"Excellent. And the colors?"

"I loved the colors in the picture," Helen said. "The deep

red of the body looked great with the off-white of the chevron pattern. Do you think you can find them?"

"I'm pretty sure I can," Lia said. "The Weber Alpaca Farm has a huge selection. You did want it made from alpaca yarn, didn't you?"

"I do. I want something to keep me warm but not be heavy and bulky. You said alpaca yarn would work for that."

"Absolutely. It's lightweight, and so much softer than sheep's wool," Lia said, delighted to have another chance to work with her favorite yarn.

They worked out the timing and deposit, and Lia hung up soon with a smile on her face. She immediately pulled out the cowl scarf she'd been working on, which, thankfully, she was close to finishing. The scarf wasn't a special order—she'd meant it as an eventual addition to the craft fair booth—but Lia never liked to leave a project unfinished. As much as she would enjoy knitting the cardigan for Helen—and she'd truly love it—the unfinished cowl scarf would tug at the back of her mind. So she got busy on the final rows while listening to her audio mystery book, a glass of iced tea on one side of her chair and Daphne dozing on the other.

She became so absorbed that the sudden ring of her phone made her jump. Daphne simply opened one sleepy eye as Lia reached for the phone. Seeing the caller's name, Lia quickly swiped to answer.

"Hello, Brady. You have something to tell me?"

"Hi, Mrs. Geiger. Yes, I'm afraid so."

Uh-oh.

"They're sticking with accident as the cause of death for Cori Littlefield. They didn't see any reason to change it or to take a second look at Jessica Ackerman's death."

Lia sighed.

"At least for now," Brady added quickly. "If you had come up with something more concrete on either one of the women, that might have made a difference."

"Yes. Kind of hard to come up with evidence of a murderous push, though, isn't it? I'm guessing there are no CCTV cameras set up on hiking trails," Lia said.

"No," Brady said. "But if it helps, I think there's something fishy about both deaths, and I think you're right to question them."

"That's good to hear, Brady."

"But I also can't recommend that you go around questioning people when you could be talking to a murderer at some point."

"So I should leave it up to the police?" Lia asked and heard a sigh.

"I know. All I can suggest is to give it some time," Brady said. "They might change their minds."

Not without more to go on, Lia thought. *And how will they get that except from me?* But she said, "Thank you for trying, Brady."

She hung up and looked at Daphne, who was staring up at her. "Never mind, Daph. I'll figure something out."

When Hayley came home that night, Lia told her about Brady's call.

"Bummer." Hayley plopped on the sofa next to Daphne, bouncing the cat enough to make her grumpily reset her position. "They're wrong, you know. When Brady makes detective, he'll show them."

"I doubt that's how it works," Lia said. "But I also don't

want to wait, not that I think that would be terribly long," she added.

Hayley grinned. "His friend Brooke is studying for the exam. But she's been on the force longer than Brady." Hayley frowned then, as though reminded of something unpleasant.

Lia guessed what that might be. "Last night it seemed you didn't like hearing about Brooke's sister showing up at the station."

"Erin," Hayley said flatly. "Yeah." She reached over to scratch at Daphne's head for a moment, then looked up. "She didn't need to go there to give her sister whatever it was. They live two blocks apart, for gosh sakes! And bringing chocolate chip cookies? The whole thing was such a ploy."

"A ploy?" Lia asked.

"To see Brady again."

"Ah."

"At the cookout last Friday," Hayley said, "she kept hanging around us but talking to him, not me. Then at badminton, it was, 'Oh, Brady, what a great shot!' and 'I want to be Brady's partner next game. He's so good!'" Hayley made a gagging gesture. "It was so obvious."

"I can see how annoying that would be," Lia said. "The important thing is how Brady reacted."

"He was fine," Hayley conceded. "Oblivious, you might say. But that kind of thing . . . if it keeps up . . . it has to have some effect, don't you think?"

"Perhaps you should talk to Brady about it," Lia suggested.

Hayley chewed her lip at the thought but made no comment. So Lia left it at that.

After a brief quiet time, Hayley said, "You said you

didn't want to wait for the police to do something about the deaths. So you're going to keep working at it?"

"I think I have to." Lia stilled her knitting to think. "I have the names of several people I'd like to talk to."

"Like who?"

"There's Tiffany Hurst. She competed with Jessica for dramatic roles all through high school and then in college. I mean *really* competed, from the sound of it."

"Enough to make her kill?" Hayley wondered.

"That's the question. But it wasn't just Tiffany. Losing good roles to Jessica apparently drove her mother wild, too."

"Hah, the classic stage mother," Hayley said.

"Sounded like it." Lia set her needles in motion again.

"But still . . . ," Hayley said, apparently ready to argue, until something struck her. "Wait! Wasn't there a case . . ." Hayley grabbed her phone and started typing rapidly. "Yes! The cheerleader mom. Some years ago she hired, or wanted to hire, a hit man to kill the mother of another cheerleader that her daughter was competing with. Think Tiffany's mom might have hired a hit man?"

"I have no idea, Hayley, and frankly that scenario didn't occur to me. Where would someone find a hit man in Crandalsburg?" Lia asked.

"I can ask Brady," Hayley said. "But hit men can travel like anybody else. If this mom had connections . . ."

"Now that I think of it, that could have happened," Lia admitted. "Technically speaking, I mean. But it still seems a bit far-fetched for Crandalsburg."

"Not really," Hayley argued. "Just because a community is small doesn't mean there's no wackos in it. Although," she added, "I guess they'd have a harder time not being noticed."

"Right," Lia agreed. "They'd have to work at it. But it's

still very possible for people to hide their darker side from others."

"So you'll put Tiffany and her mother at the top of your list?" Hayley got up and headed to the kitchen.

"For now," Lia said. "The order might shift as I dig up more about the others." Hearing the clink of things being shifted in the refrigerator, she called out, "If you're looking for something to drink, there's lemonade in the green pitcher."

"Perfect!" Hayley called back. "Want some?"

Lia declined. After Hayley had returned, they both sat quietly for some minutes before Lia said, "There's an instructor at Aymesburg College named Marc Bernard. I checked online, and he's still on the staff." She described what she'd learned about Bernard from Jessica's old friends.

"Sounds like a creep," Hayley said.

"Another example of a someone able to hide a darker side of themselves," Lia said, quickly adding, "Assuming what I've been told about the man is true. So far it's been hints and rumors. I'd like confirmation. But I obviously can't get it from him."

"Aymesburg?" Hayley asked. "There's a girl working at the Weber farm for the summer who goes there. Maybe she can help you. Want me to ask?"

Lia brightened. "Yes, please do! I was going to go there for yarn—I have a commission for an alpaca yarn sweater—and could meet with her then, if she's agreeable."

"I think she'd be fine, but I'll check with her about the French instructor and let you know what comes of it. Hey! A new sweater commission—good for you! And good for our alpacas, I guess."

"I'm always happy to keep them in the business of growing fiber," Lia said with a grin.

Hayley's phone chirped. She checked her text messages and frowned. "Bethanne King—again. Well, she can just wait till tomorrow for an answer. I'm officially off duty." With that, Hayley got up and headed up the stairs. "I think I'll go for a run as I listen to my playlist and think pleasant thoughts. Which means anything but Bethanne King!"

Chapter 13

The next morning, Lia mulled over how she could contrive to meet Tiffany, Jessica's onetime rival. She checked the high school's website and saw that although the school wasn't yet open for students, teachers were on duty for meetings and preparation. The site had a staff list with photos, and Lia studied Tiffany Hurst's. Certain that she could recognize the woman in person, Lia thought she might try waiting outside the school around three o'clock to catch Tiffany on her way out. It was iffy but it was the best Lia could come up with.

That left her several hours, which she could spend at the alpaca farm. Hayley had sent her an all-systems-go text concerning the summer worker she'd mentioned, which Lia took to mean that the girl had some knowledge about Marc Bernard and was willing to share it with her.

Lia reviewed the directions for the sweater she'd be making for Helen, checking on the required needle sizes.

Satisfied that she owned them, she slipped the pattern book into her tote to help in picking the yarn colors. Just the thought of searching through the yarn shop at the farm gave Lia a little thrill, and she thanked her lucky stars once again for leading her to the craft fair, which gave her wonderful knitting opportunities she would never have found on her own.

Lia's drive to the farm was as lovely as always, winding through miles of farmland once she left Crandalsburg. There were acres of cornfields, occasional cow pastures, and well-kept farmhouses and barns, a few looking as old and historical as the craft fair barn. She took the turnoff for the Weber farm and before long spotted alpacas in the distance, a sight that would have startled the original owners of those older farms she'd passed but which only made Lia smile in anticipation.

Lia sent Hayley a quick text through her car's Bluetooth system to announce her imminent arrival and was rewarded with the sight of her daughter walking toward her as Lia pulled into the farm's parking area.

"I hope I'm not interrupting your work," Lia said as she climbed out.

"No, I'm good," Hayley assured her.

Lia glanced around, her hand shielding the sun from her eyes. "Where will the fundraising event be set up?"

"In the pasture over there." Hayley pointed to a large fenced area where several alpacas were grazing. "We'll bring the herd into the corral next to the barn that day. People can come in a few at a time to pet them, take photos, and hear our spiel about care and feeding and such. The games and food trucks will be at the farther end of the big pasture to keep the noise from upsetting our sweet guys."

Lia caught Hayley's use of *our* when referring to the alpacas. It hinted at how close she'd grown to her job. Though Hayley had taken a salary cut when she'd switched from the big Philadelphia marketing firm, she was clearly much happier at the Weber farm. She'd talked her way into creating a position for herself that the Webers hadn't had before, and Lia knew how hard she was working to show that they hadn't made a mistake. This fundraiser could be a make-or-break event for Hayley's job, stressful enough without the added pressure of someone like Bethanne King.

"Was the text Mrs. King sent last night anything important?" she asked as they crunched over the parking lot's gravel to get to the farm buildings.

Hayley sighed. "Just another reminder for me to check on something I've already done and which, of course, she already reminded me of—making sure we'd have giant balloons to mark both the turnoff and the farm entrance." Hayley smiled then. "They'll be cute, though, with big smiley alpaca faces!"

"Sounds perfect," Lia said. As they closed in on the barn she asked about Ava, the college student she'd come to meet. "Will this be a good time for her?"

"We'll see. If not, you'll be around for a while, right? Picking out your yarn?"

"Right," Lia agreed. "And she's okay about talking to me about this?"

Hayley paused just outside the barn to answer. "I explained why you wanted to know about this French instructor. But I saw a look in her eyes when I said his name. I think there's something she wants to share."

Lia nodded and followed Hayley into the barn. Inside, two large fans were blowing, apparently there to cool the animals as several maneuvered to stand in the air stream. Lia smiled at the look on some of the alpacas' faces as they did so, their lips curling back from their front teeth with pleasure. In the spring, they had all been sheared of their fleece to make them more comfortable during the hot summer months. But by August their coats had grown enough for the animals to need help with the heat. Lia reached over a gate to rub the fuzzy head of a friendly tan alpaca.

"That's Patsy," Hayley said. "And over there's Rosie. Remember my special bud Rosie?" She pointed to a fawn-colored alpaca. She named others in the area, some a darker brown and one black with a cream-colored face. Lia knew portions of their shorn fiber would be left natural when spun into yarn, but much of it would be dyed to a broad range of colors—a boon to all knitters.

Hayley was glancing around, looking for Ava, when Lia called her attention to a young woman out in the corral who was spraying an almost-white alpaca's belly with a water hose. "That's her," Hayley said and led the way to the barn's opened back.

"Hey, Ava," Hayley called out. "This is my mom. Can you take a break soon?"

The young woman in a Weber Farm green tee and jeans shut off her hose. "Sure. Give me five minutes. I'll come inside, okay? It'll be cooler."

Lia liked that idea and went back into the barn with Hayley to enjoy the fans along with the alpacas.

"Mind if I take off?" Hayley asked. "I've got a couple of calls to make."

"Go right ahead," Lia said. "No need to wait around."

"I also think Ava might be a little more comfortable talking privately about what she knows," Hayley said. "She's a good kid. You can trust what she says. Oh, and she's a nursing student. I mentioned that you were a nurse," she added. "Just for, you know, a little connection."

"Thanks, Hayley." Lia watched her daughter go off, aware of an air of maturity in her that wasn't always apparent off the job. Hayley's referring to Ava as a kid also made Lia smile, since there might be only three or four years between them. Three or four life-changing years, she reminded herself. Ava was rolling up her hose, so Lia headed over to an alpaca that was stretching its head out of the stall toward her and petted its curly head, enjoying the friendly encounter. In a minute she saw the girl coming her way.

"Hi, Mrs. Geiger," Ava said as she drew near. "It's nice to meet you. Sorry to keep you waiting." She waved to a bench in a corner. "We can sit down if you don't mind getting a little dusty."

"Not at all, Ava," Lia said and headed over. "I appreciate your talking with me, and I'll try not to take up too much of your time."

"That's okay." Ava lifted her light brown ponytail and fanned the back of her neck. Her blue eyes stood out brightly against her tanned and slightly flushed skin. "We're not exactly punching time clocks here. As long as we get our work done, the Webers are fine with it. I love working here. It's the best summer job I've ever had."

"Hayley said you're studying nursing. You won't switch to alpaca breeding?" Lia asked with a smile.

Ava laughed. "No, I love nursing, too. But I'll keep visiting these guys after I get a hospital job."

"That's good. We need dedicated nurses. Hayley explained that I have questions about Marc Bernard, the French instructor at your college. Were you in any of his classes?"

"I wasn't," Ava said. "I had four years of Spanish in high school. But I have friends who were, and I picked up a lot of things about Mr. Bernard from them." She wrinkled her nose. "Not-so-great things."

"I've already heard from women who were high school students when he taught at that level," Lia said. "This was twenty-six years ago, and he was a young, attractive teacher. There were apparently rumors about inappropriate behavior on his part with high school–aged girls."

"Wow," Ava said. "And no action was taken?"

"Not that I'm aware of. That kind of thing was handled differently then. Rumors weren't enough, I suppose. Assuming they were true," Lia added.

"I wouldn't bet against them," Ava said. "Those friends of mine took his class in their first year. Most of the kids in it were just out of high school. He's probably in his late forties now, but still pretty hot and loaded with personality. My friends said he closed in on the most naive girls, the ones with the least defenses. And," she added with disgust, "those least likely to cause him any trouble with the administration.

"I got to know this one girl through my friend Sara," she continued. "She's been seeing Mr. Bernard for a few months. Between us we tried to convince her to break up and report him, but we got nowhere. The girl couldn't bring herself to do it."

"That's unfortunate." Lia paused. "Do you think she would talk to me?"

Ava looked skeptical. "I don't know. But maybe Sara and I can convince her."

"Thanks, Ava. I think it would be good for this young woman. But she'll have to see it that way."

"I know," Ava agreed sadly. She glanced over at the corral, where one of the alpacas was pacing near the open doorway.

Lia stood. "I shouldn't hold you up from your work any longer."

Ava smiled. "It looks like Zsa Zsa wants her turn at a hosing down." She got up from the bench. "I'll let you know if I can set anything up with this girl." She held up crossed fingers. "Wish me luck!"

Lia watched her head off to the corral and an eager Zsa Zsa, indeed wishing her luck on her mission. She dusted off her pants then, and headed off for her own, much pleasanter task—picking out yarn for her newly commissioned sweater.

Chapter 14

Lia was browsing in the yarn shop when Hayley came up to her.

"How's your shopping going? Time for a quick lunch with me?"

"Oh! Yes, absolutely. I already picked out what I need. I just couldn't stop looking."

"Great," Hayley said. "I'll grab us a table while you settle up."

A few minutes later, Lia pulled out a chair across from her daughter and dropped her bag of precious yarn on an adjoining one. After a young waitress scurried away with their sandwich and drink orders, Hayley said, "This place is small, so fast service means patrons turn over quickly."

"Makes sense," Lia said. "Will it be open during your fundraising event?"

"Nope. The food trucks will handle all the food. Oh,

that reminds me, I better check with the ice cream vendor. There was some trouble with his truck, last we spoke." Hayley whipped out her phone and dictated a reminder note into it.

"Plenty of things to keep track of, huh?"

Hayley rolled her eyes and nodded. "How did it go with Ava?"

"Quite well. She had some interesting things to share about our French teacher." The waitress brought their orders, and Lia paused. Once they were left alone, she gave Hayley the gist of her conversation with the young college student.

"Marc Bernard sounds like a creep," Hayley said. "I'm glad I didn't run into any professors like that at my schools."

"And I'm extremely glad to know that," Lia said. "Ava told me about a particular girl who has reason to report Bernard but was reluctant to. If Ava can convince her to talk to us, would you be willing to come with me? She might feel more comfortable talking to someone closer to her age."

"Absolutely!"

"Good. If nothing else, we might be able to put a stop to Bernard's behavior. Maybe we can learn something useful about him, too." She shared her thoughts on why Bernard might have had strong motives for eliminating Jessica.

"Yeah," Hayley said. "She could have been a problem. From what you told me about her, Jessica wasn't someone who could be easily manipulated."

"No," Lia agreed. "Her comment to her friend Lauren about being assured an easy A if she took Bernard's class tells me she wasn't above using what she knew about the instructor to her benefit."

"A dangerous game to play with the wrong person," Hayley said.

Indeed.

After lunch, Hayley went back to the farm office and Lia headed to her car. It was too soon to catch Tiffany at the high school, but there was time to stop at the farmers' market for more corn.

Unfortunately for Lia, shopping at a farmers' market was very close to browsing at the yarn shop, and besides corn, she ended up with several bags of fresh vegetables and fruit, including a honeydew melon that the clerk helped her choose for ripeness. As she loaded it all in her car, Lia remembered how Belinda had the foresight to bring a cooler to protect her produce from the heat. Not having planned as wisely, Lia realized she'd better get her purchases into a refrigerator. So she zipped home quickly to unload her bounty before her hoped-for talk with Tiffany.

That delay, plus being slowed by unexpectedly heavy traffic, unfortunately meant that by the time she made it to the high school, teachers were already leaving the building. Had she missed Tiffany? Lia peered through her windshield as a stream of educators walked to their cars, able to eliminate the men but fearing she wouldn't identify Tiffany in time—if she hadn't already left. Then she spotted a woman with dark blond hair worn in a shoulder-length bob, just like the photo Lia had seen on the school's website.

Lia jumped out of her car to intercept her, but Tiffany's car was close to the school building. Before Lia could reach her, Tiffany had hopped in and driven off. Lia stood helplessly watching the car head toward the exit, then shook herself. If she couldn't speak to Jessica's former rival at work, she'd do so at the woman's home. Lia hopped back into her car to catch up, assuming that was where she'd be heading.

Tiffany, however, had other plans. Within minutes Lia realized they were heading to Cranberry Hill, the large shopping mall just outside Crandalsburg. She decided to continue following and see what came up.

Tiffany pulled into the mall and parked in the Macy's lot. Lia had to circle a bit to find a spot and then hurry through rows of cars on heat-radiating pavement. As she rushed into the store, the air-conditioning was a welcome relief. Lia looked around anxiously. With no sign of Tiffany, Lia began heading toward a nearby women's clothing area but then spotted the familiar figure exiting the store into one of the mall's inner concourses.

Fortunately for Lia, who needed to quick-step to catch up, Tiffany paused once outside the store to scan passersby and seated patrons. Lia watched from several feet behind, then saw a hand wave from across the way. It belonged to an older woman standing next to a jewelry store entrance. Tiffany immediately waved back and headed over while Lia tagged behind at a discreet distance. She was close enough to hear the older woman's greeting, called out in a sharp, piercing tone as Tiffany neared.

"Tiffany! Is that how you dress for work?" Lia noticed Tiffany stiffen a moment before continuing on.

"It's only teacher preparation day, Mother."

"You should always look your best." The woman Tiffany addressed as "Mother" had certainly made the effort herself, wearing a navy linen dress with heels and pearls. Her white hair looked professionally coifed. Her makeup was tasteful and well applied, though Lia felt a pleasanter expression would have meant much more than the perfect shades of blush and lip gloss.

"Come look at this ring," the woman said, ordering, not requesting, as she turned into the jewelry store, expecting her daughter to dutifully follow, which she did.

As Lia held back, pretending to window-shop but keeping an eye on the two, she pulled up Tiffany's last name from her memory: Hurst. Lia also remembered that Mrs. Hurst had been described by Nicole and Lauren as creating major fusses with the high school drama department whenever Tiffany was deprived of what she thought was her daughter's due. From this first impression at the mall, Lia could believe it.

The mother and daughter left the jewelry store after a few minutes without buying, Mrs. Hurst complaining that she hadn't been offered a discount. "After all the business I've given them!"

"Perhaps that was a new employee," Tiffany suggested.

"If the manager had been on the premises, I would have seen to it that it was that man's last day. Incompetent fool. Let's go to that new dress shop that's opened. Maybe we can find you something more decent to wear."

"Mother—"

Lia lost the rest of Tiffany's response as they moved off, but if it was any kind of protest, it was apparently useless. She watched the two head down the concourse and decided to stay with them. Though Lia was not normally an eavesdropper, the opportunity to catch unguarded words from two women who had played a part in Jessica's life— possibly a greater one than anyone knew—overcame all proprieties.

Once in the dress shop, Lia tried her best to stay close to the pair among the racks, though all she managed to pick up from their conversation was clothes related and increasingly annoying. Mrs. Hurst tossed out multiple negative comments about Tiffany's fashion sense, or lack thereof, along with suggestions for weight loss. But Tiffany, Lia noticed, didn't seemed particularly bothered by it, responding more and more robotically, as though she'd heard most of it before, which, by the age of forty-five, she probably had.

She agreed to try on a few things that her mother pushed at her, though with little enthusiasm. Lia grabbed a dress at random to follow when the two walked off to the fitting rooms.

From her dressing room, Lia could hear the pair converse through Tiffany's door as Mrs. Hurst demanded reports on her daughter's progress. After Tiffany stepped out to model her outfits for her mother in front of the large mirror at the end of the aisle, Mrs. Hurst proclaimed two outfits to be acceptable. What Tiffany's opinion was, Lia never heard, but as the younger woman changed back into her own clothes, they discussed where they would head for dinner and agreed on a restaurant at the mall for convenience.

That presented Lia with another decision: to follow along or let them be. At that point she hadn't learned anything interesting other than the surprising meekness of Tiffany Hurst, whom she'd pictured as a combative rival to Jessica. So far, it appeared her mother was the one who'd done all the scrapping. Tiffany must have had talent to get as far as she had, but perhaps not as much as her mother thought. Obviously not enough to win Broadway or film roles. What a disappointment it must have been, a disappointment for which Tiffany was apparently still being punished.

The pair left the fitting rooms to pay for Tiffany's outfits. Lia waited a beat, then followed behind. She'd made up her mind to stay with them. But had she been noticed? Returning her dress to its rack, she glanced around, then spotted a light summer cardigan. Enough to alter her look? Perhaps, along with slipping on her driving glasses and doing something different to her hair.

Though Tiffany and her mother left before Lia paid for her cardigan, she knew where they were going and would have no problem catching up to them. After that, it might be a little harder.

Chapter 15

"Table for one?" the young hostess asked a trifle pityingly as Lia stood before her. She'd donned the new cardigan over what she'd worn to the alpaca farm, which was a pair of cutoffs and a tee, a little dusty but not too bad. But she'd pinned her hair back unflatteringly and donned the driving glasses, whose frames she'd picked some time ago by cost rather than style.

"Yes," Lia confirmed. "One." She looked past the hostess and spotted Tiffany and Mom seated in a booth. The one next to them was gloriously unoccupied. "I'd like to sit there," she said, pointing.

"We have tables—," the hostess began, probably considering a booth to be a waste of space for one person. But Lia stood firm and was reluctantly led to her place of choice, covering an overlooked, dangling price tag a little awkwardly and sliding onto the bench that backed up against Tiffany's.

She took the menu with a grateful smile and leaned back to see what she could pick up from the adjoining booth. Mrs. Hurst was spewing a string of complaints about a neighbor, nothing of interest to Lia, who was only happy that she could overhear. She pulled out her phone to text Hayley not to wait for her for dinner, then looked over the menu for something soft and quiet to eat. Soup would have to be it—not her first choice on a hot summer day, but the air-conditioning was blowing hard enough to make her glad of her new cardigan.

When her order came, Lia slowly spooned her tomato bisque, barely tasting it as she concentrated on the conversation going on behind her. For a long while, it remained uninteresting and dominated by Mrs. Hurst. At one point the older woman did go silent after saying she needed to send a text, which Lia thought must have been a welcome relief to her daughter. Apparently it gave Tiffany a little time to gather her own thoughts, because after a few moments of quiet time, Tiffany brought up a subject that perked up Lia's ears.

"You know that accident that happened last week?"

"Hmm?" Mrs. Hurst said absently. "What accident?"

"That woman who fell into Long Run Falls."

"Oh, that. What about it? It wasn't anyone we knew." Mrs. Hurst sounded irritable.

"It's just that it made me think of Jessica. You remember? Jessica Ackerman?"

"Yes, I remember Jessica Ackerman! Why would you think about her? That was years ago!"

"I know, Mother. But she died in the exact same way, falling from the same spot. It seemed so strange."

"What's strange about it?" her mother argued. "A lot of people fell from there. It's a dangerous spot. It should have been roped off years ago. But anyone with common sense would have known not to go too close to the edge."

"Jessica had common sense," Tiffany countered softly. "And it's not true, Mother, that many people died falling from that same place. Only Jessica and this latest one, Cori Littlefield."

"Since when did you become such an expert on Long Run Falls accidents? Or about Jessica Ackerman, for that matter? That girl, whether you knew it or not, was an air-headed, conniving, no-talent—"

Mrs. Hurst stopped as their waitress came up to their table. "How's everything?" the server asked, her cheery voice carrying to Lia. "Can I get you anything? Ready for dessert?"

"No, we're not ready for dessert!" Mrs. Hurst snapped. "I'll let you know when we are."

"Ohh-key dokey," the woman said, her voice a little shaky and a lot less cheery. Lia cringed, picturing a tight smile on her face.

"Speaking of airheaded . . . ," Mrs. Hurst grumbled as the waitress walked away but hadn't made it out of hearing distance.

"She was very talented," Tiffany said.

"What? Who?" her mother demanded.

"Jessica. You never liked that she won the best roles, but she did beautifully in them. It wasn't right of Miss Schiller not to spread the starring roles around more, but you have to admit Jessica was very, very good."

"I admit nothing of the sort!" her mother said. "She burrowed her way into that woman's good graces and stole all those parts from you! It was nothing but bald-faced favoritism, which continued at the college."

"College was different," Tiffany argued. "At college, we

really had to prove ourselves. I tried, believe me, but Jessica was always better."

"There you go again, putting yourself down!" her mother cried, not kindly but in anger. Lia heard accompanying table raps as she said, "How many times have I told you that in order to succeed in the arts, you have to put yourself forward with confidence! That's all Jessica had. Not talent, confidence! But once you stepped into that role of Juliet after she died, you absolutely blossomed, Tiffany. It led to even better roles that caught people's attention. That agent!"

"Yes, that agent." Tiffany voiced it with much less enthusiasm than her mother's. "Where did that get me? A few minor roles off-Broadway that led nowhere. Was it worth it, Mother?"

Instead of answering, Mrs. Hurst sharply called for the check. Their waitress left another table within a minute and hurried over, receiving a reprimand for not having been instantaneous. Mrs. Hurst settled the bill, then bustled out of their booth ahead of Tiffany, who, Lia noticed, took her time following. Leaving a larger tip, Lia wondered? But Tiffany's last question hung in the air. *Was it worth it, Mother?* Lia would dearly have loved to know exactly what she had referred to.

Wow," Hayley said after Lia returned home and described what she'd been up to. Hayley went over to Lia to give her a hug. "Thank you for never being a Mommy Dearest!"

"Horrors! I wouldn't have been able to stand myself," Lia said. "Or forgive myself. Not to mention that your father would have been appalled."

"Saved on all sides," Hayley said with a grin. "But poor Tiffany. What she must have had to put up with. Does she still live at home?"

"I doubt it. I got the impression they were meeting for a regular, dutiful dinner. Frankly, I felt awful listening in on most of it, but at the same time I just might have learned something important."

"That Tiffany's mom is our murderer?"

Lia shook her head. "Not enough for that, but there was enough to make me want to find out more. Mrs. Hurst definitely had, and still has, a lot of anger toward Jessica."

"And Tiffany asked her, 'Was it worth it?' which sounds to me like she knows her mother did something awful."

"It could mean that," Lia agreed. "And it could mean a lot of other things, too. We just don't know."

"We need to know more about Mrs. Hurst. Have you looked her up?" Hayley asked.

"I haven't," Lia said. "I had expected to talk only with Tiffany today."

"Then let me get to work on that while you have something more to eat. It doesn't sound like you had a decent dinner at the restaurant."

"No, it wasn't much," Lia agreed. "But I can do the search. You've got other things to do."

"But I'd rather do this," Hayley said, laughing. "Have some salad. I made one from those tomatoes and cucumbers you picked up. Or have some ice cream."

Lia acquiesced. She was still hungry and the tomato salad sounded good to her—which she might top off afterward with the ice cream. No reason she couldn't have both, right? She set down Daphne, who had worked her way onto Lia's lap during the discussion, and went to the kitchen while Hayley trotted upstairs to her laptop.

Hayley had made a delicious-looking tomato salad, with onions and herbs added along with a vinegar dressing. Lia spooned a good-sized serving into a bowl and toasted a slice of sourdough bread to go with it.

She was enjoying her food at the dining table when Hayley came tromping down the stairs as she called out, "You're not going to believe this!"

"What?" Lia asked, her fork midway between bowl and mouth. She quickly set it down.

"You kept calling Tiffany's mother Mrs. Hurst," Hayley said, pulling out the chair across from Lia to sit.

"Yes? I assumed that was her name. Was I wrong?"

"It threw me off," Hayley said. "But I finally got it straight. She was Mrs. Hurst when Tiffany was born and for a few years after. But she divorced Mr. Hurst—Ed—and remarried. Brace yourself for what her name is now." Hayley paused dramatically before saying, "King!" At Lia's non-reaction, Hayley said, "Bethanne King! Tiffany's mother is my fundraising event nemesis!"

"Oh!" Lia said. "Oh dear!"

"Yes. Now you understand what I've been dealing with."

"Yes, I do," Lia said. "And I'm so sorry." Lia thought back to her time at the restaurant. "Did you get a text from her about an hour ago?"

"I certainly did."

"I heard her say she was sending one. I had no idea it was to you. Wow!"

"Yeah, wow." Hayley leaned back in her chair. "So now I know exactly who I'd love to send to prison for murder. Can you come up with the evidence?"

Lia laughed. "You might not be the only one who feels that way, but I'm sorry—no guarantees. Thank you, though, for finding that out about her."

"You're welcome," Hayley said. "It's a start. My research, I mean. Next I want to find Bethanne King's hit man and some rock-solid proof that links the two. C'mon, Daph." She picked up the ever-willing cat. "Come with me and bring me good luck. Maybe I can finally get this woman off my back."

Chapter 16

The Ninth Street Knitters settled down in Jen Beasley's living room, each woman pulling out her knitting project as they chatted with one another. Lia displayed the beginning rows of her newly commissioned sweater along with the pattern book photo of what it would eventually look like.

"Ohhh, alpaca yarn," Maureen said, reaching out to squeeze the skein.

"Love the pattern," Tracy said as the others murmured agreement.

"And that's not all I've been busy with," Lia said. She gave a summary of her week's investigative activities, from her chat with Nicole and Lauren at the Ale House, through her talk with Ava at the alpaca farm, and finally to listening in on Tiffany and her mother.

"Wow," Maureen said. "And you managed to knit besides all that?"

"I always find time to knit," Lia said with a smile. "And

it gives me quiet time to mull over what I've learned about Jessica. Remember, that's why I'm looking into Jessica's death in the first place, because of Cori's claim that her ongoing nightmares were an actual memory."

"Right," Maureen said. "And if Cori saw Jessica pushed to her death, Jessica's murderer might have caused hers."

"But why would he or she have waited so long?" Diana asked. "If they knew Cori was a witness all those years ago, why not eliminate her right away?"

"That's something I've struggled over as well," Lia said. "I don't claim to have the answer, but I've thought of a few possibilities. First, that the murderer either didn't know there'd been a witness, or if they did, they might not have known who she was. Perhaps by the time they realized and identified Cori, enough time had passed to feel assured she either didn't understand what she saw or was too trauma-tized to say anything. On the other hand, maybe something in their own life prevented them from acting. It could also have been that our murderer felt differently about killing a child than a grown woman."

"Then what changed, other than Cori growing up, of course?" Maureen asked. She loosened a length of blue yarn from her skein to begin knitting on the sweater sleeve in her lap.

"There was the publicity about Cori and her crochet art," Jen reminded her.

"Yes," Maureen said. "But why would this person fear that she would now speak out?"

"That I don't know," Lia admitted.

Tracy lowered her slim, baby-sweater-sized needles. "Maybe," she offered, "this person accidentally ran into Cori and saw recognition on her face. Or they could have shown up at the craft fair as a kind of a test and got that reaction from Cori. Did you see any of our suspects there, Lia?"

"I wouldn't have recognized them if they'd shown up," Lia said, shaking her head. "The only ones I've seen in person since Cori's death are Tiffany and her mother."

"I like Tracy's theory," Jen said. "It would explain why Jessica's murderer suddenly felt threatened by an adult Cori, whose memories could be taken seriously." Jen then winced. "How sad that the publicity—which must have made Cori so happy—might have led to her murder."

"Well, whatever brought about her murder," Maureen said, "we all promised to help Lia look into it, and I haven't come up with a darned thing!"

"Me neither," Tracy said. She was echoed by Diana and Jen.

"Just getting your feedback helps tremendously," Lia assured them. "Really! But I'd love it if one of you could help me figure out a way to meet and talk with Jessica's old boyfriend. His name is Kevin Shaw, and he's now a practicing dentist in Crandalsburg. That's convenient, in one way, but I don't see myself asking him about Jessica while he's holding a drill in my mouth."

Silence fell on the group for several moments until a male voice asked, "How about coming to the photography club meeting?" Bob Beasley stood just outside the kitchen, having helped himself to some of the snacks the women brought to Jen's house each week, as he was always invited to do.

"Oh!" Jen cried. "Is he a member?"

"Been one as long as I have. Five years, at least." Bob popped the last half of one of Diana's stuffed mushrooms into his mouth.

"They meet once a month," Jen said to the group, then turned to Bob. "When is the next one?"

"Tomorrow night. If you want to come, Lia, I can introduce you to Kevin. Nonmembers are welcome. Jen comes with me sometimes."

"I'd be glad to go again," Jen said. "What do you think, Lia?"

"Absolutely," Lia said. "Chatting with the man in a social situation would be much better."

"Just don't go accusing him of murder during the meeting," Bob said with a sly grin.

"I'll try to hold back," Lia said, returning the grin but wondering at the same time what she *would* say to Kevin Shaw. How does one bring up suspicious deaths while discussing cameras and photos? Fortunately, Lia had time to think about that.

By Friday afternoon, Lia had done enough knitting and thinking. She wouldn't be meeting Jen and Bob for several hours, so there was time to do something else she'd decided on. She wanted to talk with Cori's sister, Robin. So far, Lia had been hearing a lot about Jessica. Now she wanted to hear more about Cori.

Catching comments at Cori's funeral, she'd learned that Robin had her own interior decoration business. A quick look online gave Lia the address. She thought she'd take a chance and just drop in.

Robin's business was on the ground floor of a two-story office building at the end of a strip mall. The rest of the mall held a coffee shop, a liquor store, a hair salon, and a fast-food restaurant. The sign on the door for Wendt Interior Design invited Lia to walk in, so she did, entering a room with a large table, stacks of catalogues, and rows of hanging fabrics. Room photos covered the walls along with a couple of framed certificates.

Lia heard a voice coming from the back of the shop. Robin leaned out of a doorway with a phone pressed to her ear. She held up an index finger, indicating she'd be with Lia in a minute. That gave Lia leisure to look around. She strolled past the photos, admiring them but feeling no sudden urge to redecorate. She was content with her modest but comfy home. The newer styles she saw would be fine for others.

She turned to finger through the racks of upholstery fabrics. She had paused at a particular dark blue sample, picturing it decorated with Daphne's tan-and-white fur, when Robin clicked into the room on three-inch heels that added to her already significant height. Her somber funeral suit had been exchanged for a pale green linen dress, tastefully accented with a multicolored beaded necklace.

"Hi!" she said, holding out her hand. "I'm Robin. How can I help you?"

Lia shook Robin's hand and gave her name. "We met briefly at Cori's funeral," she said. "I knew Cori through the craft fair."

"Oh yes," Robin said. "I remember. How nice to see you again. Are you thinking of redoing some rooms?"

"I'm afraid not." At Robin's puzzled look Lia added, "I wanted to talk to you about Cori. You see, I've been struggling with the way she died."

"Oh?"

"Do you mind? If this a bad time, I could come back," Lia said.

Robin glanced at her watch. "No, I have a few minutes. Why don't we sit down?" She indicated a pair of skirted chairs that flanked a small glass-topped table. "Can I get you something to drink? Coffee?"

"No, thank you," Lia said as she pulled out one of the chairs. "I'll try not to take up too much of your time. At the funeral home," she began, "I spoke with one of Cori's school friends. She told me about Cori's nightmares."

"Ah, the nightmares," Robin said, nodding. She settled into the seat across from Lia. "I'm guessing Cori told this friend they were about something that really happened."

"She did."

"I'm afraid that idea plagued Cori most of her life," Robin said.

"You didn't believe it?" Lia asked.

"No, nor did our mother. Yes, Cori's babysitter did die from a tragic accident at the falls, when Cori was around six. But Mother and I kept that information from Cori at the time, deciding she was too young to deal with it. We told her Jessica had moved away."

"But the nightmares?"

"They appeared years later. Cori must have learned what really happened to Jessica from someone at school. Maybe it was our mistake not to tell her ourselves. I don't know. But Cori . . . well, you must have noticed. Cori struggled tremendously with her emotions."

"Pressures at the craft fair did seem to overwhelm her occasionally."

"Yes. Things that most of us can deal with were much more difficult for Cori. Sometimes it seemed our mother was too . . . well, never mind. Luckily Cori took to crocheting. It turned out to be soothing."

Lia's brows went up. "She created amazing art with it."

"They were pretty, weren't they?"

Robin glanced at her watch again, prompting Lia to

quickly ask, "I wondered why Cori moved to York. A friend of mine told me Cori had briefly worked as a temp at her office there. Work like that doesn't seem much of a draw."

Robin grimaced. "It wasn't her best decision. We knew, Mother and I, that Cori would have a hard time of it. She worked similar jobs here in Crandalsburg, but that was always with our support." Robin uncrossed and recrossed her long legs, smoothing the skirt of her dress. "Cori got it into her head that she needed to prove she could do it all on her own—not just live on her own, which she certainly could have done here. There was a lovely efficiency available in my apartment building that she could have taken. But she insisted on going off to a totally new town. Of course, it didn't work out."

"She had lived at home until then?"

"With Mother, where she eventually needed to return."

"Did Cori mention any worries after she returned to Crandalsburg? Had she been contacted by anyone who made her feel threatened?"

"No, not at all!" Robin leaned toward Lia. "Look, I know you want to find another explanation for Cori's death besides accident. I understand that, because I didn't believe it myself."

"Oh?"

"But I'm accepting it, for my mother's sake, and I hope you will, too. You see, it would be very hard on my mother if she thought Cori had killed herself. But that's exactly what I believe happened."

Reading skepticism on Lia's face, Robin said, "Think about it. She's had these nightmares about Jessica falling or being pushed into the falls, an image that plagued Cori for years. She struggled with depression brought on by her limitations, and it finally caught up with her, maybe as she was reliving her nightmare. It's tragic, and I feel terrible that I couldn't prevent it, but that's truly what I believe happened. But for my mother's sake, I'm going along with the ruling of accidental death." Robin looked at her watch. "Now, if you'll excuse me, I'm expecting a client very soon."

"Yes, of course." Lia stood. As they headed to the office door, she said, "I hope your mother is recovering well?"

"Little by little. Of course, being with her as often as I am, it's hard for me to see it, but they assure me there's progress."

"I'm glad to hear it. Thank you for talking with me." Lia stepped out into the heat of the parking lot and, once in her car, turned on the air-conditioning and sat, thinking over the conversation.

Was she mistaken about Cori? She thought she'd seen joy in the young woman over her burgeoning success at the craft fair. During Lia's visit at the house, Cori had seemed upbeat and interested in the new project presented by the photo Lia had brought. The Jack and Jill shadow box had upset her, true, but she seemed to have rallied fairly well. Lia hadn't felt she'd left Cori in deep gloom.

She thought about what her hairdresser, Crystal, had said about Robin, that as an eleven-year-old she'd distanced herself from her much younger sister. Understandable, of course, at that age. But had they ever been close? Did she really understand Cori—enough to be right that it was suicide?

Sitting in the parking lot for some minutes as she faced Robin's building, Lia gradually realized no one had gone into the interior decorator's office. A client running late, or had Robin simply wanted to end an uncomfortable conversation? Lia supposed she couldn't blame her.

She put her car in gear and drove off. She needed to get a few facts about photography into her head before the meeting that evening.

Chapter 17

"Y ou're going to a photography club meeting?" Hayley leaned against the kitchen counter munching on the sandwich she'd thrown together after dashing in from work. She planned to meet Brady soon for the tennis clinic Terrell Smith offered at Gunther Park.

"I'm going with the Beasleys," Lia said. "Is Brady sure he's up to playing tennis?"

"It was his left shoulder that was shot, remember? Brady's right-handed. He's also nearly a hundred percent back in shape. So what's this about the photography club?" Hayley asked. She took another bite of her ham and cheese.

"Kevin Shaw will be there, the man who was Jessica's boyfriend at the time she died," Lia explained. "I hope to talk with him."

"Oh wow!" Hayley cried, then her flash of excitement faded. "But how are you going to go from chatting about photography to asking about Jessica?"

"That I haven't figured out. Any suggestions?"

Hayley scrunched her lips. "I don't suppose 'Nice to meet you—got any good photos of your old girlfriend?' would be the best idea, huh?"

"Probably not," Lia agreed with a smile.

"Well, I've got to get changed," Hayley said. "I'm sure you'll think of something." She popped the last of her sandwich into her mouth and hurried out of the kitchen.

Lia heard her thump up the stairs and turned to Daphne. "I wish I were as sure about that." The fluffy cat offered a purring ankle rub but little else.

A short time after Hayley took off, Lia left to meet Jen and Bob. The photography club convened at a library in Meadowview, a community midway between Crandalsburg and York, convenient, Bob had explained, for members coming from surrounding areas. As she pulled into the parking lot, she saw her friends already waiting near the door and waved.

When Lia joined the two, Jen informed her that Kevin Shaw had arrived and was inside. "I was worried because there was no guarantee he'd show up, but we couldn't think of any plausible excuse to check on that. I'm so glad you haven't wasted a trip."

"Well, I would at least have learned a little about photography," Lia said. "But I'm still struggling with a way to bring up the subject of Jessica with him."

"There'll be a speaker first," Bob said. "That might give us all time to think of something." He held the door for them, and Lia followed Jen to the library's meeting room.

About thirty people milled about the room, men and women who were predominantly middle-aged or older. Bob briefly greeted a few, then pitched in on setting up chairs. Jen pointed out Kevin Shaw, standing by the projector and talking with two other men.

"He's the one in the blue-and-white-checked shirt," she said.

Lia studied Shaw for a while, but other than a general impression—average height, in apparent good shape—she gathered little about the off-duty dentist before Bob reappeared and suggested they take seats. They chose the last row, which gave Lia a way to keep Shaw in view as he sat down a few rows ahead.

The club president, a slim woman wearing a long skirt, stood at the head of the gathering to introduce Pete Sullivan, their speaker of the evening. Sullivan, it turned out, was one of their newer club members and had photos taken on a European trip to show and discuss.

Polite applause greeted him, someone dimmed the lights, and Sullivan launched his PowerPoint show of medieval churches and historic castles while describing camera angles, light, time exposure, and technicalities beyond Lia's understanding or, frankly, concern. She was much more interested in Kevin Shaw, whose profile she caught as he turned toward the presentation, apparently paying rapt attention.

Bob seemed absorbed as well, nodding occasionally in agreement with a point the speaker made, but Lia caught Jen stifling a yawn. Lia wondered if her friend occasionally accompanied her husband to these meetings in return for his good-natured acceptance of the weekly living room takeover by the Ninth Street Knitters—though he did benefit from a share of their appetizers.

Lia spotted a refreshments table off to the side, which gave her hopes of a chat with Shaw later on. At the end of the talk, an announcement by the club's president concerning an upcoming club activity, an outdoors nature photo opportunity, gave her an idea for leading that conversation in the right direction.

As the lights went up, Bob stood and stretched his back. "Let's get over there," he said, gesturing toward the side table. "I'll introduce you to Shaw."

Lia and Jen headed over with him, and each picked up one of the already-poured cups of punch. Bob grabbed a large pretzel before leading them through the gathering crowd toward his prey.

"Hey, Kevin!" he said, stepping up to the dentist. "Enjoy the talk?" Before Shaw had a chance to answer, Bob said, "You already met my wife. This is her friend Lia Geiger." After Kevin and Lia nodded to each other, Bob added, "Kevin has a dental office in your town, Lia."

"In Crandalsburg?" Lia said, hoping she looked surprised. "That's good to know. I'm fairly new to the town and still learning about it," she added truthfully. "Where is your office?"

"In the Barkley Building, over on Pine Street."

"Ah," Lia said, nodding.

"Are you a new club member?" Shaw inquired.

"No . . . ," Lia began, then hesitated.

"She's like me, Kevin," Jen broke in, "mostly enjoying a chance to get out and learn something new."

"The club does seem to have interesting activities," Lia said. "Like the nature walk that was just mentioned."

"Right," Bob chimed in, probably guessing where Lia was heading with that. "The club's visited areas that are great for scenic shots. We're always looking for more."

Lia was ready to mention Long Run Falls, but as she drew breath, the evening's speaker, Pete Sullivan, walked up and Kevin turned to him. "Hey, Pete. Great stuff tonight."

The others added their compliments as well, which Pete modestly brushed off. "It's my devious way of conning people into looking at my vacation photos," he joked. "Captive audience."

The group protested genially, and Kevin brought up a point Pete had made during his slide show, something that had gone over Lia's head at the time, and before she knew it the three men were deep into a lively discussion of the various uses of a UV filter. She glanced at Jen, who shrugged helplessly.

After some minutes of standing silently and noticing other club members taking off, Lia was ready to write off the evening as a loss. But when a voice over the library's public address system announced it would be closing soon, Bob piped up with, "Say, what do you all think of continuing this at Angelo's? I could do with a beer instead of this library punch. Pete? Kevin?"

Both men nodded agreement, and Bob shot a look at Jen and Lia, who both responded with enthusiasm. The men helped Pete gather up his equipment, and Bob gave Lia directions to the restaurant, adding, "Or just follow me," and before the entire library went dark, they were all on their way.

The last to arrive, Lia was glad to find Angelo's half-full and relatively quiet when she finally joined the others at the table. Though the place wasn't far from the library, she'd been caught by a red light that she'd watched the others sail through. They were seated at a round table, and somehow Bob and Jen had managed to save her the chair next to Kevin. Pete sat on Kevin's other side, with Bob and Jen completing the circle.

"We ordered a pizza to go with our beers," Bob cheerfully informed her, and soon a waiter appeared with a large pitcher and five glasses, which he began to fill. When he got to Lia's, she asked for a half fill.

"Not a beer drinker?" Pete asked. "We didn't give you much of a choice, did we?"

"I'm fine with it," Lia said, "especially along with pizza. But I have a longish drive home and should stay alert."

"Good idea," he said, taking a long, thirsty draw from his own glass, but Pete didn't strike Lia as a major beer drinker himself. His knit shirt outlined a trim build with no hint of a beer belly. His age was difficult to pinpoint, with his silvery hair contrasting with a smoothly tanned face and an air of high energy, though he was not exactly unique in that. Tom's hair had turned gray quite early, a Geiger family trait.

Ordinarily Lia would have politely asked for more details about Pete's European trip, but it was Kevin whom she wanted to get talking. Unfortunately the men quickly resumed their photography discussion, which grew too technical for either Lia or Jen to participate in. When the pizza arrived, though, Jen took advantage of the break to bring up the club's outdoor excursions. "Have you been to Long Run Falls yet? It's supposed to be quite picturesque."

Nobody answered. Pete had just taken a bite of his pizza, but Kevin, Lia noticed, stared down at his plate. Finally Bob said, "I don't think so, but maybe we should. Is the climb doable for average hikers?"

"From what I've been told," Lia said, "there's a range of trail choices, from easy to more challenging. But there's some risk to be aware of. A young woman died from a fall there less than two weeks ago."

"That's right!" Jen said. "I heard about that."

"There's another place I was going to recommend," Pete broke in. "It's in Amish country." He went on to describe the location and photo possibilities, totally changing the subject Jen had managed to raise. Kevin perked up and asked questions that prolonged the discussion. Even Bob weighed in, apparently unable to resist any club-related talk, much to his wife's exasperation, as she displayed to Lia with a subtle eye widening.

But Lia waited patiently, and by the time the last pizza slices had been transferred to plates, she'd found her opportunity.

"That young woman I mentioned who was killed at Long Run Falls is someone I happen to know." She explained about the craft fair and their side-by-side booths. "Cori Littlefield wasn't an outdoorsy person. She spent most of her time working on her crochet art and had just received a commission for a new project that she was eager to start. That made it hard to understand why she would have suddenly gone on a hike like that, alone. The curious thing is, there was another fatality at the same spot, some twenty-six years ago. It was a young woman who happened to be Cori's babysitter."

"Gosh," Jen said. "What a coincidence. Twenty-six years ago? Kevin, were you in Crandalsburg at that time?"

Kevin nodded. "I was." He glanced at Pete before turning to Lia. "And I know who you mean. Jessica Ackerman. She was a friend."

"I'm so sorry. It must have been as much of a shock for you, then, as Cori's death was for me," Lia said. "Did you know Cori back then, too? I mean, since Jessica babysat for her?"

"I remember the name. It's unusual enough, and I guess Jessica must have mentioned her. When I read about the accident, I figured it must be the same girl."

Lia paused as she tried to think of what to say next. Jen jumped in to help. "Didn't you say there was a feature story about Cori and her crochet art in the *Crandalsburg Gazette*?" she asked Lia.

"Yes, just two days before she died."

"Was there?" Kevin took a swallow of his beer. "I guess I missed that."

"Well, maybe the club members would rather not go to Long Run Falls, at least not just yet," Pete said. "I say we look into the Amish place," he added, once again pulling a switch on Lia's carefully laid track. "I'll throw that out to the group on the Facebook page. Maybe there'll be other ideas."

Kevin then brought up sports, which Pete jumped in on as Lia and Jen could only sit helplessly by, silently sipping their beers. When the pizza disappeared and the beer pitcher had been emptied, Bob posed the idea of another round but got no takers, and Pete and Kevin began pulling out their wallets to take care of their share of the bill.

Bob insisted on covering Lia's, and soon everyone was heading out the door as a group. Lia said her good-byes, unable to talk privately to Jen or Bob before walking to her car, which was parked at the opposite end of the lot. Pete, she soon noticed, followed behind.

"Lia," he asked after some steps. "May I have a word?"

She turned to him and smiled, curious.

Pete cleared his throat. "Bob might not have mentioned this. Or maybe he doesn't know. I'm fairly new to the club."

Lia waited.

"Besides being an amateur photographer," he said, "I happen to be the Crandalsburg chief of police."

"Oh!"

He nodded. "I picked up on what you and Jen were trying to do in there."

Chapter 18

Lia watched Bob and Jen's car exit the restaurant's parking lot as she stood facing Pete Sullivan, chief of police. There was nothing to worry about, of course. Pete was being perfectly polite. But she'd felt herself tense, though she couldn't say exactly why.

"I was on the force when the young woman you mentioned, Jessica Ackerman, took her fall," he said. "Not as chief, of course, but I can assure you we looked into her death very carefully at the time before concluding it was accidental." He shifted his weight. "Officer McCormick spoke to me about your concerns. He'd mentioned your name, but it didn't click tonight until you brought up Jessica in there."

Lia lifted her chin. "Did Brady, that is, Officer McCormick, tell you about Cori Littlefield's nightmares? That she believed she had seen Jessica pushed into the falls?"

"He did." He looked at her sadly. "I'm afraid it just isn't enough to change my mind and reopen the cases. Two similar deaths that many years apart, even when the victims knew each other, doesn't point to anything other than coincidental accidents, without further evidence of wrongdoing. Believe me, both were investigated thoroughly." Before Lia could speak he added, "And Kevin?"

"Yes?"

"He was questioned at the time of Jessica's death, along with many others, because of his association with her. Nothing suspicious was uncovered."

"I was told by Jessica's friends that there had been problems between the two," Lia said. She shifted her stance slightly to get out of the direct beam of an overhead light shining in her eyes. "A few minutes ago, Kevin referred to Jessica simply as a friend, but they had dated seriously."

Pete sighed. "There was no evidence that anyone was with Miss Ackerman at the time of her fall. Kevin's statement that he was fishing with a friend was verified. My advice, Mrs. Geiger—Lia—is to let this go. I'm sorry about your friend, but accidents do happen."

Lia nodded. She thought about bringing up Tiffany Hurst's mother, Bethanne, or the teacher, Marc Bernard. But she had nothing more on them than she had on Kevin. Just the beginnings of suspicions, which she knew wouldn't go far with the Crandalsburg chief of police.

"Thank you, Pete," she said. "That's pretty much what Officer McCormick suggested to me."

"He's a good man," Pete said. "Have a good night." He began to turn, then stopped to add with a smile, "And drive carefully."

Lia smiled back. "I will."

*   *   *

Lia called Jen as soon as she got home to tell her about the parking lot conversation, which Jen immediately shared with her husband.

"Bob says he had no idea Pete was a police chief! He said Pete just joined the club a couple of months ago, and he never talked to the man about anything other than cameras and photos. He's so sorry he set you up."

"Please tell him it wasn't a problem at all," Lia said. "Pete was perfectly nice about it."

"He did seem very pleasant," Jen agreed.

"And he might have saved me some trouble." Lia ruffled Daphne's fur as the cat cozied up to her. "I mean since he let me know Kevin had an alibi for Jessica's time of death."

"Well, that's something. It narrows the field. Now we'll see what we can come up with on the others."

Lia heard Hayley's voice outside as a car door closed, and she finished her call with Jen. In a minute Hayley walked in, announcing breezily and unnecessarily, "I'm home." She dropped her tennis bag near the stairs before heading over to flop on the sofa. Daphne immediately jumped down from Lia's lap to scurry over.

"Brady's not coming in?" Lia asked as she brushed cat hair from her skirt.

"He had things to get done before his shift tomorrow. Laundry, for one." Hayley patted her lap to invite Daphne up. "We stopped for ice cream on the way home."

"How was the tennis clinic?"

Hayley blew a few strands of hair from her face. "You're not going to believe this."

"What?"

"Erin showed up."

Lia reached for the knitting beside her chair. "Coincidence?"

Hayley made a face. "Doubtful. Brady thinks he mentioned something to Brooke about his plans."

"Did Brooke come as well?"

"She did."

"So maybe Brooke was the one interested in the clinic?" Lia suggested. She loosened a length of yarn to start stitching.

"Maybe," Hayley said with little conviction. "But after the drills were over, it was Erin who made a big deal about the four of us staying for a set of doubles. It couldn't be with anyone else in the clinic—and she obviously knew some people—it had to be us."

"I see," Lia said, which she did. Erin wasn't terribly subtle. "So afterward, did you talk it over with Brady? The sisters didn't come along with you for ice cream, did they?"

"No, and no." Hayley shifted her position on the sofa, causing Daphne to protest with a soft squeak. "Mom, I think I need to get my head straight first. When Brady and I first started going out, I made a big deal about wanting to keep things casual. Meaning, for one thing, no strings. So how do I have any right to be annoyed when another woman starts batting her eyes at him? But I *am* annoyed. And that's annoying!"

Lia nodded gravely.

"I don't know, maybe it's just Erin herself," Hayley continued. "That she's being so, so . . . I don't know . . . so . . ."

"Annoying?" Lia supplied.

"Yes! But then I tell myself that's not fair. She likes Brady. She has a right to show that, I suppose."

"She could be more subtle," Lia said.

"You think?" Hayley laughed, though it had a touch of sharpness to it.

"From what you've told me," Lia said, pausing her needles to look up, "Brady hasn't been encouraging Erin. Is that right?"

"Well, he hasn't been discouraging, either. But no, I guess he's just been friendly, like he would be to anyone."

"Then I'm wondering if you're annoyed with Erin because she's pushing you to decide how you feel about Brady."

Hayley stared at Lia. After several moments she nodded. "That might be it. I don't like what she's doing because I don't want to be rushed. I made too many bad decisions by being impulsive, as you well know, Mom."

Lia only smiled.

"But I did take my time deciding to quit my job in Philadelphia to come work at the alpaca farm," Hayley pointed out.

"Yes, you did." Lia said, though she thought some might quibble that two weeks wasn't particularly lengthy for that kind of decision.

"And it's been working out—so far, at least. I also want to take whatever's developing between Brady and me slowly."

"I think that's very wise, Hayley."

Hayley moved Daphne off her lap to the next sofa cushion. "So how do I get Erin to butt out?" she asked as she stood.

"That, I'm afraid, I have no answer for." That would have to come from Hayley.

Hayley turned to head to the kitchen. "I'll figure something out. Want anything? I'm getting ice water." When Lia declined, Hayley asked, "How was that photography club thing you went to?"

"Well . . ." Lia waited until Hayley returned, glass in hand, to give her a summary of the evening.

"Oh my gosh! That was Brady's boss listening in as you grilled one of your suspects?"

"I don't think I was exactly grilling," Lia protested. "Though Kevin Shaw did look uncomfortable being asked about Jessica."

"Aha!"

"But Pete, that is, Chief Sullivan, said Kevin's claim of having been with a friend when Jessica fell was confirmed."

"Well, then, that's that, I guess."

"He also referred to Brady as a good man," Lia said.

Hayley beamed. "Did he? That's great." She gulped some of her water, then reached over to lift the ever-willing Daphne back onto her lap. "Did you tell him about Beth-anne King?" she asked hopefully.

Lia shook her head. "There's nothing much to tell, is there? Nothing concrete, that is. That's all that would matter to the police."

"Yeah, I suppose. Bummer." Hayley stroked Daphne for a bit, then said, "I'll bet that daughter—Tiffany?—knows something. Maybe, after all these years, she's ready to spill it."

"I don't know," Lia said. "That would be a pretty major shift for a person who was raised by such a controlling mother."

"It sounded to me like she was starting to speak up for herself," Hayley said. "Maybe Cori's death will be her tipping point."

Lia was thinking that over when her phone rang. It was Olivia asking if Lia had any of the dark blue knit place mats she remembered seeing. "My sister-in-law mentioned she's been looking for that color, and I said I might be able to get them for her from you."

That reminded Lia that she had two busy craft fair days ahead of her. After she assured Olivia she did indeed have a set of dark blue place mats, she folded up her knitting and bid Hayley a good night. Thoughts of murder and suspects would have to be set aside, if possible. Lia needed a good night's sleep.

Chapter 19

As crafters gathered at the barn the next morning, Lia unpacked her knit place mats from one of the boxes she'd brought. "I actually have two sets of dark blue," she told Olivia, who hovered closely. "One has a white daisy worked into a corner." She pulled it out to display. "And this set is edged with two thin red stripes." Lia smoothed both and looked inquiringly at her friend.

"Oh! I don't know which Jeanie would like," Olivia said, worry lines gathering.

"Why not take a photo of each to send to her?" Lia suggested.

"Good idea!" Olivia pulled out her phone, took the shots, then tapped at the screen to send them. "I'll let you know as soon as I hear back," she promised.

"And I'll set them aside till then," Lia promised, gathering up the mats to slide beneath her counter. She was tidily folding one of Tracy's knit baby sets when Nicole came through the barn's side door, pulling a handcart piled high with handwoven baskets of many sizes. She paused at Lia's booth to say hi.

"Your wares may be as lightweight as mine," Lia said, looking down at Nicole's load, "but at least I can compact my things. You must have to make a lot of trips."

"Tell me about it," Nicole said, rolling her eyes. She wore a gauzy red blouse over a printed knee-length skirt that day, the colors matching those in many of her baskets. "With my booth way over there, I probably put in miles going back and forth." She looked at Cori's still-empty booth. "I'd be interested in this one, but not just yet. I think it needs to stay as Cori's for now."

Lia nodded.

"Any progress on your investigation?" Nicole asked.

"Only of a negative sort." Lia explained about Kevin Shaw having had an alibi from a friend for the time Jessica took her fall.

"Well, that's something at least." Nicole grinned. "And good news for his patients, right? I mean, who'd like to find out that the guy who's been drilling in your mouth was a secret murderer?"

"Not me!" Lia agreed with a smile.

Bill Landry called out a five-minute warning for the front doors to be opened, and Nicole lifted the handle of her cart. "Better go!" she said before hurrying off.

Lia got busy with her own booth, though she generally had additional minutes before early-arriving customers made their way to her. She was pleased to see a good-sized crowd once Bill let them in, which showed further recovery from the craft fair's negative publicity of some weeks before. Cori's good publicity had helped enormously, a thought that saddened Lia as she glanced toward the now-vacant booth. But she set that aside for the time being, especially as she noticed a familiar figure hurrying her way, with a second woman in tow.

"Helen, good morning!" Lia greeted the woman whose alpaca sweater she was currently working on. "You're here bright and early." A worrying thought occurred that Helen had come to cancel her commission, but Helen's broad smile quickly eased that.

"I've brought you another order," Helen said. She turned to the woman next to her. "My friend Kim was highly jealous when I told her about the sweater you're making for me." That caused her shorter, fair-haired friend to burst into laughter. "So," Helen continued, "I told her she should just get one for herself. Not exactly the same, of course, but something nice."

Kim stepped forward. "I've heard about alpaca sweaters," she said, "and always thought I'd love to have one, but I'm not much of a knitter myself and didn't know about you. Helen said you have pattern books to look through?"

"I do!" Lia said, delighted that her initial fear was not only wrong but corrected so pleasantly. "But if you want it soon, I'll have to turn the order over to another Ninth Street Knitter. But as you see"—Lia waved toward the several beautiful sweaters hanging at the side and behind her— "they're all highly skilled."

Kim reached up to finger an airy pink pullover with an open-weave design. "Yes, that would be fine."

Lia pulled out several pattern books that she suggested they spread out on Cori's empty counter and thought about who in her knitting group would accept the commission. She'd throw it out to all, of course, and she smiled to herself at the thought of the excitement it would cause.

Kim made her choice, and after a discussion about colors, Lia took a deposit on the order as well as all the necessary information. Later, after having taken a seat to knit during a lull in the number of shoppers, she saw Nicole heading her way. Lia set her needles and yarn aside and stood to meet her.

"I just had a chat with Lauren," Nicole said as she came up. "I called to tell her what you said about Kevin Shaw, since she's the one who knew him when he was dating Jessica back then. I thought she'd like to know about his alibi." Nicole drew a long breath. "You might want to think again about taking him off your suspect list."

"Really?" Lia said, surprised. "Why?"

"Lauren said the alibi must have come from her old boyfriend Rick, since he was the one Kevin always fished with. They were both really big on fly-fishing. Lauren said she wouldn't consider an alibi coming from Rick as being rock-solid, that he was the kind of guy who'd do anything for a friend."

"To the point of lying to the police?"

Nicole nodded gravely. "Lauren says yes. One of the reasons she broke up with him was that he was such a pushover. At first she thought he was just a really nice, thoughtful kind of guy. But she came to see how excessive his need to please could be."

"But still," Lia said. "Lying to the police? I'm struggling with that."

Nicole shrugged. "All I know is what Lauren said. She believes Rick would have justified it to himself as saving a friend from a lot of unnecessary trouble, someone he was sure had done nothing wrong."

"Is Rick still in the area?" Lia asked.

"I don't think so. Lauren said she lost touch with him long ago and thinks he moved out West somewhere."

The police could certainly find him, Lia thought, but they'd probably need a better reason than a former girl-friend's skepticism of his long-ago statement to them.

"Thanks, Nicole," Lia said. "Although this puts me in a quandary."

"I know. Who to believe, right? If it helps, I'd say Lauren is a pretty good judge of people."

"Maybe so, but that still only tells me what she thinks Rick might have done, not what he *actually* did for his old friend."

"Right." Nicole glanced toward her booth and spotted a shopper browsing at it. "Sorry, I have to go." She took off, leaving Lia to mull over what change this made, if any, in her thinking about Kevin Shaw, which she did until shoppers showed up at her own booth. It was a welcome inter-ruption, since she seemed only to be going in circles with her deliberations.

Toward the end of the day, Lia had started to close up her booth when she saw a pleasantly rotund, slightly bald-ing gentleman heading her way. A last-minute sale? She mentally ran through her inventory for male-oriented items—which were limited. Perhaps something for a spouse?

It turned out to be neither. "You must be Lia, Belinda's friend," he said after glancing at the overhead sign.

"I am," Lia said with a surprised smile. "And you must be . . . ?"

"Chad Hoover." He held up a book. "I picked this up for Belinda. We're reading it for the next book club meet-ing."

Aha! "How nice to meet you, Chad," Lia said sincerely as she quickly checked him over for anything that might worry her about her good friend's new, um, friend. Finding nothing immediate, she said, "Belinda's probably in her office. I'll be happy to take you there."

Chad smiled agreeably, and Lia slipped out of her booth to lead him down the side hallway. She gave two quick raps on the office door and opened it to lean in. "Chad's here," she announced.

"Oh!" Belinda jumped up, her hands flying to her hair as Lia stepped aside to allow Chad access. "You're early," she said.

"I am, but this nice lady showed me the way."

Lia grinned inwardly at Belinda's fluster, which her friend covered by formally introducing the two.

"I've heard so much about you," Chad said to Lia, "that I feel I already know you."

Unable to say the same, since Belinda had barely mentioned Chad's name to her, Lia shot a glance at her friend, who picked up on its meaning.

"There's plenty more to learn, of course," Belinda said, looking apologetically at Lia. "This would be a good time to get into it. Lia, why don't you join us for dinner? We were going to grab something after I closed up the craft fair."

"Great idea!" Chad said genially.

Lia hesitated. "If you're sure I won't be—"

"Please come," Belinda said, warmly.

When Chad seconded that with enthusiasm, Lia relented. "I'd love to."

They discussed where to meet up, deciding on Louisa's Country Kitchen, known in Crandalsburg for comfort food.

When Lia went back to her booth to finish closing it, Olivia was waiting for her, having information about her sister-in-law's big place mat decision. "She'd like six of the daisy-trimmed ones," she announced, looking pleased.

"We can settle on it tomorrow, though, okay? She's in no rush. I just wanted you to know before I left."

"Thanks, Olivia. That works for me." Lia was happy about the sale but also eager to be on her way. There was an interesting—and unexpected—evening awaiting her.

Chapter 20

When Lia walked into the restaurant, she saw Chad sitting by himself in one of the booths. He spotted her and waved her over, rising to meet her.

"Belinda got a last-minute call," he explained as Lia slipped in opposite him. "She should be here in a minute."

"Great!" A waitress came up with water and a menu for Lia. After learning a third person would be joining them soon, she left, and Lia said to Chad, "So, you and Belinda are in a book club."

"Yes." Chad's eyes danced. "The group has been established for a long time and is pretty set in its ways. But we're working to shake it up, little by little."

Lia grinned. "Literary infiltration. Sounds dangerous."

"We're constantly on alert," he said, returning the grin. "Actually, we're just trying to broaden their tastes to include something we'd enjoy reading. I feel woefully behind on my fiction, having been immersed in numbers for so many years." At Lia's questioning look, he explained, "I'm a math instructor."

Before Lia could ask more, Belinda came rushing up to join them. "Sorry, that took longer than I expected." She slid in next to Chad.

"No problem," Chad assured her. "We were just getting started."

Their waitress reappeared to run through a recitation of the day's special, which gave Belinda a chance to catch her breath. They all then turned to study their menus.

After giving their orders, they began to chat casually, Belinda reaching for and nibbling on one of the breadsticks their waitress had left. Lia was pleased to see strong differences in Chad from Belinda's late ex-husband, Darren. Obviously Belinda had had more than enough of self-centered deceitfulness, an attribute that, unfortunately, hadn't become clear until well into their marriage. Lia, of course, couldn't be sure of Chad's honesty at this point, but his interest in all topics beyond himself and his few self-deprecating jokes led Lia to believe he was far from narcissistic. The more they chatted, the more Lia liked him.

"I'm going to have to make a decision about Cori's booth," Belinda said after their food had arrived. Her last-minute call, it turned out, had been from an interested vendor. "I'm getting new applications, good ones."

Lia nodded sympathetically. "When you do decide," she said, "Nicole expressed interest in trading her current booth for Cori's."

"Who's Cori?" Chad asked.

Belinda reminded him of the crochet art vendor whose death she'd told him about and whose name he'd obviously forgotten. Then she turned to Lia. "Are you convinced by now that it was accidental?"

"I wish I were," Lia said, shaking her head. "But all I can say is that I'm not satisfied. Cori's nightmares about Jessica and her own identical manner of death? The connection is too disturbing."

"Jessica?" Chad asked.

Belinda explained about Cori's babysitter. "Lia was extremely helpful with digging up the truth when my ex-husband was murdered," she said. "But if there's anything at all to dig up about this situation, I wish she'd leave it to the authorities."

"I'd be most happy to," Lia said, "if they were ready to move on it. But they considered Jessica's death accidental and are sticking with that. I'm wondering if they had all the information they needed at the time."

"Have you found anything new?" Chad asked. He took a sip of the pinot grigio he'd ordered for the three of them.

"Nothing concrete, I'm afraid. I have more questions than answers." Lia explained about the threats in Jessica's young life, coming from Tiffany Hurst and her supercompetitive mother, Bethanne, and from Kevin Shaw and French teacher Marc Bernard. "Though I don't know if any of those threats led to murder."

"Marc Bernard?" Chad set down his fork. "The same Marc Bernard I know at Aymesburg?"

"You know him?" Lia asked.

"Chad teaches at Aymesburg," Belinda said. "Math."

"How well do you know Bernard?" Lia asked, hoping not to hear they were best pals, which could affect her positive opinion of Belinda's budding relationship.

"Only as a colleague," he said. "I don't read French, and he's not into numbers"—he paused—"unless they have dollar signs in front of them."

"Hah!" Belinda laughed. "Why do you say that?"

Chad grimaced. "I probably shouldn't have. Not very nice and none of my business—except Lia mentioned she was concerned about the man. I've heard rumors about him, too. There's never been anything official brought up against him that I'm aware of, but he's the kind of oily personality I don't care for and wouldn't trust."

"But the 'dollar signs'?" Belinda prompted.

Chad laughed. "Just my observation of what's important to Marc. He dresses quite well, vacations impressively, and drives a new, top-of-the-line car almost every year. And I can verify that the salary of a small college instructor doesn't support that."

"So what does?" Lia asked.

"My guess is his wealthy wife."

"How nice for him," Belinda said with a touch of snark.

"And again," Chad said, "none of my business if it works for them. No law about who has to bring more money into a marriage. But there should be at least some equality of commitment and caring between the two, at least to my mind."

"And you think that's missing?" Lia asked.

Chad blew out a lungful of air. "Not only missing, but the opposite was apparent the few times I was with both, mostly at college functions. Melanie—that's his wife—is a sweet person. A little older than Marc, I'd guess, and not what some might call a beauty—which shouldn't matter, though it seems to, to her—but very nice. She's obviously besotted with him, even after many years. But he . . . he's much less so, often to the point of outright rudeness. I've felt sorry for Melanie on many occasions. But she seems to take it as the most she has a right to expect from him."

"How sad," Belinda said.

Lia agreed. "How long have they been married?" she asked.

"Twenty-five years," Chad said. "I only know because they had an anniversary celebration a short time ago. A big bash. Almost," he added, "as though they felt a need to prove something."

"Twenty-five years," Lia mused. "He must have gotten married shortly after being hired by the college," she said.

"That's how long he's been there?" Belinda asked.

"According to my sources, not too long before her death Jessica joked about taking one of his classes at Aymesburg for an easy A. That was twenty-six years ago."

"An easy A," Belinda said. "Like she had something on him."

"The rumors from high school that connected the two," Lia reminded her. "They might have been true."

"So if Jessica spoke up," Belinda said, "it could have put the kibosh on both his upcoming marriage—which brought him a nice lifestyle—*and* a job that gave him access to a steady stream of vulnerable girls."

"And, assuming we're right about this," Lia said, "all because of Jessica, a young woman he might have underestimated."

"Well, the vulnerability," Chad said, "might have been Bernard's. If he was putting himself in compromising situations with his female students, it could have got him fired."

"And yet he's still there," Belinda said. "All these years."

"I still think of the students as the vulnerable ones," Lia said. "Many are young and inexperienced. If he was in fact behaving inappropriately—highly so—he's been very careful, choosing young women he could be sure wouldn't cause him any problems."

"Maybe so," Chad conceded.

Lia picked at her food for a few moments, thinking. "I'm hoping I'll get to speak with one of those young women."

"Tell her to speak up against this sleazeball!" Belinda said.

"First be sure she's being truthful," Chad cautioned. When he got a glare from Belinda, he defended his comment. "Just saying that guys have rights, too. Even sleazeball guys."

"They do, though statistically speaking, these accusations are most often true," Lia said, "and I will, as best I can, anyway." The thought of what she might hear was not a happy one, and she finished the last of her wine silently, mulling over the possibilities and what she would do about them.

Chapter 21

Sunday morning, Lia was pleased to arrive at the craft fair barn at the same time as Maggie. Her quilter friend's liveliness would be a needed lift. After the discussion the previous night with Belinda and Chad, Lia had awakened that morning feeling down. While all she had on Marc Bernard were rumors and hearsay, the thought of what he might be getting away with was still disturbing. Maggie's smiling face helped push some of that away.

"How's my favorite knitter today?" Maggie asked as they met up at the barn's doorway. Maggie's mass of bright red hair seemed to have doubled in the August humidity, but it only complemented her large frame and ebullient personality.

"Pretty good," Lia said. She held the door for her friend. "I've picked up two commissions for sweaters lately, which I'm happy about. How about you?"

"Oh, I can't complain," Maggie said. "Full-sized quilts

don't exactly fly off the line, of course, but the baby ones have been doing well. Business has been recovering nicely since the slowdown back in May."

"It has. I'm glad for everyone's sake, but particularly for Belinda's."

Maggie paused as they reached Cori's vacant booth. "Nice that someone's still bringing fresh flowers," she said, noting a pretty arrangement of purple coneflowers brightened with yellow marigolds on the front counter.

"Zach Goodwin brought them yesterday," Lia said, glancing across the way toward the genial beekeeper, who sold jars of honey along with his wife's homemade jams and jellies. "He said Florrie put it together from her garden." A good thing, Lia thought guiltily, as it kept slipping her mind to do so herself.

Maggie gazed at the bouquet silently. "I hated that Cori's funeral was private and all we could go to was the wake," she said after a few moments. "Not that I enjoy funerals, but I still missed it. I'm not sure why."

Lia had to think about that. "Maybe" she offered, "because at funerals you get to hear eulogies that share things about the person you might not have known."

"Right! And over here, we were just getting to know Cori. There weren't any speeches at the wake, just everyone offering condolences to her sister."

"I suppose it was the best Robin could manage." Lia explained about Cori's mother still recovering from a bad accident. Maggie shook her head sympathetically. "But I did learn a few things about Cori," Lia added. "From a school friend of hers, Amanda Briggs."

Maggie brightened. "Oh, Amanda was there? I missed her. Amanda works at the shop where I buy most of my fabrics. She's a sweetie."

Lia considered sharing what the young woman had told her about Cori's nightmares, but Olivia walked in just then.

"I can take those place mats for my sister-in-law now, if you're ready," she said to Lia.

"Sure!" Lia said, and Maggie took off, wishing them a great day as Lia slipped into her booth to pull out the daisy-decorated place mats.

Pleased to make a sale even before the doors opened, Lia bagged the place mats for Olivia, then got to work readying her booth for the day. She caught Belinda as her friend stepped out for her usual last-minute checkup to say, "I liked Chad a lot."

Belinda's cheeks pinked. "I'm glad you got to meet him."

"But there was one very important question I never got around to asking him," Lia said, assuming a serious tone.

"Yes?" Belinda asked, her eyes narrowing cautiously.

"What book did he bring for you to read for the book club?"

Belinda laughed. Her phone rang, and she pulled it out to check on the caller. "Gotta take this," she said and walked away, the phone to her ear, and Lia turned back to her work, smiling to herself.

The craft barn doors opened to admit an encouraging number of shoppers, who fanned out among the booths. Several stopped at the Ninth Street Knits booth, and by the time lunchtime rolled around, Lia had sold a satisfying number of items. Ready for a break, Lia grabbed her insulated lunch bag as soon as Olivia returned and headed outdoors in search of a shady table.

She was in luck. A small group were vacating a table as she neared, and Lia gratefully took their place, settling in to relax and recharge. She spread out her food and enjoyed her view of the barn, its white-painted trim setting off the red sides nicely as the sun caught the metal rooster perched high on the cupola. Shoppers dotted several other tables, enjoying cool drinks and snacks picked up from the outdoor food vendors.

She had finished her sandwich and was nibbling lazily at cut melon slices when Maggie appeared, winding her way toward Lia.

"You looked like you were enjoying yourself too much," Maggie said as she approached. "Somebody needed to put a stop to that, so I guess that'll have to be me."

"Please join me," Lia said with a grin, and she waved her friend over, then set about brushing a few crumbs from the table.

Maggie plopped onto the opposite bench with a slight groan. "I got myself caught in a long conversation with a customer. My fault. She's bought from me before—nice lady—but I made the mistake of asking about her grandchildren. Now I know everything there is to know about them— and then some." She took a long sip from the tall drink cup she'd brought with her, then opened up her lunch bag.

"I do that myself," Lia admitted. "It's hard not to when someone is buying baby items."

Maggie nodded vigorously. She pulled the lid off a yogurt cup and stirred it with a plastic spoon. "This morning you mentioned talking to Amanda about Cori at the wake. Anything you can share? I'd be interested in knowing more about that poor girl."

"Actually, that conversation spurred me to learn as much as I can about Cori." Lia told Maggie about the nightmares Amanda had described, the Jack and Jill diorama Cori had made, and Cori's years-ago babysitter, whose death so eerily mimicked her own and whose name Cori had blurted out concerning the diorama.

"Oh my gosh," Maggie said, her yogurt spoon paused midway to her mouth. "You think Cori was murdered!"

"I strongly suspect that," Lia confessed. "But I haven't been able to come up with any solid proof."

"Wow," Maggie said, obviously struggling to wrap her head around that. "It's a whole different ball of wax from when you came across Belinda's ex, lying in the craft barn with his head bashed in. No doubts about murder there. But Cori? Wow." She looked at Lia through the splayed fingers she'd dropped her face into. "You're sure?"

"Enough to keep looking into it," Lia said. "But it's like trying to prove a negative. I can't believe Cori committed suicide, as her sister suggested. Cori's life had just taken a huge upward swing, you know, with her crochet art becoming so popular. And accidental? The likelihood of Cori suddenly hiking up to the spot she'd been having nightmares about is hard to believe, and leaning over so precariously as to fall is downright preposterous."

Maggie's mouth curled one-sidedly. "Wasn't it Sherlock Holmes who said, 'Once you eliminate all the things it can't be, what's left is the truth'? Or something like that."

Lia smiled. "You're a Sherlock Holmes fan?"

"Who isn't?" Maggie returned to her yogurt, scooping up a spoonful. "I like to listen to audiobooks while I quilt."

"I knit with them myself," Lia said. "But as far as the quote, I doubt the police would go along with that. They need more."

"Picky, picky," Maggie said, reaching for her drink cup. She took a long sip, then said, "I'll be heading to the fabric shop tomorrow. How about I chat with Amanda while I'm there? She might have more to say than she did at the wake."

"That would be great," Lia said. She began packing up

her lunch bag. Olivia was keeping an eye on her booth for her.

"And let me know what else *you* come up with," Maggie said as Lia stood. "The more heads working on this, the better. Our sweet Cori shouldn't have her life taken from her without at least getting justice."

"I promise," Lia said. "And thank you!"

She was making her way back to the barn when she was surprised with a phone call from Hayley.

"Mom!" she said. "I just heard from Ava. She's been talking to that girl who got mixed up with the French teacher. Her name's Megan. Guess what? Ava's convinced her to meet with you."

Chapter 22

Before Hayley left for work the following morning, she and Lia discussed the upcoming chat with Megan, which was set for later that day at the alpaca farm.

"Why is she meeting me at the farm?" Lia asked. "Is it because Ava will be there?"

"Partly," Hayley said. "But Megan also lives around there, and she works at a coffee shop in Crandalsburg, where she'll have to head afterward. Instead of her regular ride, Ava will get her there after you talk."

Lia nodded and saw Hayley off, then brewed a second cup of coffee, which she carried out to the living room to enjoy while knitting and catching the news on TV. Daphne took her usual place by her side, sighing contentedly as she settled down.

After half listening to events in far-flung countries, Lia was glad when the news anchors switched to local happenings. Mention of the upcoming school year made Lia think of Tiffany. Hayley was right, Tiffany must know something and might be ready to spill it.

She recalled how Tiffany had brought up Jessica at the restaurant, after previously only repeating "Yes, Mother" to everything her mother said. That flare of independence had upset Bethanne enough to stalk out of their booth, effectively putting an end to the subject. Perhaps Lia could prod Tiffany a bit?

Lia set down her knitting and picked up her phone. She pulled up the Crandalsburg High School website she'd consulted before and found a phone number. That connected her to the school's office, and within a short time Tiffany picked up her call with a polite, "This is Miss Hurst."

Lia explained who she was and asked if she could come to speak with her. "It's about Cori Littlefield's death. And Jessica Ackerman's."

Into the long silence that followed, Lia prompted, "Miss Hurst?"

"Yes, I'm here," Tiffany answered. "Sorry, I just had to think about that for a minute. Sure, we can talk, but not here. On teacher prep days, I have some flexibility. I've been taking walks at Gunther Park during my lunch breaks. Can you join me there at noon?"

"Absolutely."

"Good. Wear your walking shoes. I'm there for exercise. We can meet at the entrance, okay?"

Lia agreed and described herself briefly. She let Tiffany do the same, despite knowing she'd have no problem recognizing the drama teacher. Then she ended the call.

Highly satisfied, Lia set down the phone and picked up her needles. She had plenty of time to make progress on Helen's cardigan, which also gave her time to get her head together about the best way to approach her meeting with

Tiffany. The knitting, she knew, would be the easier of the two.

By eleven fifty, Lia was already waiting at the park entrance, not willing to take a chance on missing Tiffany. She'd donned her tennis shoes, the sturdiest walking pair she owned, and in deference to the ongoing heat, wore shorts and a loose tee. She also carried a large water bottle. Who knew how long and how brisk this walk would be?

Shortly before noon she spotted Tiffany approaching, dressed similarly in shorts and a tank. Lia assumed the teacher had changed at school to the appropriate but also youthful ensemble, an outfit Lia could picture Bethanne disliking. Besides the clothes, Tiffany's bearing was different than it had been when Lia followed her at the mall with her mother. More relaxed but with shoulders farther back and head held higher. It might have been because of the exercise, but Lia suspected other reasons as well.

"Miss Hurst?" Lia asked, stepping out of her shadowed spot.

"Mrs. Geiger?" Tiffany answered. Barely slowing, she turned into the park and jerked her head for Lia to join her. "Call me Tiffany, please. I'm off duty," she said with a grin.

"And I'm Lia. Thank you for meeting me."

"No problem." They settled into a steady, brisk pace, passing moms leisurely pushing strollers and others less interested in working up a sweat. "So," Tiffany said, "you knew Cori Littlefield?"

"From the craft fair," Lia said. "She brought her crochet art there a few weeks ago. Her booth was next to mine."

"I saw the newspaper article about her," Tiffany said, now swinging her arms as she walked. "She made some beautiful things."

"She did," Lia agreed. "And she was so happy about all

the shoppers the publicity brought to the craft fair. She also got a special commission that clearly interested her. The morning of her death, Cori was eager to get to work. That's why I can't understand why she suddenly went off on that hike up to Long Run Falls, a place I've been told had bad memories for her."

"Jessica," Tiffany said, her tone flat.

"Yes, Jessica," Lia said, beginning to puff from the effort of talking while walking at a near trot. "Jessica was Cori's babysitter."

Tiffany's head snapped toward Lia. "She was?"

"You didn't know?"

Tiffany turned back to the path ahead. "I wasn't friends with Jessica, just a classmate. I thought you meant Cori knew about Jessica's fall, just as the rest of Crandalsburg did."

"Cori was only six when it happened. Her sister said they told her at the time that Jessica had moved away. But Cori's school friend said Cori had ongoing nightmares about Jessica's fall, as if she'd seen it happen."

Tiffany fell silent. After several moments she asked, "Do you think she did?"

"Jessica's death clearly affected Cori greatly, much more than it would have if she'd only learned about it years later. If that had been the case, I think it would have had little impact on her. I saw evidence that Jessica was in Cori's thoughts until the day Cori died." Lia described the crocheted diorama.

Tiffany frowned as she stared down at the walking path. "The scene she created had a figure at the top?"

"Yes, looking down at the fallen figure," Lia said. She screwed the cap off her water bottle for a drink. "When I first saw it, I was puzzled because I took it to be a depiction of the Jack and Jill nursery rhyme. But instead of Jack having fallen, it was clearly a female figure below, one that Cori called Jessica."

Tiffany picked up her pace. "This is all very interesting—and disturbing," she said. "But why are you sharing this? What do you want from me?"

"Help," Lia said. When Tiffany looked at her, Lia gestured toward an empty park bench up ahead. "Could we sit for a minute? It'd be easier for me. Just a minute."

"Sure." Tiffany veered toward the bench.

When they'd settled, and each had taken a swallow of water, Lia said, "I don't believe Cori's death was accidental, or Jessica's, either. The more I've found out about the two, the closer I get to believing Jessica was pushed to her death and that Cori witnessed it. I think Cori might have been murdered because of what she knew."

"You *think* that," Tiffany said after a few moments. "I'm guessing you can't actually prove it."

"No. The police found no evidence, and neither have I. It's near impossible when the murder weapon is a steep, rocky waterfall."

"Of course," Tiffany agreed. "So why try? What do you want from me? I certainly wasn't a witness."

Lia shook her head. "I'm trying because a young woman, who was struggling hard to have a successful life, had it taken from her just as she was nearing her goal. And I'm talking to you and to everyone I can who knew Jessica, because I'm more and more certain that Jessica's death led to Cori's. Something must have been overlooked. Someone didn't speak out all those years ago about what they knew."

Tiffany leaned forward, holding the water bottle between her bouncing knees, staring at the weedy grass below. After several silent moments she looked up at Lia.

"I'm sorry," she said. "I'm not that someone." She jumped to her feet. "You've wasted your time. And mine's running out. Sorry, but I have to go."

Tiffany abruptly jogged off, leaving Lia behind on the bench. Lia watched until she disappeared around a curve, then picked up her bottle, took a swig, and stood to head back to the park's entrance.

That's that, she thought to herself, then added, *Or maybe not. We'll just have to wait and see.*

Chapter 23

Once back home, Lia realized that with so much else on her mind, she hadn't done anything about the sweater ordered by Helen's friend, Kim. She immediately sent off a group email to the Ninth Street Knitters to announce the commission and describe the pattern, emphasizing that it would be knitted with alpaca yarn. "Who wants it, ladies? Let me know," she wrote.

Knowing the excitement that would cause, Lia smiled as she hit *send*, wondering which of her friends would ask for it. Her guess was either Maureen or Diana. If both, well, she knew they'd work it out between them.

As it grew close to four o'clock, Lia checked her phone one last time for any cancellation texts about the meeting with Megan. Finding none, she gathered her purse and keys and headed off to the alpaca farm.

As she drove, Lia thought about what lay ahead. She could only guess at the turmoil going through the mind of the young woman she was about to meet. Megan was taking an important first step toward regaining control over her own life. The last thing Lia wanted was to say the wrong thing and set her back. But Lia also needed to get a clear picture of Marc Bernard. Would that be possible without prodding Megan too much? Without upsetting or scaring her off?

Lia's thoughts flew back to their go-to solution whenever seven- or eight-year-old Hayley clammed up about anything that was bothering her. Jigsaw puzzles. Being able to look down at the pieces instead of directly at Lia or Tom helped, and as a *Kittens at Play* or *Map of the United States* puzzle slowly took shape, Hayley's story would gradually come out.

Megan, of course, wasn't eight, and jigsaw puzzles were out of the question. But alpacas weren't. A few minutes spent with those gentle animals with their huge, trusting eyes just might be helpful, or so Lia hoped. Feeling encouraged, she made her final turn into the Weber farm, parked, and texted Hayley that she had arrived.

Ava came to greet Lia as she was heading to the alpaca barn. "Hayley passed the word," she called out, her boots crunching down the gravel path. "She said she'll see you before you go."

"Megan's not here yet?" Lia asked.

"She's on her way."

Lia let Ava catch up to her. "Has she been here before?"

Ava shook her head. "I don't think so. Why?"

"I thought it might be a good idea to let her look around the farm awhile instead of rushing into any deep discussion."

"Good idea," Ava said. "She's on the shy side and will be nervous, I know, which is why I've asked her to come here, where I can be with her. I told her how easy you are to talk to, but you're still a stranger."

"Of course," Lia said. "And thank you, Ava, for being such a good friend to her."

Ava shrugged. "If I were in her shoes, I'd want someone to do the same." A soft ping sounded, and she looked at her phone. "She's here."

"Good. How about I give you two a few minutes while I hang around the barn?"

Ava agreed and headed to the parking area, while Lia followed the gravel path in the opposite direction. Clouds had moved in since she'd walked in the park with Tiffany, lowering the temperature nicely, though some of the clouds looked ominously dark. If it was going to rain, Lia hoped it would hold off, at least until Megan needed to leave. This might be Lia's only chance to talk with the girl, and interruptions of any kind weren't welcome.

From her vantage point inside the barn, Lia watched the alpacas wander about the corral until she heard voices approaching. She turned to see Ava with a girl about her age with dark hair tied similarly in a high ponytail. In contrast to Ava, who wore jeans and a bright green tee, Megan was all in black. Lia guessed it was her coffee shop uniform, which might have a colorful logoed apron added later on. Lia smiled at her.

"Mrs. Geiger," Ava said as they walked in, "this is my friend Megan Burke."

"Hi, Megan," Lia said, stepping forward. "I'm glad to meet you. And please call me Lia."

Megan's large, dark eyes were similar to those of the animals Lia had just been watching, but not nearly as trusting. Her gaze darted around uneasily until finally meeting Lia's. Her "Hi" came out softly.

"I was just trying to put names to the alpacas out there," Lia said. "I've met some of them before. Have you?"

Megan shook her head, but her expression brightened as she looked out at the corral.

"Come on," Ava said. "I'll introduce you." She led the way out and was quickly surrounded by the friendly, curly-headed animals. "This is Patsy," she said, rubbing the back of a tan alpaca, then pointed to a black one. "That's Lulu, and Rosie's the super-friendly one," she said of the fawn-colored alpaca who'd begun nuzzling Megan.

Megan laughed and patted Rosie tentatively. "Their furs are all different colors!" she said.

"Alpacas run from black, brown, and beige all the way up to white," Ava said. "And it's not fur," she added. "It's fleece, like sheep, except no lanolin. You should see them in the spring before we shear them. They're like big, fuzzy teddy bears. But they'd be too hot in the summer with all that."

"Rosie is my daughter's favorite," Lia said as the alpaca circled Megan. "Hayley works here, too."

Megan giggled as Rosie nudged her hand for more petting. "She's like my dog," she said. "Buster always wants attention."

"They're really easy to get along with," Ava said. "Just don't get between a mom and her baby. The moms can be very protective of the crias—not that they'd hurt you. More like you'd upset them a lot."

"Any moms around here?" Megan asked, and Ava pointed to one keeping her distance from them with her little one snuggling close by.

"Oh!" Megan cried, startled. "Rosie likes my bracelet." She laughed and pulled her hand out of Rosie's reach, the silvery charms glinting as the animal tried to nip at it.

"She's also our curious one," Ava said, grinning. "We have to watch out for her."

Another worker began dragging a hose out of the barn, and Ava drew Megan and Lia toward a gate in the fence, saying, "We'd better get out of the way." Once out of the corral, they leaned on the top rail to watch the alpacas enjoy a cool hosing down, one by one.

After a few quiet minutes, Lia caught Ava's eye when Megan bent down to brush a bit of alpaca fleece from her pants leg.

Nodding, Ava said to her friend, "Megan, what do you think? Shall we get into it?"

"Sure," Megan said, straightening, but she seemed to have trouble getting started as she frowned toward the activity in the corral.

"I know this is difficult for you, Megan," Lia said. "But I promise to keep whatever you say confidential as long as you want me to."

Megan sighed and tucked a loose section of hair over her ear. "The difficult part for me, Mrs. Geiger—Lia—is admitting how really, really stupid I've been."

Ava put a hand on Megan's shoulder and squeezed. "You're not alone in that, Meggy, believe me. We all do stupid things."

"You're not stupid, Megan," Lia said. "You're young and inexperienced. But you're recognizing it now. That's the important thing."

"In the beginning, I was so flattered," Megan blurted. "Marc was so . . . so, everything! Handsome, sophisticated, even funny! I didn't know he was married," she added, glancing at Lia as her cheeks flushed. "Not until just recently when somebody—not him—clued me in. And then when I asked about it, he claimed they were separated and on the verge of divorcing. I believed him. I really thought he cared about me." She grimaced. "But it was all lies. I know that now. And I stupidly fell for it."

"He's the one to blame for lying," Lia assured Megan. "You're young, and I'm guessing you've grown up around people who were generally truthful." When Megan gave a weak smile, Lia said, "He obviously played on that. And," she added, "he's done it before."

"He has," Ava said. "Starting years ago, right, Lia?"

"I'm sure he did," Lia said. "And it might have led to the deaths of two young women, the latest just two weeks ago."

Megan's head jerked. "What? How?"

"That's what I'm trying to find out. And it's only conjecture at this point, Megan, so I'll need you to keep it to yourself, okay?" When Megan quickly agreed, Lia said, "You may have heard about the young woman who fell to her death at Long Run Falls?"

"I did. I recognized the place."

"She's someone I knew well enough that I found it hard to believe she would have gone to the falls on that day—or ever. Cori had ongoing nightmares about her babysitter, who'd fallen from that identical spot twenty-six years ago. That babysitter hinted to her friends about having a secret relationship with Marc Bernard—her high school teacher at the time."

Megan was silent for a long time as she stared at the alpacas. Eventually she said, "I recognized that spot because Marc liked to hike in that area. He took me there once, to see it."

"He did?" Ava threw Lia a look.

"It was the middle of the week, when I guess he figured no one would see us together." She paused. "It was before your friend Cori had her fall," she said. "But I'm sure it was the same spot. You know why?" She turned to face Lia, who waited silently. Megan said, "Because he told me about that other girl having fallen from there, the babysitter. He didn't say her name, but he said it was someone who'd been a student of his."

Megan turned back toward the corral. "We had had an argument on the way up there," she said. "Nothing important, just something silly. But I'd never argued with Marc before, and I could tell he didn't like it. Halfway through our hike, he changed our route. All of a sudden he wanted to show me the falls. I balked. We'd been walking for a while already, heading in another direction altogether, and I was getting tired. But he insisted. By the time we finally got there, I was exhausted."

She was quiet for a while again. "He apologized afterward. Said he didn't realize how far it would be. But he must have, mustn't he? He'd been there before. But me? As usual I fell all over myself taking the blame, saying I should be in better shape and all that." She hit the fence rail with her fist. "I hate when I do that."

"He's a creep," Ava said, giving Megan a quick squeeze. "And you're way too nice to be treated like that."

Lia gave her a moment, then asked, "Did Marc ever mention Cori? Perhaps after the news of her death?"

"No." Megan turned and leaned back against the fence. "But you said she had a booth at the craft fair?"

"Yes, next to mine."

Megan held up the bracelet that Rosie had been so intrigued by—silver links with a dangling heart. Her eyes softened as she fingered it. "Marc bought me this. He said he'd thought of me when he saw it." She looked up at Lia. "He said he got it at the craft fair."

"*Our* craft fair?" Lia asked. When Megan nodded, she asked, "When?"

"About two weeks ago."

"That would have been the weekend that a story about Cori was published in the paper," Lia said. "Would he have gone there because of that?"

"I don't know," Megan said. "He said he also bought a couple of framed photos for his office, that he'd been thinking of them from another trip there. So maybe it was just a coincidence?"

"Maybe," Lia said, though she wasn't convinced.

"Megan," Ava said, "you've got to make a clean break from this guy. What he's been doing—seeing you, a student of his, and who knows how many others—is wrong for so many reasons. You know that. He shouldn't be getting away with it. You need to speak up. To report him."

Megan looked stricken. "I can't. I know I should, but I just can't. Not yet."

"Megan—," Ava began, but Lia stopped her.

"It's your decision," Lia said. "Nobody's forcing you. Just think about it."

Megan looked at Lia gratefully. "I will." She pulled out her phone to check the time. "But I have to get to my job now. Can you still drive me to Coffee Beans and Bakes?" she asked Ava.

"Of course." Ava smiled. "And I promise not to nag you on the way."

Megan smiled back. She reached over the fence toward Rosie, who'd wandered close by. "One last pet?"

Rosie was more than fine with that, and Lia watched the two obviously enjoy the interaction, glad to see some of Megan's stress melt away before she had to work. But it would return; of that Lia was quite sure.

Chapter 24

Ava and Megan took off, and Lia lingered, petting Rosie idly as she remained deep in thought.

"Thinking about adopting her?"

Lia glanced up to see Hayley walking toward her. "I don't think there's room for one more creature in my house," Lia said, smiling.

"Probably not. At least not until I get all my junk out of there." Hayley laughed. "Maybe not even then. How'd it go?" she asked, tilting her head toward the parking area.

"Well enough," Lia said. "Megan's obviously conflicted. She's angry, but more at herself, I think, than at him. It's a start, though. She had some interesting things to say." Lia gave Hayley the gist of the discussion.

"So our French instructor was at the craft fair on one of Cori's last days," Hayley said, frowning.

"Yes," Lia said.

"Sounds ominous," Hayley said.

"It does to me, too. Was he there to identify Cori? We can't know for sure. But the timing is suspicious." Lia then told Hayley about her talk with Tiffany that afternoon.

"Hmm, interesting that she agreed to talk to you," Hayley said. "But then she didn't say much, did she?"

"No, but she listened to what I had to say. I think I stirred some thoughts in her, but she wasn't ready to share them with me. At least not then."

"Well, my vote goes to the French teacher," Hayley said before she grinned. "But mostly because I don't like him." Her phone pinged, and she read a text. "By the way, don't hold dinner for me tonight. I've got a few things to take care of. One of them is this." She waggled her phone. "I could be late."

"Go do what you need to do," Lia said. "I'm done here." They hugged, and Lia watched as Hayley strolled away, her phone to her ear. Lia felt a nudge at her elbow and saw Rosie leaning toward her.

"Feeling neglected?" Lia asked as she scratched the friendly alpaca's head. A fly tickled Lia's ankle, and she bent down to swat it away. As she did, she noticed something sparkling in the grass, just inside the fence. It was Megan's silver bracelet. It must have slipped off while she was patting Rosie good-bye.

"What a shame," Lia said. She reached between the rails to pluck it from its nest of grassy weeds, then brushed off dust as she straightened and considered what to do. One impulse was to immediately put it back and hope Megan would never think of the piece again. But Lia remembered the expression on Megan's face as she showed them the bracelet. She wasn't ready to emotionally separate herself from Marc Bernard. She'd want the bracelet back.

Where did she say she worked? Coffee Beans and

Bakes? Lia could return it on her way home. After that, she sincerely hoped Megan would trash it, but that'd be up to her.

In her car, Lia did a search on her phone and found the website for Coffee Beans and Bakes. Its location wasn't far from the central Crandalsburg restaurant area. Confident that she could find the place easily, she put her car into gear and drove off.

When Lia walked into the coffee shop, the aromas of both coffee and cooked bacon made her stomach rumble. She glanced at the overhead menu and saw several choices that would do nicely for a dinner—stacked sandwiches, entree salads, and more. And Hayley had said she might be late.

"Lia!" Megan's voice from behind the counter startled her, apparently as much as Lia's presence had startled Megan.

Lia dug into her pocket for the silver bracelet and held it out. "I found this in the grass next to the fence."

"Oh! Thank you." Megan reached for it. "I didn't realize I'd lost it."

Lia noticed that instead of putting it on, Megan slipped it into a pocket. "Walking in," Lia said, "I suddenly got hungry. The menu looks pretty good. I think I'll get something for myself."

"Great! What would you like?"

Lia ordered a chicken wrap along with a fruit assortment. "And hazelnut coffee, if you please."

"Got it. I'll give a call when it's ready," Megan said, putting in the order.

The shop was less than half-full and Lia easily found a table next to the window where she could wait. Megan took another customer's order, then puttered around her work area. Glancing her way as she waited, Lia saw Megan stiffen as the door opened and a new customer walked in. It was a good-looking man who appeared young at first, dressed as he was in trim jeans and a tee. But Lia caught clues that added on several more years—facial lines, flecks of gray in his dark hair—none of which actually detracted from his looks, but they adjusted the original impression. From that, along with Megan's reaction, Lia could only assume this was Marc Bernard.

He went up to the counter and leaned toward Megan—possessively, Lia felt as she watched. He reached for Megan's hand, but she pulled it back, though she remained where she was. He spoke too quietly for Lia to pick up more than an occasional word, but he seemed to be urging Megan toward something, an invitation of some sort. Lia was pleased to see Megan shake her head. Bernard continued coaxing until another worker appeared from the back and set an order in front of Megan, who then turned to work the coffee machine. She called out to Lia that her order was ready.

When Lia went up, Bernard sidled left but only slightly, clearly intending to stay as he continued to lean on the counter. As Megan rang up Lia's bill, she said, "Marc, this is a new friend of mine, Lia Geiger."

Marc turned startlingly blue eyes on Lia as he straightened and smiled engagingly. "How do you do, Lia. Will you help me shake some sense into our mutual friend here?"

"She's already been doing that," Megan said. "We had a good talk just this afternoon."

"Really?" Lia saw Marc's eyes narrow, but he quickly recovered and flashed Lia a bright smile. "Then all should be very well."

"Lia," Megan said, "I forgot to ask. Did you want this to take out?"

"I think I'll have it here," Lia said. She reached for the tray holding her meal and smiled benignly at Marc. "Good to meet you," she said, before heading off to her table. She sat where she could continue to keep Marc and Megan in view.

Customers arrived more steadily, keeping Megan busy, but Marc continued to linger and talk to her whenever she came near, though his tone, from what Lia could pick up, grew increasingly annoyed. Finally, as enough customers appeared to prevent further conversation, he bought a coffee and turned away from the counter. To Lia's surprise, he came over to her table.

"May I join you, Lia?" he asked.

"Yes, of course," Lia said, then watched as he took the chair across from hers.

"So," he said after a quick sip from his cup and flashing his amazingly bright smile again, "we have a friend in common. But I know nothing about you other than your name. Tell me, who is Lia Geiger?"

Lia smiled politely. "Nobody in particular. Just a woman who lives in Crandalsburg."

"In Crandalsburg? And why have we never met? I've been here for many years."

"Perhaps because I've only been here for a few months. And you live in Crandalsburg?" Lia asked, preferring to turn the questions away from herself. "I suppose that's convenient to the college?"

"Aha, see! You know so much more about me. Yes, I teach at the college. Now tell me what you do."

"I'm retired," Lia said. She decided not to bring in her work at the craft fair. "I was a surgical nurse."

"A surgical nurse?" Marc's eyebrows rose. "How interesting. But how does that bring you and Megan together? Did she have surgery? You saved her life and you've been friends ever since?" He said it jokingly, but Lia noticed a new edge to his tone.

She shook her head. "No, nothing like that. Just through mutual friends. And you know her through her classes, I presume?"

Marc nodded but continued his focus on Lia. "Just mutual friends, you say, and you're new to Crandalsburg. So you haven't known each other long?" When Lia agreed, he added, "Or very well? And yet," he said, the edge in his voice sharpening, "you feel you have the right to tell her how to run her life?" His smile had also disappeared.

Lia lifted her chin before answering and returned his gaze directly. "Merely offering a new perspective, which, of course, she's free to ignore."

"It didn't seem that way to me," he said, actual anger now seeping into his voice though he seemed to be struggling to keep it down. "It seemed like someone poking their nose into something that is none of their business." He scraped his chair back and banged his coffee cup into a nearby trash receptacle, the noise causing several heads to turn and Lia to jump, though she did her best to cover it.

"I'm sorry you see it that way," she said evenly.

Marc got to his feet and stood over her, the wide smile back but now more sharklike than friendly. "I'd advise you to stick to your knitting," he said. "Good night, Lia Geiger. Perhaps we'll meet again."

He turned and left the shop, leaving Lia shaken. How did he know about her knitting? Or was it simply a guess, an assumption that all older women knit as they watched their soap operas? And were his last words about meeting again a veiled threat? Or was she reading too much into it?

Megan, she saw, continued to bustle about behind her counter, working to keep up with the dinner-hour rush. Lia watched for a while, giving her nerves time to settle—and Marc Bernard time to be completely gone. When she felt better, she headed on out to her car, telling herself there was nothing to be worried about. At the same time she scoured the area carefully with her eyes.

Chapter 25

As she walked into her little home, everything felt wonderfully calm and normal to Lia. Daphne met her at the door, offering welcome comfort with rumbling purrs as Lia picked her up for a hug. Lia's phone rang, and she set the cat down to answer.

"Please, please, please let me have it." It was Maureen responding to Lia's notice about the alpaca sweater commission, pretty much as Lia had expected.

"You're the first to call, so it's yours," Lia said.

"I did check with Diana," Maureen said. "She won't be finished with the sweater she's working on, so she's okay if I take this one."

"Good. I'll get all the information about the pattern and colors to you on Thursday."

"Wonderful!" Maureen then asked, "How did it go at Bob's photography club on Friday?"

Friday? Only three days ago, though to Lia it seemed

like ages. "It was interesting," she said and launched into a description of the evening, leading to her talk with Kevin Shaw when they all went out for pizza afterward. "When I asked him directly about Jessica, he seemed evasive. But it turned out that the other man at the table, besides Kevin and Bob, was Crandalsburg's police chief. He spoke to me privately and told me about Kevin's alibi for the time of Jessica's death."

"Wow! That must have been awkward, I mean about questioning Kevin in front of a police chief."

"It was, once I realized it, but he was perfectly nice about it."

"So Kevin's off the suspect list?"

"Not necessarily." Lia explained about the possible weakness in the man's alibi that she'd learned about from Nicole.

"And the police didn't see that?" Maureen asked.

"Well, at the time, they weren't looking into Jessica's death as a possible murder," Lia said. "As Pete said, there was no evidence to suggest that."

"Pete?"

"Pete Sullivan, the police chief. And I don't have anything concrete to take to him."

"Yet."

"Yes," Lia agreed, but would she ever have it? With no witnesses and the murder weapon being a waterfall filled with rocks, what could she reasonably expect to come up with?

She heard a car door slam out front. Certain it must be Hayley, she ended her call and went to the kitchen to pull out an assortment of leftovers. In a few moments, the front door opened, and Hayley called out, "I'm home," as she headed straight to the kitchen.

"Hungry?" Lia asked.

"Ravenous. Did you eat?" Hayley eyed the covered dishes spread across the counter.

"I did," Lia said. "At Coffee Beans and Bakes. Which I'll get to in a minute. Choose what you want for your dinner first. There's plenty to pick from, as you see."

Hayley checked each container and quickly filled a plate. She warmed it all in the microwave, while Lia poured out glasses of iced tea for both of them and carried them to the table in her dining area. When Hayley joined her, Lia smiled at the mix of food—a slice of ham buried under gravy-topped mashed potatoes under dabs of various leftover vegetables.

"When you were little, you insisted that nothing on your plate should touch," she said, reminiscing.

"Did I?" Hayley said, digging in. "I must not have been very hungry back then."

"You ate less," Lia agreed. "But you were little, and you didn't have a job with such long hours."

"Which I love," Hayley said, "but particularly today."

"Oh?"

Hayley held up one finger. "In a minute." She shoveled in another forkful, and Lia let her be, sipping at her iced tea. She also steered Daphne away from bothering Hayley, coaxing her onto her own lap.

Eventually, Hayley slowed down. When most of the flower pattern on the plate became visible, she reached for her glass and leaned back in her chair for a break.

"It's my boss who made it clear to me today why I picked the right place to work," she said before taking a drink.

"Mr. Weber? Why, what did he do?"

"He took a call from Bethanne King."

"About the fundraising event?" Lia asked.

"About me." Hayley grinned at Lia's puzzled expression. "She wanted to know if I was related to Lia Geiger. Mr. Weber said she was clearly angry about something, though she didn't say what. He guessed it had something to do with you and decided it was none of his—or Bethanne's—business."

"So what did he say to her?"

"He said he had no idea who I was related to and didn't care and pointed out that Geiger was a pretty common name in this area. He then changed the subject to the fundraising event. Fortunately, it's too late for her to pull it away from us."

"Was that the end of it?" Lia asked.

"She didn't press him, so I guess it was. If she believed him or not, I can't say. He told me afterward that now he understood what I must be dealing with, which was nice of him."

"Thank goodness!" Lia said. "I'm so sorry. I should have thought about how this might have affected you."

Hayley scraped up some mashed potato. "If you had, I would have still insisted that you keep working at it. What if Bethanne King is our murderer! Her threatening my job wouldn't be any reason to let her off the hook."

"Tiffany obviously told her about our meeting this afternoon," Lia said. "But Bethanne's reaction doesn't necessarily mean she's guilty of murder. She's a controlling woman and could have simply been angry over my intrusion."

"Yeah, maybe," Hayley admitted. "But what if Tiffany suspects her mother of murdering Jessica and Cori? Even though she didn't say so to you, she might have asked Bethanne pointed questions that she didn't like."

"I think that's very possible," Lia said. "I mean Tiffany's suspicions. I just wish she'd shared them with me instead of going to her mother, if that's what she did."

"I know. A lot of ifs. What will you do? Talk to her again?"

"I'm not sure," Lia said, shifting Daphne a little more comfortably on her lap. "It might be best to let her work it out for herself awhile."

Hayley carried her empty plate into the kitchen and slipped it into the dishwasher. "Any ice cream left?" she asked. She opened the freezer and pulled out a carton. "Want some?" she asked, reaching for a bowl in an upper cabinet.

"No, thanks. The dinner I had at Coffee Beans and Bakes was very filling."

"Oh, that's right. You said you ate there. How come?"

Lia explained about the dropped bracelet and how she'd decided to return it right away.

"Did you talk to Megan some more?" Hayley began scooping out ice cream, and Lia waited until she came back to the table.

"The French teacher, Marc Bernard, showed up while I was at the coffee shop."

"He did? Wow." Hayley slid back onto her chair. "What's he like?"

Lia described Bernard and how he hung around Megan while she worked, though she seemed to be resisting whatever he was proposing. "I wasn't close enough to hear."

"Too bad, but good for her," Hayley said, digging into her chocolate peanut butter blast treat. "Maybe her talk with you and Ava is working."

"I hope so." Lia decided not to say anything about Bernard turning his anger toward her. No use worrying Hayley when it might be a big nothing.

"By the way," Hayley said, "Brady said Chief Sullivan mentioned you."

"He did? Whatever about?" Something to do with Kevin Shaw?

"Seems he's going to be in our neighborhood tomorrow. I think you signed a petition for the playground to be fixed up, is that right?"

Lia had to think back. "I may have. I do remember somebody coming to the door with a clipboard once. Yes, that must have been it."

"Well, the mayor and Chief Sullivan will be doing a ribbon cutting and making speeches. Brady must have mentioned where we live. He figures they want to stir a good turnout—you know, in case TV cameras show up. What do you think, Mom? You might get on TV!"

Lia grimaced. "I can do without that." She thought about the time she was caught by the cameras after having called police to a crime scene. Not a pleasant experience. But a playground ribbon cutting would be totally different. "I might go," she said, "just to see and maybe meet more of our neighbors. What time is it?"

Hayley grabbed her phone and shot off a text. After a few minutes she got an answer from Brady. "One o'clock."

Lia nodded. She saw Hayley continue her text conversation with Brady, so she picked up Hayley's empty ice cream dish and carried it to the kitchen for her. One o'clock the next day would be convenient. Perhaps Sharon would like to walk over with her. Lia had never been to a ribbon cutting of any kind before. And seeing Pete Sullivan in an official role would be interesting, too. Yes, she'd definitely go and help fill out the crowd.

Chapter 26

The next morning, Lia was about to call Sharon when she spotted her outside, working on her flower garden. On the verge of stepping out, Lia remembered the milk sitting out and went to put it back in the refrigerator, sure that Sharon would be weeding for a while. But when she returned, her neighbor was heading back to her house.

"Sharon!" Lia called, leaning out her door. "Do you have a minute?"

"Sure." Sharon set down her gardening tools carrier, then said, "Careful!" She pointed to Lia's open door. "Your cat is joining us."

Lia quickly scooped Daphne up to put her safely back inside. "Thanks," Lia told Sharon as she pulled the door shut. "She's been getting more curious about the outdoors lately for some reason."

"She probably wouldn't go far," Sharon assured her. She

pulled off her gardening gloves to toss into her tool carrier and wiped her brow, asking, "What's up?"

Lia trotted down from her porch. "There's going to be a to-do for the refurbished playground over on Fourth Street, today at one. The mayor and our police chief, cutting a ribbon and making speeches. I'm going. Want to come along?"

"Hmm. I remember the struggle to get that project into the budget. I'd like to see what they did with it. The speeches? I don't know. I might not hang around too long for those."

"I'll see how it goes myself," Lia said. "But great! Glad to have your company. Probably a fifteen-minute walk, right? I'll meet you out here at a quarter to." She went back to her house to find Daphne sitting queen-like on the sofa.

"Don't look so innocent," Lia mock-scolded. "Trying to sneak out like that." She picked up the cat for a hug, knowing how bad she would feel if anything happened to her. The outside world could be a dangerous place for a house cat, and Daphne had wormed her way firmly into Lia's heart during the few short weeks she'd been with her.

Lia's phone rang, and she returned the cat to her throne to answer. It was Maggie.

"Hey, Lia, just wanted to tell you I went to the fabric shop yesterday and managed to chat with Cori's friend Amanda while I was there."

"Did anything new come up about Cori?"

"Well, Amanda talked a lot about things she and Cori did together in school, most of them not too unusual. But there was one thing."

"Yes?" Lia sank into her knitting chair to listen.

"Once, when they were about twelve, Cori asked Amanda to come with her when she had to go to the dentist. Cori's mom had made an appointment for her for a regular checkup, but with somebody new. That made Cori nervous, seeing a different person, but he was at the same dental office she'd gone to before, just a new partner. Her mother told her she was old enough to go by herself, but Cori begged Amanda to come with her.

"Amanda said everything was going okay. The hygienist, who knew Cori, let Amanda come back with her and sit in the corner while she did all the cleaning stuff. But then the new dentist came in to introduce himself, and Cori suddenly went ballistic."

"Wow. Did Amanda know why?"

"She didn't, other than maybe because the new guy was a stranger. She said Cori just had a meltdown, and they had to call her mother to come get her. Everybody was upset, of course, with Cori's mom apologizing like crazy and hustling Cori out of the place. Amanda didn't see Cori for a while after that, and when she finally did, the last thing she wanted to do was bring it up."

"Sure," Lia said. "She was only twelve. About that new dentist. Did Amanda give his name?"

"Not exactly," Maggie said. "But she's gone to him herself since then and thought he was perfectly nice. He apparently took over the practice after the older guy retired, so I'm pretty sure it was Dr. Shaw."

Kevin Shaw. Lia had half expected that and wasn't shocked to have his name confirmed. She *was* disturbed to learn about Cori's reaction to him. It would have been six years after Jessica's death, an event that Cori had nightmares about. Had she recognized Shaw as the person she claimed to have seen push Jessica to her death? Was the memory—or perhaps imagination—of a six-year-old trustworthy?

"Is that any help?" Maggie asked.

"Yes," Lia said, "I think it is, but I can't say exactly how, for now."

"Well," Maggie said. "Maybe one piece of the puzzle, huh?"

"It could be. Thanks, Maggie."

"No problem. I picked up some great fabric in the process. Keep me updated, okay?"

Lia promised and ended the call, remaining in her knitting chair to do some thinking.

S haron had changed out of her gardening clothes into a sundress and sandals. "I might try to speak to our mayor afterward about an issue or two," she explained. "Thought I'd do better looking presentable."

On the walk over, she chatted about those issues, which had to do with protecting a particular stream and its surrounding area. Normally, Lia would have been interested in the environmental subject, and she tried her best to pay attention. But her thoughts kept wandering back to what Maggie had told her about Kevin Shaw. Fortunately, Sharon didn't seem to notice, and they arrived soon at the playground area to merge into a gathering crowd.

A podium with a microphone was set up at the gate to the playground, and a man in a short-sleeved white shirt and tie fiddled with the wires as other office types milled nearby. Lia didn't see Pete Sullivan or the mayor but thought they might have been part of a small group on the far side of the playground, close to a line of cars, including police cars. She glanced around, wondering if Brady might be there, but didn't spot him.

She did see a local television station van, so Hayley was right about the TV coverage. Lia smiled to herself. Twenty seconds' worth, max, would be her guess, unless it happened to be a slow news day. She also saw an ice cream truck farther down, taking smart advantage of a gathering that included children.

"Wow! They did a pretty good job!" Sharon said, looking at the new playground equipment, whose brightly colored slides, swings, and climbing apparatuses sparkled in the sun.

"My kids have been drooling over it for weeks," a young woman said, turning to them. "Hi, Sharon! How are you doing?"

"Rachel!" Sharon said. "I didn't see you there. Lia, this is my gardening club friend, Rachel Stokes." She introduced Lia, and the two exchanged greetings.

"Where are your children?" Lia asked.

"Down there," Rachel said, pointing to the ice cream truck. "Third and fourth in line." She laughed. "A small price to pay to keep them quiet until the speeches are over and the gates are opened."

Lia glanced at her watch. "It should begin in a couple of minutes."

They chatted as more people gathered, Lia's back to the houses across the street. At one point, Lia noticed Rachel staring over her shoulder.

"That's Robin Wendt," Rachel said. Lia turned to see Cori's half sister climbing several steps toward a brick house, newer and larger than Lia's but with early-twentieth-century charm. Robin held thick, interior decorating–type books, possibly wallpaper or paint samples, and fabric pieces. With the street currently lined with cars, Lia guessed she must have had to carry her load some distance from her parking spot.

"My neighbor used her," Rachel said. "She did a nice job

on their living room. I used to see her coming and going a
lot. But that was some time ago. I'd heard her business had
slumped lately. But it looks like she might have a job at that
place. Good for her."

"I've met her," Lia said. "Glad to hear it." She watched
as Robin pressed the doorbell, then turned to look at the
playground crowd. From the distance it was difficult to be
sure, but Lia felt like Robin had zeroed in on her in particular, and that her posture had stiffened in annoyance.
The door to the house opened, and as Robin disappeared
inside, Lia shook herself. Likely she'd only seen frustration
in the woman over the loss of a handy parking spot.

The ribbon-cutting ceremony was about to begin. Lia
turned back toward the podium, finally seeing Pete Sullivan as he stood to the left and slightly behind the mayor,
Allen Johnson. Pete looked very official in his formal blue
uniform and hat, different from the man who'd given a talk
about his photos and later shared a table of pizza and beer
with her. His bearing at this event was stiff and serious, at
least at first. Lia smiled as she caught him winking at a
group of small children standing in front.

Mayor Johnson spoke first. Bald-headed, rotund, and with
a lively manner, he kept his speech brief, thankfully, possibly
in deference to the hot sun many in the crowd were enduring
and the beads of perspiration appearing on his own pate,
which he dabbed at with a white handkerchief. He then
turned the microphone over to Pete, who said a few words
about safety and monitoring. After that, the large scissors
came out to ceremonially cut the playground's ribbon.

The crowd clapped and the mayor grinned and waved.
A flood of children were welcomed in, followed closely by
a television cameraman.

"I'm going to try to catch Johnson. Wish me luck," Sharon said and took off. Lia wandered closer to the fence to watch the excitement of the youngsters, enjoying the squeals of joy as they tested the slides and swings.

"Makes you want to be a kid again, doesn't it?"

Lia turned to see Pete at her shoulder. He'd taken off his hat and unbuttoned his uniform jacket, which Lia guessed must be uncomfortably warm.

"It does," she said. "You gave a very nice speech."

"Thank you," he said, grinning. "It's pretty much my standard, adjusted for the occasion as needed."

"I hung on every word," Lia assured him with a matching grin.

"Nice of you to come. We never know if we'll be delivering speeches only to our own staff and maybe a stray dog or two."

"Brady, that is, Officer McCormick, passed the word to my daughter about the ceremony. Otherwise I might not have known."

Pete nodded. His face grew serious. "I, uh, hope I didn't come on too strong at our last meeting. I mean about your looking into the deaths at Long Run Falls."

"Not at all," Lia said. "I know from your perspective that I must appear to be an interfering loon." When Pete chuckled and shook his head, she added, "You were perfectly polite as you gave me good advice." She paused. "Which I have to admit I've been ignoring."

Pete sighed at that, but Lia rushed ahead. "Because I believe I have a bit of an advantage, being a nonofficial person. People tell me things that they might not think of mentioning to the police."

"And they've done so recently?"

"They have. Things that might change your mind about those two deaths being accidental."

Pete was silent for several moments. An aide came up to say the car was waiting for him. Pete nodded. "I'll be right there." Then he turned to Lia. "Have you ever been to that area of Long Run Falls we're talking about?"

Surprised, Lia said, "No, I haven't."

"I already planned to take the rest of the afternoon off. If you're free, I'd like to show you the spot in question. We could discuss your new information then."

Lia had to think for a minute. All that time, she'd been imagining the area where both Jessica and Cori had slipped to their deaths, seeing it through others' eyes. Perhaps it was time to see it through her own. She never expected to do so accompanied by the Crandalsburg chief of police. But who safer to be with? She saw the aide fidgeting nearby, waiting for Pete. She nodded.

"Yes, I'd like to."

"Good. Give me an hour. I'll pick you up." With that, Pete walked off toward the car, Lia watching, then realizing he'd never asked for her address. She laughed. Of course, being who he was, Pete either knew or could find out easily. She wasn't sure how that made her feel. Reassured or uneasy?

Chapter 27

After a brisk walk home, during which Sharon described the few points she'd managed to make with the mayor, Lia bid good-bye to her neighbor and hurried into her house. Daphne received a quick pat as Lia rushed by and up the stairs. She needed to exchange her sandals for the sturdier shoes she'd worn on her walk with Tiffany the day before. Those soles would be worn thin before long at the rate things were going. She also decided to change her long pants for shorts and her blouse for a tee, then slathered on sunscreen as a precaution. Further thought reminded her that the day's high temperature called for water. Would Hayley mind if she borrowed her small insulated backpack? To be sure, Lia texted her, then added why she needed it. Hayley shot back a quick OK, so Lia got the backpack out of the hall closet. She filled it with a water bottle and two bananas she had planned to let ripen a little more for banana bread. That could wait for another time.

She was ready when Pete pulled up in a silver Equinox. Lia stepped out to save him the trouble of coming to the door but then noticed Daphne close at her heels. By the time she'd managed to gently push her back and close the door, Pete was already out of his SUV. Lia waved him to stay put and hurried over.

Pete had changed to hiking clothes, too, and he noted her backpack as he held the car door for her. "You brought water. Good idea."

Lia smiled and showed him the bananas. "My Girl Scout training," she explained. "To be prepared."

Pete got behind the wheel and buckled himself in. As they took off, he asked, "So you were a Girl Scout?"

"And a Brownie leader," Lia said. "For my daughter's troop. Were you in Boy Scouts?" she asked, remembering Brady's tale of his scouting activities and how they had influenced his decision to join the police force.

Pete surprised her by shaking his head. "No troops in my area. We were pretty rural. But I picked up most of those skills anyway, out of necessity."

They chatted more as he drove, Lia learning, among other things, that Pete grew up in Colorado, and before she knew it, he was pulling into a small parking area.

"I didn't realize it was so close," she said, unbuckling, but then thought of Cori, who at six had managed to make her way to the falls on foot, at least if her nightmares were to be believed. "Will the hike be long?"

"Not the way we'll go," Pete said. He grabbed his own backpack from the back seat. "There's plenty of trails that crisscross each other. We'll take the most direct route."

Lia spotted a large trail map and walked over to check it out. Pete joined her and pointed out their trail, which Lia studied. She then saw the blue line of Long Run Falls and traced it with her finger to what looked like a wide, flat area. "Is that where they found Cori?" she asked, and Pete nodded. She winced and stepped back, hitching up her backpack. "Okay, let's go."

The path was wide and heavily mulched—easy walking. As the trees grew denser, their shade lowered the temperature comfortably, and Lia almost felt out for a leisurely stroll, enjoying glimpses of unusual plants near the path edges and the occasional twitter of birds overhead.

They came to a fork, and two hikers descended toward them from the trail on the right. The four greeted one another genially as Pete veered toward the left path, Lia following. Before long, she could hear water sounds, and as the trees cleared, Pete pointed ahead. "That's it."

Lia stepped forward. She guessed they were at about the midpoint of the waterfall, not a rushing river but a steady flow coming from somewhere above. As she moved closer to the rocky edge, she could see the stream drop steeply until it gradually turned out of sight.

"There's no fence," she said. "Just these rocks that anyone could climb over."

"Warning signs are posted everywhere," Pete said, pointing to one near Lia. "And those rocks are at least knee-high and uneven, not tempting to walk or stand on."

Lia glanced around. They were in a good-sized clearing, perhaps four hundred square feet. The walking path skirted it beyond a line of trees. Nicole—or was it Lauren?—had described it as a make-out location, and it did offer a modicum of privacy. Lia pictured Marc bringing Megan there to show her where Jessica had fallen to her death and shook her head in disgust. What had been in his mind at the time?

To frighten her? Warn her? As Megan described the incident, it certainly hadn't been for anything of a romantic nature.

Then Lia pictured Cori there on her final day. "What makes you sure Cori fell from this point?" she asked Pete.

"We found her sunglasses," he said. "Prescription glasses. Her sister identified them, as did her optometrist."

Lia nodded. She walked along the edging rocks. "The ruling was accidental," she said. "But I found the fact that Cori was here at all very odd. How was *accidental* explained?"

"It wasn't, at least not in detail. Nobody witnessed her fall. But there were no signs of a struggle, here or on her body, that is, nothing that couldn't be explained by the fall. All we could prove was that it was possible for her to have stepped onto those rocks and to slip. Lacking evidence of a deliberate jump, what was left was accidental."

"Her sister told me she believes Cori killed herself," Lia said. "But I didn't see any signs in Cori of wanting to end her life."

"So you've talked to the sister? Want to tell me about the others and this new information you've come up with?" Pete went over to a large, flat rock several feet back from the edge and invited her to sit.

Lia did, pulling out the water bottle for a drink but leaving the bananas in the backpack. Pete waited as she gathered her thoughts.

"Okay," she said. "First of all, you told me Kevin Shaw had an alibi for Jessica Ackerman's time of death. The former girlfriend of that friend who provided the alibi strongly believes that he would have said anything to help out his buddy."

Pete frowned. "Lying to the police is serious stuff."

"It is. Perhaps the young man didn't realize that at the time. Or he might have rationalized it as simply saving Kevin from a needless hassle since, to his mind, Kevin couldn't possibly have caused Jessica's death.

"But there's more," Lia said. She told him about Cori's panicked reaction on seeing Kevin in the dentist's office.

Pete thought that over. "Was that ever explained?" he asked.

"Not by Cori. Her mother could only guess."

"So it might have been simply a troubled young girl's inflated fear of a dentist?"

"It could have," Lia conceded. "But along with the other things we know about Shaw, I'm skeptical of that." She drew a long breath. "Then there's Jessica's high school French teacher, Marc Bernard. Did you know about him? That there might have been a highly inappropriate relationship between the two?"

"His name came up," Pete acknowledged. "*Might have been* never became *actual* in our books."

"He's still teaching—at the college level now—and still preying on young female students. I spoke to one who has been lured into an inappropriate relationship. To me that makes the rumors of the same with Jessica believable. And he had reasons to keep Jessica from exposing him."

"Is this female student you spoke with willing to talk to us?"

"Not yet," Lia admitted.

"Well, then . . ." Pete shrugged helplessly.

"I'll see what I can do." Lia paused. Should she bring up Bethanne King? She had very little to offer Pete concerning her, and the repercussions, if it got back to Bethanne, could be a problem. Hayley was already on Bethanne's watch list. "There's another person," she said carefully. "Someone I consider a strong person of interest, but I'm not ready to give a name yet. This person considered Jessica a roadblock to their own daughter's success and might have acted, or arranged, to remove that block."

"Pretty vague," Pete said.

"Yes. But there's a good chance more might come up soon. All three of these people, Kevin Shaw, Marc Bernard, and that third person, would have been aware of Cori's return to Crandalsburg from the publicity she received. If one of the three believed she had witnessed and remembered them murder Jessica, that person might have come after Cori."

Pete sighed. "A big *if* in that statement."

"But there's also my new information," Lia said.

"Some," Pete agreed. "Nothing I could take to the DA."

"But something to look into?"

"Possibly. I'll think about it."

"Thank you," Lia said. She stood. "And thank you for showing me this spot." She went back to the rocky edge. "I still can't imagine Cori leaning precariously enough to lose her balance and fall. Or coming here at all, for that matter."

"But she did—come here, at least," Pete said, picking up a small branch and tossing it into the brush.

"Yes, you said her sunglasses were here."

"And they were clean enough not to have been here long."

"Where, exactly?" Lia asked.

"We found them on that flat rock we were sitting on."

Lia turned to consider that. "Why would she have taken them off? It was a sunny day, wasn't it?"

Pete nodded.

"And they were prescription glasses. People usually leave those on until they go indoors or it gets too dark outdoors to wear them. Which it hadn't."

Pete coughed. "There's an odd thing that also happens—very often." He paused, and Lia looked at him. "When someone intends to take their own life, they tend to carefully set aside things they're used to protecting—watches, glasses."

Lia shook her head.

"It's not proof," Pete said. "There was no note, no witness. I'm just saying that could be the explanation you're looking for."

"No," Lia said. "It's not. Cori wasn't intending to take her own life." She felt sure of that.

Pete sighed but nodded. "Ready to go?"

Lia glanced around one last time. Then she picked up Hayley's backpack and slipped the water bottle into it. "I am," she said and headed away from the waterfall, toward the trail.

Chapter 28

Lia mulled over Pete's words off and on for hours. Was his implication that Cori took her own life correct? It was what Robin believed. But Pete's viewpoint was a policeman's, which went by statistics, and those were never one hundred percent. Robin was Cori's sister, which should have been reliable, but it was still an opinion. But Lia wanted another viewpoint.

She thought back to Cori's wake, where she'd spoken to a longtime friend of Cori's mother. They'd only managed a few words. Lia would like a few more.

The next morning Lia did an online search and discovered Shirley Dunn lived next door to the house Cori grew up in and where she'd returned to live with her mother after briefly striking out on her own. Certainly an ideal location to know the family well. Would Shirley remember Lia and be open to talking with her? She'd soon find out.

Lia called and got a landline's answering machine. She

left a message, explaining as concisely as she could who she was and why she'd called, then left her own number and hung up with fingers crossed. She didn't have long to wait. Within minutes, Lia's phone rang, showing Shirley Dunn's phone number.

"I'm so sorry, dear," Shirley said. "I get so many—are they called spam calls?—that I thought you were another one. Then I listened to your message. Of course I remember you! We had that nice chat over by the punch bowl. Your message said you wanted to talk about Cori. Why don't you come here, dearie, and we can visit over coffee. Much better than over the phone, don't you think?"

Lia readily agreed. Shirley gave her an address and directions, which Lia didn't need, and told her to come whenever she was ready. "I don't get out that much," she said. "So I'm delighted to have company."

Lia gave her half an hour and when she pulled up saw Shirley waiting at her door. The house was as lovely as Judith Littlefield's, next door. Old, but well kept up and with a similar large, welcoming porch. Lia glanced over to the Littlefield house as she climbed out of her car and saw that Cori's crocheted wreath was gone from the door. It made Lia sigh, but she set that feeling aside as she headed toward Shirley and her bright smile.

"Come in, come in!" Shirley said, pushing her screen door open for Lia, then stepping back to make way for her. Her yellow flower-printed dress reached down to sturdy orthopedic shoes, and she held a rubber-tipped cane, which she lifted to display. "Two more weeks with this thing . . . maybe," she said. "Turned my ankle chasing after a piece of mail that blew out of my hand. Serves me right," she said with a laugh. "It was just junk mail!"

She waved Lia into the living room, where a silver tea

set waited on the coffee table. "I couldn't resist pulling it out," she said, following Lia and taking the hostess spot on the sofa. "It's so seldom I have an excuse anymore. It was my grandmother's, and I know she'd love to see me using it."

"It's beautiful," Lia said as she sank onto a nearby chair. "I have a few special things that were wedding gifts that I don't bring out often enough."

"We should force ourselves every day," Shirley said. "They weren't given just to look at." She poured coffee into a flowered china cup. "Cream and sugar?"

"Just cream. Thank you," Lia said as she took it, then reached for a cookie as Shirley held out a small silver plate. "I feel transported to another time," she said with a smile. "And one not that long ago."

Shirley nodded, the curls of her silvery hair bobbing. "It's a shame, isn't it? How things change and sometimes get lost? Well!" she said, in a getting-down-to-business tone. "What was it you wanted to ask me, dear?"

Lia took a sip of her coffee, which was delicious, and set the delicate cup and saucer down carefully. "At Cori's wake, you said you were a good friend of Cori's mother."

"Judith," Shirley said, nodding. "We've lived side by side for years."

"When Cori came back to Crandalsburg to live with her mother, did you see much of her?"

Shirley poured her own coffee and stirred it as she thought back. "Off and on. Cori was a shy girl, not one to run over and visit, at least not on her own. But she'd hang around if I stopped in for a chat with Judith."

"How did she seem to you?" Lia asked. "Happy? Sad?"

"Oh, definitely happy, that is, after she was given a booth at the craft fair." Shirley's eyes lit up. "Then, when that story came out about her in the paper, she was really excited—well, her version of excitement, I mean. You'd have to know her well to recognize it."

Shirley reached for a cookie and bit into it, catching a few crumbs. "I'd been looking after Cori a bit after Judith's accident, you know. When that reporter asked to stop by and interview her, Cori was at first reluctant. But I told her I'd come over and be with her, if she liked, which I did. And I know Cori could see that the reporter was impressed, especially when she saw all the crocheted pieces laid out. That helped Cori relax, and she posed quite nicely with it all for the photos. I was so proud.

"But even then, Cori worried until the story was finally published. That was the first and only time she came knocking on my door on her own. To show it to me!" Shirley laughed. "So, yes, she was very happy those final days." She looked down at her hands quietly a moment before bringing back her smile. "I'm so grateful she had that."

Lia sipped her coffee, giving Shirley a few seconds, then said, "I spent some time with Cori the morning of that last day. Did you happen to talk to her later on?"

"No." Shirley shook her head sadly. "I wish I had. Maybe I could have stopped her. Who knows? But my granddaughter took me to my doctor's appointment." She pointed downward. "The ankle, you know. It took a long time. I think somebody had to be squeezed in at the last minute—some kind of accident. I didn't mind at the time. Things happen. I remember I told my granddaughter the next time it could be me needing to be squeezed in. But afterward, when I heard . . ." Shirley sighed.

"More coffee?" she offered, and when Lia declined, she refilled her own cup.

"Cori's sister, Robin . . . ," Lia began.

"A very different girl," Shirley said. "Half sister, you know."

"Yes. I wondered—"

There was a knock at the door.

"Now, who could that be?" Shirley struggled to her feet, her cane tapping as she walked over to answer it.

"Hi, Grandma!" Lia heard a high-pitched, girlish voice.

"Darcy!" Shirley cried. "What brings you here today?" A dark-haired girl in her late teens bounced in, and Shirley, looking pleased, introduced her to Lia. "What do you have there, sweetie?" she asked her granddaughter, nodding toward the white plastic bag in her hand.

"Mom sent over these tomatoes," the girl said, holding the bag up. She laughed lightly. "Please take them, Grandma! We've got so many, we're all sick of eating them. And I'm supposed to bring you back, if that's okay? Mom got some quilting fabric, and she wants you to help lay it all out. She says you should stay for lunch."

"Oh! Well . . ." Shirley looked uncertainly toward Lia, who quickly popped up.

"Please go ahead," she said. "We can finish our talk anytime."

"If you're sure?" Shirley said, then took the bag from Darcy and looked into it. "Oh, these are lovely. Here," she said, pulling out a big ripe one to hold out to Lia. "To make up for cutting things short, with a promise to pick it up again."

"Thank you," Lia said. "Enjoy your quilting!"

Lia headed out the door, then paused for a minute on the porch to gather her thoughts. A car pulled up to the curb just then, and Lia was surprised to see Robin climb out.

Dressed in a businesslike pencil skirt and loose top, Robin squinted as she looked toward Lia.

"Good morning," Lia said. She stepped off the porch. "Or is it almost afternoon?"

"Almost," Robin said. She glanced up at the house Lia had just left. "I didn't realize you were friends with Shirley."

"New acquaintance," Lia said. "She's a nice lady. And"—she held up her gift with a smile—"she gave me a tomato. Taking a break from the office?" she asked.

"Just a quick one. Picking up a few things for my mother."

"How is she?" Lia asked.

Robin grimaced. "As well as can be expected, I guess." She sighed. "Cori's death set her back, I'm afraid. I do what I can, but there's no way I can bring Cori back."

"No. I'm sorry. You've had quite a lot to handle lately, I expect."

Robin nodded and made a move to go until Lia said, "I noticed Cori's crocheted wreath is gone."

"Her wreath? Oh, the one on the door. Yes, I took it down. Hated to see it suffer from the elements." She took a step, then turned back. "A word of caution, if you don't mind?" Lia waited, curious. "Shirley . . . well, I hate to say it . . . but, wonderful neighbor as she's been all these years, unfortunately she's getting older and tends to get things mixed up sometimes." Robin paused as though searching for the right words. "Like, at Cori's wake? Shirley seemed to have forgotten how old Cori was, and she spoke about her as if Cori was still a teenager. And there've been other signs. Just so you know."

Lia wasn't sure how to respond to that but acknowledged the statement with a nod. Robin bid her a good day and headed over to her mother's house. Lia watched for a few moments, then climbed into her own car, carefully stashed her gift tomato in the console, and sat for a minute.

Chapter 29

Lia gave Belinda a call before starting her car. "Have you had lunch yet?"

"No. Is it lunchtime?"

Lia smiled. "It is. I'm out and about. How about I pick up something and bring it over?"

"Yeah. Okay. That sounds good!" Belinda's voice livened as her mind seemed to catch up from wherever it'd been. "Anything at all."

"See you in a few," Lia said. She set her phone down and turned on her ignition. Hamburgers and shakes? Sushi? Chinese? She grinned, knowing her friend well. Chinese it was. She grabbed the phone again, put in a take-out order, then pulled away from the curb with one last look at Judith Littlefield's house. No sign of Robin, whom she pictured gathering whatever items her mother needed, and had a sympathetic thought for both.

Before long she was knocking on Belinda's door, a bag

filled with aromatic cartons in hand. Belinda answered within seconds.

"Funny thing," she said, welcoming Lia in. "I wasn't the least bit hungry when you called. Now I'm famished."

"Good," Lia said, "because we have lots." She headed back to Belinda's kitchen.

"I recognize that smell," Belinda said, following. "General Tso's chicken, right?"

"What else?" Lia said, pulling cartons out of her bag and lining them up on the table. "You never order anything else. But then, I should talk. I always have moo goo gai pan."

"Of course you do. We should probably branch out sometime, shouldn't we? But once you find what you like, why bother?" Belinda opened the door to her pantry. "Coffee or tea?"

Lia thought. "Green tea if you have it."

Belinda shuffled through her shelves and triumphantly held up a small box. She filled two mugs with water and started them heating in the microwave.

They bustled about, laying out plates and utensils, dishing out food, and finally digging in until their first hunger pangs had been satisfied.

Belinda leaned back, smiling contentedly, and picked up her mug for a first sip of tea.

"So, what have you been up to since Sunday?" she asked.

Lia set her fork down. "Quite a bit, as a matter of fact."

"Hmm." Belinda took a second sip. "That sounds like a lot more than just knitting."

"It was." Lia told about her walk with Tiffany and how the drama teacher claimed she had no help to offer. "But later her mother, Bethanne, called Hayley's boss and demanded to know if she was related to me."

"Wow! So Tiffany squealed to Mom." Belinda scooped more food from the carton onto her plate.

"Squealed or confronted," Lia said. "I have a feeling Tiffany has had questions all these years about what happened to Jessica and finally wanted answers from her mother."

"That must have been interesting," Belinda said with a small smirk. "From what you've told me about the woman, I'm guessing she wouldn't take that well."

"As proven by her call to Hayley's boss," Lia said.

"Right. Did that cause Hayley any trouble?"

Lia shook her head. "She said Mr. Weber was totally on her side." Lia scooped up a forkful and ate while thinking. "I'd like to know what came out of Tiffany's questioning, of course. Maybe nothing or maybe the beginning of something."

"More tea?" Belinda asked. When Lia shook her head, she got up to fix herself another mug.

"Then there was Marc Bernard," Lia said. "I spoke to a student of his and found her very believable regarding his highly inappropriate behavior. In my opinion, you can tell Chad the rumors he's heard are likely true." She then described seeing Marc interact with a much less pliable Megan than he was used to at the coffee shop, then turning his frustration and anger on Lia as the cause. "He was right, of course," she said. "Although not totally. I think Megan was ready to stand up to him before she spoke with me."

"Good for her." The microwave pinged, and Belinda dropped a fresh tea bag into her mug and returned to her chair.

"She's not yet ready to break things off and report him," Lia said. "I'm hoping that will come."

"One step at a time," Belinda said, and Lia nodded. "Well, you *have* been busy," she said.

"Yes," Lia said, wrinkling her brow. "But yesterday I began to have doubts about what I was doing." She pushed around the remains of the moo goo gai pan on her plate.

"Why? What happened?"

Lia described her hike at Long Run Falls with Pete Sullivan and their discussion at the spot where both Jessica and Cori had fallen. "Pete and his detectives have investigated both deaths thoroughly. He's convinced that Jessica's fall was accidental, and Cori—" Lia's voice broke slightly. "He thinks it's likely that Cori took her own life."

"No!" Belinda cried. "I don't believe that."

"I don't want to, either," Lia said. "But you have to admit we didn't know Cori that long. Her sister, Robin, though, told me the same thing."

"Oh." Belinda's face fell.

"However," Lia continued, "this morning I spoke with the family's next-door neighbor, an older woman named Shirley Dunn, who I met at Cori's wake. She saw no signs of depression during the many times she'd been with Cori and assured me that Cori was quite happy and upbeat, especially since taking the booth at the craft fair and getting the great publicity."

Belinda frowned. "I've read that people with serious depression are able to hide it quite well."

"I have, too." Lia frowned into her tea mug, though there were no tea leaves sitting at the bottom to read. "But I still feel," she said, "just my strong, gut feeling, that Cori was looking forward to her future, not planning to end it."

And, Lia thought to herself, *Shirley might be confused on some things*, as Robin claimed, but Lia leaned toward trusting the older woman's ability to see what was going on

with her young neighbor—as she watched her closely for so
many years.

Lia did some grocery shopping before heading home.
Not surprisingly, food ran out twice as fast now that
Hayley had moved in. As she carried her bags into the
house, Lia's phone started ringing, and she hurriedly set
things down to answer.

"Hi, Mom," Hayley said. "Just wanted to tell you I'll
probably be late again tonight."

"That's fine," Lia said. She could revise her meal plan
easily.

"Notice anything different in the house?" Hayley asked.

"Well, I just came in . . ." Lia glanced around. "Oh! I can
see more of my floor!"

Hayley chuckled. "I came home during my lunch hour
and took away some of the boxes."

"Yes, I see now. What a pleasant surprise! So things are
going smoothly for the fundraiser? No more trouble from
Bethanne King?"

"No, she's been quiet. It's nice but almost feels weird.
Like, when you sort of get used to the sound of jackham-
mers on your street, and it finally stops. It feels like something's missing."

Lia smiled. "Enjoy it while it lasts."

"I will. Gotta go," Hayley said. "See you tonight."

Lia put down her phone and carried her grocery bags
into the kitchen to unpack. She'd cook a hearty vegetable
soup for that night, she decided, which Hayley could enjoy
whenever she arrived home. She lined up the produce she'd
picked up, along with pasta and seasonings.

As Lia worked at the dish she'd made dozens of times

before and could probably put together in her sleep, she listened to an audiobook, chosen deliberately to give herself a break from murder thoughts. She'd had a string of highly intense days. Her mind needed a change. Listening to an Erma Bombeck book that Tom had given her years ago offered that needed relief, and she snickered over lines she'd heard before but still enjoyed.

The time flew by, and her soup was ready to simmer. She set the burner and cleaned up, then fixed herself a coffee, carrying the mug into the living room to her knitting chair. She'd reached a section in Helen's sweater that would require concentration, an intricate part of the pattern that would continue to keep her mind busy. Lia pulled out her knitting, took a quick sip of her coffee, and got contentedly down to work.

It wasn't until she'd moved on to more routine stitches that Lia missed Daphne. The cat wasn't always close by. She occasionally picked an out-of-the-way spot for a private nap. But Lia realized she'd been home long enough for Daphne to come out of hiding.

Lia set aside her knitting and went to the kitchen, where she checked on her soup, giving it a stir. Then she went in search of Daphne, uneasiness beginning to creep over her.

The downstairs area was an easy check, especially with fewer of Hayley's boxes around. Besides, Lia knew if Daphne were there, she'd be on the sofa or next to Lia's knitting chair.

Lia headed upstairs, stopping first in her bedroom. There was no sign of Daphne on the bed or underneath. The closet door was closed, but Lia checked inside anyway, finding nothing besides shoes and a small dust ball on the floor. She checked the bathroom quickly, then went to the office–slash–storage room, calling out by then but getting no response. The office took more time to search because of multiple hiding spots, though none of them were particularly enticing to a cat. No Daphne.

"Daphne," Lia called, growing concerned. "Where are you?" She went into Hayley's room, glad to see it was relatively tidy, which made it easier to find a missing cat. But the cat was nowhere to be found.

By that time, Lia was seriously worried. She remembered Daphne's recent attempts to slip out of the house. Could she have done so when Hayley carried her boxes out earlier? But wouldn't Daphne have lingered nearby? She was not an adventurous cat, eager to go dashing off, merely a mildly curious one. If Hayley hadn't noticed her outside before she left, Lia believed Daphne would have hung around to be found mewing at the door by the time Lia came home.

So why wasn't she there? Lia went out to her backyard, calling, then circled around to the front. No Daphne. Lia chewed at her lips, thoroughly frightened by then and unsure what to do next.

Where could Daphne have gone? she asked herself. What had happened to her?

Chapter 30

As Lia heard Hayley's car pull up that evening, she struggled to get herself under control. But when Hayley walked in, it took only one look at Lia for her to cry, "Mom, what's wrong? What happened?"

Lia slumped back in her chair. "It's Daphne. She's missing."

"Missing? How?"

"All I know is that she was gone when I came home this afternoon. I've searched the house, the yard, anywhere I could think of." Lia didn't add that she'd also driven through the neighborhood, fearing to come upon the worst—Daphne injured or dead by the side of the road. "I can't find her anywhere."

Hayley stared openmouthed. "How can that be? How could . . ." She sank onto the sofa. "Oh gosh! When I was home today. Carrying those big boxes . . . I had to prop open the door. She must have got out then. Oh!" Hayley's face had gone ashen. "What did I do?"

"It's just lately that she's started trying to sneak out," Lia said. "You didn't know. But why wouldn't she stay around? Or at least come back soon? I just don't understand that."

"Maybe something frightened her," Hayley offered. "Or . . ." Hayley's expression darkened. "Maybe someone took her."

"Took her!" That hadn't occurred to Lia, but she saw the possibility. Daphne was an easygoing, friendly cat. She'd never been skittish with strangers.

"I'm calling Brady," Hayley said, pulling out her phone.

"Hayley, I don't—"

"He'll know what to do."

Brady, who was off duty and at home, advised Hayley to report the missing cat. "But don't say she was stolen. You don't know that yet. Just missing."

Hayley had put her phone on speaker, and Lia asked, "Will the police care about a missing cat?"

"Pets are property," Brady pointed out. "And Daphne's a purebred, right? That ups her monetary value. If she was in fact stolen, it's at least a misdemeanor—could be more. We will take action to find her and discover what happened. Does she have a microchip?"

"I don't know," Lia said. "I'll find out from her first owner."

"Then there's plenty of online pet sites for reporting a missing pet," Brady said. "Those could mean more eyes looking out for her."

"Good. I'll find them," Hayley said. "But we should keep looking around here, shouldn't we?"

"Absolutely," Brady said. "I'll help. You have photos on your phone?"

"Yes," Hayley and Lia answered in unison.

"Perfect. I'll be right over."

As they waited for Brady, Hayley got busy on the online missing-pet sites, and Lia called Jen about the microchip, then reported Daphne missing to the local police. The call to Jen was the more difficult one, since Lia knew how much Jen cared about Daphne, having only given her up because of Bob's allergies.

"No, we never got a microchip," Jen told Lia. "I'm afraid it never occurred to us with Daphne being an indoor cat. Please don't feel bad on my account," she added. "I know whatever happened was accidental and that you care as much about Daphne as we do. I'm sure you'll have her back, safe and sound."

Lia dearly hoped Jen was right and blessed her friend for her super-kind response.

When Brady arrived, they mapped out a plan for canvassing the area. "It's getting late, though," Brady warned. "Nobody wants to hear a knock on their door as they're getting ready for bed."

"Then we'd better get started," Hayley said and hurried out the door, Brady and Lia not far behind.

They split up to cover more ground, with Lia thinking ruefully that she'd wanted to meet more neighbors but not this way. Lia's canvass area was two blocks over, and her first couple was welcoming and sympathetic. With a small boy peering from behind, they studied Daphne's photo and were clearly sorry that they couldn't help Lia. But they took her contact information and promised to be on the lookout.

Most of the rest were the same—caring but unhelpful— though she ran into a few who simply went through the motions, and one clearly impatient person who was border- line rude.

Lia got text updates from both Hayley and Brady, but none were what she hoped to see. One man, Hayley reported, actually offered her a kitten if she didn't find Daphne. *Can u imagine?* she'd texted.

As the hour grew late, the three agreed by text to suspend their canvassing and meet back at the house. Lia was the first, and she hated the silence that greeted her instead of her sweet cat. Hayley trudged in glumly within minutes, with Brady soon following.

"We've covered a lot of territory," Brady said, obviously trying to be upbeat. "There'll be a lot of people on the lookout for her. I think you'll hear something soon."

Hayley nodded but looked morose, barely managing a faint smile.

"Coffee anyone?" Lia asked. "Or something cold? It was pretty muggy out."

"No, thanks, Mrs. Geiger," Brady said. "I'd better get home."

Hayley got up from the chair arm she'd perched on. "Thanks so much for helping," she said and walked out with him, returning shortly to flop on the sofa. "I feel awful thinking about how scared Daphne must be, outside, at night, in some strange place."

By this point Lia only hoped she was alive but didn't say so. And if some stranger decided to keep her, Lia would rather think of Daphne as well treated and happy, though it would still break her heart to have lost her.

Sleeping that night was difficult. Dreadful dreams kept shaking her awake whenever she dozed off, but she managed to catch an hour or two. She was awakened around seven by Hayley's screech.

"Hayley?" Lia called groggily, propping herself on one elbow.

Hayley came rushing into her room, her phone in hand. "She's found!"

"Daphne?" Lia was instantly upright.

"She's in this lady's backyard! She heard her mewing. We can come get her!" Hayley sank onto Lia's bed, relief and joy on her face. "Mom, she's okay!"

"Thank goodness." Lia threw back her covers. "Let me get some clothes on. You have an address?"

"Yes." Hayley hurried back to her own room to dress, calling as she did. "I remember this woman. Older, very nice, wanted to fix me some iced tea. I wasn't all that sure she understood, frankly. She didn't have a cell phone, so I wrote down my number for her expecting she'd probably lose it."

"Never underestimate a person because of age," Lia called back as she slipped on her shoes.

Hayley met Lia in the hall and held up her keys. "I'll drive. I know where the house is."

That was fine with Lia, whose excitement hadn't totally conquered her grogginess. She buckled into Hayley's Nissan, then held on as her daughter took off with screeching tires. Thankfully, all the visible cars on the block were currently motionless at the curb.

"I just had a terrible thought," Hayley said as she slowed for a stop sign. "What if it isn't Daphne? What if it's someone else's cat that looks like her?"

"That *is* a terrible thought," Lia said. "But don't hold on to it. We'll find out soon enough."

Hayley drove another few blocks, then slowed, pointing to a white house on the corner. "That's it." She parked, and they unbuckled and climbed out.

"Daphne came all this way?" Lia said. They'd ridden close to a mile, maybe more. Hayley's worry that it might not be Daphne wormed its way back before Lia could block it.

"Good morning!" An elderly woman, fully dressed and every white hair in place, greeted them at the front door. "I do hope I didn't call too early," she said as she ushered them in. "I'm an early riser, but I know not everyone is."

"Not at all," Lia assured her. "We were so happy to get your call." She glanced around the tidy living room, searching for Daphne but not finding her.

"May I offer you some coffee?" the woman said. "By the way, I'm Muriel Burgess."

"And I'm Lia Geiger. This is my daughter, Hayley."

"How do you do?" Muriel said, and determined, apparently and frustratingly, to be the perfect hostess, offered coffee again.

"No, thank you, Mrs. Burgess—," Hayley began.

"Miss Burgess," their hostess corrected.

"Miss Burgess," Hayley said with a nod. "That's very nice of you. But we need to get Daphne right away. Is she in your backyard?"

"Oh no!" Miss Burgess said, causing Lia's heart to skip a beat. Had Daphne got out again?

"No," Miss Burgess explained, "I brought her inside as soon as I found her. I hope it was all right, but I gave her a little food. The poor thing acted like she was starving. All I had was a little hamburger—I don't have pets myself, you see. But she gobbled it down right away. Was that okay?" she asked worriedly.

"That's fine," Lia said. "So she's in your kitchen?"

Muriel laughed. "Not anymore. As soon as she had her food and a little water, she made herself quite at home. She went upstairs to one of my bedrooms, but I moved her to the bathroom. I don't have a litter box, you see. Let me get her." She turned to go, then stopped. "You're sure you wouldn't like some coffee first?"

Hayley and Lia declined in unison, each struggling to resist doing an end run around Miss Burgess to dash up the stairs themselves. The older woman took the steps cautiously, while claiming she'd be right down.

Hayley gave Lia a wide-eyed look of impatience as the woman crept upward. Lia patted her arm, encouraging a calm that she herself grappled with.

In a few moments they heard a door open and Miss Burgess say, "There you are, you little dickens. I have a surprise for you downstairs."

"Daphne?" Hayley called, unable to restrain herself anymore, and was rewarded with a loud, answering mew. In seconds, they saw Daphne's fluffy tan-and-white face peer around the corner before she came scrambling down the stairs and into Hayley's arms.

"It's her!" Hayley cried.

Lia grinned happily. "It definitely is."

Daphne's purrs were near deafening as she wiggled joyfully in Hayley's grasp, then leaned over to be transferred to Lia's.

"Well," Muriel said, smiling as she stepped carefully down. "It looks like she missed you!"

"We're so glad to have her back," Lia said. "Thank you so much for rescuing her."

"No trouble," Muriel said. "No trouble at all."

"One thing," Lia said, handing Daphne back to Hayley. "You discovered Daphne this morning, right?"

"That I did," Muriel said, nodding. "As soon as I came down here, I heard her mewing. And I knew it must be this young lady's cat," she said, smiling at Hayley. "So I let her in right away, and I started looking for that piece of paper with your number on it, which I didn't need right away, of course. It was much too early to call you right then. But I'd forgotten where I put it, until—"

"Is your yard fenced?" Hayley broke in, having picked up where Lia's question was leading and less patient than her mother.

"Fenced? Oh yes. It's always been fenced. Living on a corner like this, it's too tempting for people, well, children, mostly, to want to cut through to save a few steps. I've always had a garden, you see, and I don't like—"

"Is it the kind of fence that would keep out small animals as well as people?" Hayley asked.

"Well, come see for yourself." Muriel genially led them to her kitchen, where she opened a back door. Lia stepped out onto a small stoop to see a backyard not much bigger than her own but with a tall wooden privacy fence surrounding it.

"I don't like car headlights shining at me when I sit out there in the evenings," Muriel said, explaining the height of the fence.

"I don't think Daphne could climb that, do you, Mom?" Hayley asked, clutching the cat.

Lia shook her head. "No, I don't think she could."

"So how did she get in?" Hayley asked.

It was a rhetorical question, but Muriel responded to it. "I have a gate on the side," she said, pointing in that direction. "It's not locked, but there is a latch that can be worked on both sides. Of course," she said musingly, "a cat couldn't have handled it."

Lia shook her head. "No, she couldn't. So how," she asked, "did she get into your yard?"

Muriel, Hayley, and Lia stared at one another, none of them having an answer for that. Only Daphne seemed unconcerned as she snuggled contentedly in Hayley's arms.

Chapter 31

They were finishing their coffee back at the house after throwing together a quick breakfast when Hayley said, "Someone had to have put her there."

"I agree," Lia said. She had called Jen with the good news about Daphne, who currently snuggled on Lia's lap after switching from Hayley's a minute ago. "And I think that particular someone has sent us a message."

"What do you mean?"

Lia held Daphne upright for Hayley, the ragdoll cat falling into her usual do-whatever-you-want-with-me limpness. "Look at the fur on her chest. A square section has been clipped out of it."

Hayley leaned closer. "You're right! I never even noticed! It's definitely clipped. Miss Burgess wouldn't have done that. It had to be Daph's kidnapper. But what's the message?"

"A warning, I think." Lia settled the cat back down.

"Letting us know it could be worse next time." *Unless I stop asking questions.*

"Next time!"

"But there won't be a next time for Daphne," Lia said, gently scratching the cat's ears. "We'll see to that."

"Absolutely," Hayley said. She carried her mug into the kitchen and slipped it into the dishwasher. "We'll watch her like a hawk. She'll never get outdoors on her own again." Hayley headed to the stairs.

"But I can't watch you like a hawk," Lia said softly.

"What? Me?" Hayley paused on the first step.

"Yes, you. Daphne's not the only one in this household I care about. And I can't hover over you."

"No, but nobody's going to kidnap me." Hayley scoffed. "Least of all if it's Bethanne King who did this. She might be able to snatch a cat, but she'd have a lot more trouble with me."

Hayley trotted on up as Lia watched, remembering the frightening episode not so long ago that Hayley seemed to have already put out of her mind. It hadn't left Lia's. Had she put Hayley in danger once again? Lia couldn't live with herself if anything happened to Hayley because of her.

When Hayley reappeared, ready to leave for work, Lia said, "Please promise me you'll be on special alert from now on."

Hayley seemed on the verge of making a joke but stopped when Lia's expression showed she was all seriousness. "I promise, Mom," she said. "Don't worry. I'll be careful."

Hayley left, clearly thinking that was enough. But it wasn't for Lia. The best protection she could see was for the person who'd sent this warning to be behind bars. That meant finding out who he or she was. As Lia got busy cleaning up the remains of their breakfast, she thought of her next-door neighbor, who might be able to help with that. She put down her dish towel and gave Sharon a call.

"Did you find Daphne?" Sharon immediately asked.

"We did, and in interesting circumstances." Lia described Muriel Burgess's tall privacy fence and how Daphne had to have been deliberately left in the yard by whoever had taken her. "Did you see anyone hanging around yesterday afternoon when I was out, or coming into our yard?" she asked.

"Gosh, no, I'm afraid I didn't," Sharon said. "What an awful thing to do! Could it have been kids? Their idea of a prank?"

"Possibly," Lia said, "but I don't believe that was the case. You know I've been looking into Cori Littlefield's death? I think someone sent me a warning to back off." She described Daphne's clipped fur.

"How dreadful," Sharon said. "I really wish I'd seen something. Lia, I know this is after the fact, but do you think you should get one of those outdoor security cameras? I never thought I'd be recommending something like that in our little town."

"I might look into that. Do you suppose any of our neighbors have one?"

"Hmm," Sharon said. "Worth checking on. I'd be happy to call around if you like."

"Would you? If just one house had it and caught one of the people I have in mind lurking, it could make all the difference."

"Though a camera could be iffy, there's also the possibility someone noticed a stranger to the neighborhood hanging around and can give a description. I'll let you know what I find."

Lia settled into her knitting chair, grateful to have that task taken care of for her after the canvassing she'd gone through the night before. Instead of picking up her knitting, Lia patted her lap for Daphne to hop up. She then hugged the purring feline, who soaked up the extra attention, as she'd been doing all morning.

"Who had you?" Lia asked. "What did they do with you all those hours?"

Daphne's blue eyes blinked at Lia, but all she could offer was a furry head for Lia to rub.

Lia arrived at Jen's for the weekly Ninth Street Knitters meeting, toting her work-in-progress cardigan and happy to see her knitting friends. Jen met her at the door with a hug.

"How are you doing?" she asked.

"Much better than I was twenty-four hours ago," Lia said. "And Daphne doesn't seem any worse for the wear."

Jen nodded and stepped aside for Maureen and Diana, who arrived at that time, chatting up their usual storm. Further discussion of Daphne's cat-napping would wait.

As everyone settled in Jen's living room, Maureen held up her alpaca yarn, newly purchased for the commission Lia had passed on to her. They all oohed and aahed over the soft robin's-egg blue yarn. "I'll edge the sweater with this dark blue," Maureen said, waving that skein. "I think it should be very striking."

Tracy displayed the white baby sweater that she'd worked a yellow and tan bunny pattern into. "Almost finished," she told Lia. "I should be able to give it to you next week for the craft fair."

After a few more catching-up comments, Jen took advantage of a pause to say, "Lia had a disturbing day yesterday."

All heads turned to Lia, who cleared her throat, then shared her tale. The room filled with cries of, "Oh, Lia! Poor Daphne!"

"She's fine," Lia assured them. "And we're none the worse for several hours of worry, other than a few more gray hairs showing up," she joked. "But I'm taking what happened very seriously." She described Daphne's trimmed section of fur. "I believe because of that and because of how she was left that it was a warning."

"A warning?" Diana asked.

"For me to stop snooping into Cori's and Jessica's deaths."

"But it seems to me," Maureen said, "to do something like this is to admit that you, Lia, are on the right track. That you're not just imagining a murder occurred when everyone else thinks it was accidental."

"She's right," Diana said. "That means someone is definitely worried."

"But who?" Tracy asked.

"That's the tricky part," Lia said. She took a sip of the lemonade she'd poured for herself. "If any of my neighbors had been able to tell me who was lurking in my neighborhood yesterday afternoon, my job would be nearly done. I've already gone over the possibilities, but it hasn't narrowed down the field. Kevin Shaw's dental office is closed on Wednesdays, so I can't automatically eliminate him. All the others seem to have flexible schedules, which means they're still on the list."

Lia brought the group up to speed on what she'd learned since they last gathered—her meeting with Tiffany in the park, which led to Bethanne's angry call to Hayley's boss, and Lia's uncomfortable interaction with Marc Bernard after talking with Megan.

"Will you tell Pete about Daphne?" Jen asked.

"Pete?" Tracy asked.

"Pete Sullivan is the Crandalsburg chief of police," Lia said and explained how they'd met. She turned to Jen. "I went with him to Long Run Falls, to the spot where Cori and Jessica fell."

"You did?" Jen asked, surprised.

"We ran into each other on Tuesday, and he suggested showing the area to me after I admitted I'd never been there. I shared what I'd learned up to then, but it didn't impress him. He needs proof, of course, which I don't have yet, so he's sticking with the official ruling of accidental." Lia took a breath. "I didn't think Daphne's cat-napping would impress him either, so, no, I haven't gone to him about it, though I did report to our local station when Daphne first went missing."

The group discussion broke up into separate conversations, and Lia pulled out her knitting, listening as she got busy with her needles. She hadn't reported to the knitters Pete's suggestion that Cori might have taken her own life. She'd struggled with the thought at the time and still did. Robin believed it to be true, but Shirley Dunn vehemently didn't. How did one know for sure?

Breaking into her thoughts, Jen asked Lia, "Have you ever spoken with Cori's mother?"

"Her mother? No, I haven't. She's going through recovery after a car accident and couldn't even make Cori's wake. I wasn't sure I should disturb her."

"It's been over two weeks since Cori died," Jen said. "Not a terribly long time, but the initial shock will have worn off by now. When my aunt was in rehab, she said after a while she felt forgotten by the world. Mrs. Littlefield might actually appreciate having someone to talk to about Cori, besides her other daughter, that is. Someone she could share old memories with that a family member already heard a million times. Those old memories might be useful to you."

"A good point," Lia said. "Let me think about that." She did so, as she kept on with her knitting.

The time flew by, as it always did. When fingers grew tired and all that could be said had been said, the knitters tucked away their work and helped Jen tidy up. Good-night calls blended with the sound of car doors closing, and Lia pulled away along with the others. She'd decided by then to at least find out which facility Judith was in. After that, she'd consider whether to visit or not—though Jen's argument had her leaning toward doing it.

Chapter 32

When Lia got home from Jen's, she found Hayley sitting quietly in the living room, Daphne on her lap and a mug beside her on the end table. Hayley had texted Lia much earlier that she'd be having dinner with Brady that evening, which pleased Lia, as much for the safety of it as anything else.

"Have a good evening?" Lia asked. She dropped her knitting bag next to her chair.

"Uh-huh." Hayley's response was distracted, as she seemed absorbed in her thoughts. Lia went to fetch a glass of ice water and carried it back to her knitting chair.

After a stretch of quiet, during which Hayley idly ran her hand over Daphne's fur and Lia took sips of water, Hayley said, "Brady and I had a good talk tonight."

Lia set down her glass. "Oh?"

"I'd been doing a lot of thinking. About Erin, for one thing. Remember how you said that I might be so annoyed with her because she's pushing me to make decisions I didn't want to make?"

"I do remember. You weren't sure you wanted to, well, stake a claim on Brady."

"Stake a claim?" Hayley grinned. "Not how I'd put it but, yeah, that's about it, I guess. I wanted to keep things casual, but I didn't like the thought of him maybe getting pulled away."

Lia nodded and waited quietly for more.

Hayley shifted Daphne slightly. "I guess your meeting with Megan was what got me thinking."

"Megan? In what way?"

"Well, she's been letting the guy she's mixed up with, the teacher, call all the shots. She's been passive, and look where it's got her. Going with the flow hasn't been so good for her, has it?"

"It hasn't."

"So it occurred to me that I was being pretty passive." Hayley raised a hand against Lia's expected protest. "I know, I know. It's not the same sort of situation. Brady is not in the least controlling. No way. But I was just kind of floating along as though I never had to decide one way or the other where we were heading."

She laughed to herself. "And I still haven't. Not for sure, anyway. But we talked about that tonight, and it was good. I explained how I was feeling, that I wanted to take this slowly, but that I thought we were good together. And Brady is fine with it, though he did ask that we'd be exclusive, you know, not see anyone else."

"And you said . . . ?"

"I said no problem!" Hayley grinned again. "That takes care of my *Erin* issue. She can bake all the chocolate chip cookies she wants and show up at all the tennis clinics, and it won't bother me a bit anymore."

Lia smiled, happy for Hayley and pleased with these signs of growing maturity. "You might bake a few cookies for Brady yourself, once in a while," she suggested. "I mean, not cookies, necessarily, but do your part and not take him for granted."

"I won't take him for granted," Hayley said, smiling. "He's a great guy and deserves a little fussing over. Probably a lot. Look how he stepped in right away over Daphne."

"He made a big difference," Lia agreed.

"But," Hayley said, frowning, "I still wish Megan could see how lopsided her relationship is and how hurtful that is for her."

"I think she's starting to get it." Lia took a sip of her water, thinking back to Marc's reaction when he picked up on that, and how he'd turned on Lia as the cause. Hayley had zeroed in on Bethanne King as their cat-napper, but Marc was high on Lia's list. For her, Marc was a person who put himself first and who saw anyone who felt otherwise as an obstacle to be dealt with. Exactly to what extent, Lia didn't yet know.

The next morning, Lia called Robin's office. She'd decided she wanted to talk to Judith Littlefield. Robin could tell her where to find her and perhaps give her mother a heads-up about Lia's visit. But the call went to voice mail.

Lia hung up without leaving a message. There were other ways to track down Cori's mother without bothering Robin, who had a business to run. She logged onto her laptop.

Her initial search online brought up several rehab facilities, and Lia began checking those closest to Crandalsburg. To her surprise, after a few calls she found Judith in a place much less convenient to Crandalsburg. But convenience wasn't everything, she reminded herself. She learned what the visiting hours were and decided to drive the twenty miles to Paxworth Rehabilitation and Nursing that morning.

Paxworth sat in a rural location northwest of York, from which it likely drew most of its staff. A low, square building, it appeared cold and institutional to Lia as she approached on the long, treeless driveway. But she'd never been fond of streamlined architecture. Low greenery softened the edges, though she would have liked to see a bit of color mixed in, especially near the benches that a few mobile patients had been walked to. Some might consider flower-filled landscaping a waste of money better spent on health care, but mental health was important, too. Lia was sure Sharon, for one, would agree on the emotional benefits of a blooming garden.

After leaving her car in the visitors parking lot, Lia stepped into a light-filled lobby dotted with comfortable-looking chairs. She smiled at a wheelchair-bound resident who looked over at her, one of several, then headed for a reception window on the left.

"I'm here to see Judith Littlefield," she told the woman working there.

"Just a moment, please." The woman tapped at a keyboard, then spoke a few words into a phone. "Alice will be with you in a moment to escort you," she said and invited Lia to take a seat.

Lia thanked her and chose a blue-upholstered wing chair to settle into. She was checking her phone for messages when a woman about her age in a pink aide's uniform came up to her.

"Mrs. Geiger? I'll take you to Mrs. Littlefield."

"Thank you," Lia said, quickly tucking her phone away. She followed Alice out of the lobby and into a bright hallway that led past offices, then, after a right turn, down a long row of residents' rooms.

"She might not be able to say much," Alice warned as they walked. "But she's awake and she can hear you."

"Oh!" Lia said. "I didn't realize. I had the impression she'd been steadily recovering."

Alice greeted another aide, who passed them with a cart, then she said, "I'm afraid Mrs. Littlefield hasn't been responding as well as we'd hoped. But she'll be glad to have a visitor." They crossed a wide lounge area, then passed another row of rooms until Alice stopped at a door that was slightly ajar. "Here we are." She tapped at it lightly before stepping in. "Mrs. Littlefield?" she called cheerily. "Judith? Someone to see you!"

Lia followed her into the room and saw a thin woman lying in a bed whose head was partly raised. She was pale and, along with her white hair, nearly blended in with the sheets. Her eyes were a startlingly vivid blue, however, and they searched Lia's face. "Robin?" she asked.

"No, not Robin," Alice said, going over to straighten Judith's pillow. "This is Mrs. Geiger."

"Lia Geiger," Lia said, moving closer so that Judith could see her better. "I was a friend of Cori's."

"Cori?"

"Yes, from when Cori was at the craft fair. We had a booth next to each other."

Alice quietly left the room, and Lia pulled a chair over to the bed to sit.

"The craft fair." Judith's voice was weak, but she seemed to understand. "Crochet."

"Yes, Cori filled a booth with her beautiful crocheted pieces. People loved them. That made Cori very happy."

Judith smiled at that. "Beautiful . . . work," she said.

"Yes, they were quite beautiful." Lia glanced around the room but saw no crocheted items. There were no photos, either, or anything personal, making the room look quite sterile. "Were you the one who taught Cori how to crochet?" she asked, hoping to stir something positive.

It seemed to do that. Judith's eyes brightened. She looked at Lia for a long time but clearly was seeing something else. Something back in time. "Cori took to it," she finally said. "A duck." Judith grinned, and Lia smiled back, pretty sure what she meant. Cori had taken to crochet work like a duck to water. "Better than me," Judith said.

That amount of talking seemed to tire her, and Judith closed her eyes for several moments. Lia waited, and when Judith's hand moved restlessly she took it in her own and patted it. Eventually Judith came back.

"Robin," Judith said.

Lia wasn't sure what that meant. Had Judith confused Lia with Robin again?

After a few more moments, Judith said, "Shouldn't sell."

"Shouldn't sell what?" Lia asked gently.

Judith started to speak but began to cough. When it continued, Lia held a water glass for her to sip from, which helped. But the coughing obviously tired her again. Lia waited but soon realized Judith had fallen asleep.

What had she meant when she said "shouldn't sell"? That Cori shouldn't have sold her crocheted pieces? Something else? She had said "Robin," but Lia didn't know if the two thoughts were connected.

Alice peeked in after a few minutes of Lia sitting quietly

at Judith's bed, still holding one of the woman's hands. "Sleeping?" she asked, and Lia nodded.

"She'll be that way for a good while. You were lucky to catch her when you did."

Alice held the door, waiting, and Lia stood. There was nothing more she could do there. They walked back down the hall together, Lia thinking, and after a few moments Alice broke the silence. "It was good of you to visit, even though I take it you don't know Judith?"

"No," Lia said. "Only her daughter. Her younger daughter."

"Oh, wasn't that a shame, her being killed while poor Judith was confined here! It really set her back, I could tell."

"Yes, I can imagine. She's in much worse condition than I expected."

They'd reached the lobby area, and Alice paused. She'd accompanied Lia as far as required, but instead of a brisk good-bye, she asked, "Can you wait a minute?" When Lia nodded, Alice went behind the reception area and through a door. In a minute she came out, followed by another woman in a dark suit.

"This is Ms. Morgan, our facility manager," Alice said, introducing the two.

Ms. Morgan smiled and asked, "You've been to see Mrs. Littlefield? Thank you so much. She's had few visitors lately. I wonder if you can help us, Mrs. Geiger?"

"Yes, of course. If I can," Lia added, wondering what in the world that might be.

"We've had a little trouble reaching her daughter, Ms. Wendt. I'm presuming you know her?"

"I do—," Lia began, intending to explain how slight their acquaintance was, but Ms. Morgan had heard what she needed.

"If," she quickly said, "you could have her call us, please, it would be very helpful. Decisions need to be made about Mrs. Littlefield's future care. They need to be made soon."

After what Alice had said about Judith, and from what she herself had seen, Lia suspected hospice was what Ms. Morgan was referring to. "I'll do what I can," she said.

Ms. Morgan nodded and thanked her, then returned to her office, where more business apparently awaited. Lia headed out to her car, feeling sad about Judith and wishing she'd come to see her much sooner.

Chapter 33

Lia drove to Robin's office in Crandalsburg but found it closed. Out on a client house call, she presumed. She called the number on her cell phone and this time left a message. Robin needed to call the Paxworth facility immediately.

It didn't feel like enough, but Lia had no idea how else to reach Robin. Then she thought of Shirley Dunn. Perhaps, as Judith's longtime neighbor, Shirley would know. Unfortunately, that call went to an answering machine. She left a detailed message for Shirley, along with her own cell number. Then she climbed back in her car and went home.

That evening, Lia felt restless. Hayley had gone back to the alpaca farm with a few more boxes of items for the upcoming fundraiser. That freed up more space in the downstairs area, though boxes of Hayley's personal items still lingered. After tidying up the kitchen, Lia realized she hadn't thought about lunch for her upcoming two craft fair days. She checked out the pantry and refrigerator and found slim pickings. There was canned tuna she could turn into a salad—if she only had fresh celery. Plus the mayonnaise in her jar was low. Her fruit bin held only one sad, overlooked, and shriveled plum.

A run to the supermarket was clearly needed. The evening had cooled down and it was plenty light out. Instead of driving, a walk appealed to her. Lia grabbed her purse and a reusable shopping bag and set off after making sure Daphne was settled safely on the sofa. No more frightening adventures for the cat—Lia would see to that.

The walk through her neighborhood was pleasant, and Lia encountered more than one person whose door she'd knocked on when searching for Daphne. She was glad to report to them that the cat was safe and sound. One upside of the frightening incident was that she'd come to know several very nice neighbors. But discussing that incident brought back all the fears and questions about it. Who had taken Daphne? Who had apparently been watching Lia's house long enough to pounce on that unexpected opportunity?

The questions looped through her mind, and before she knew it, she'd arrived at the supermarket. Though smaller than the ones Lia had grown used to in York, it carried almost everything she needed. Conveniently located close to Crandalsburg's main street, it usually did a brisk business, and that Friday evening was no exception.

Lia picked up one of the green carry baskets and headed over to the produce section. She chose her celery, dropped it in her basket, then glanced around for fruit. A woman with multicolored spiked hair standing in front of a bin of bright red tomatoes caught Lia's eye. As she drew closer, she smiled. "Crystal?"

The woman who'd cut her hair some days ago turned, a bright smile lighting up her face as she recognized Lia. "Hi! Good to see you again!" Her eyes automatically ran over Lia's hair, making Lia grin. Sure that the hair stylist couldn't possibly remember her name, what with all the clients she must deal with, Lia supplied it, then added, "We talked about Jessica Ackerman and Cori Littlefield."

"Right, I remember." Crystal's face grew serious. "I thought about that a lot, afterward. You were going to tell me if you found out anything, I mean, anything that changed things."

Lia looked behind her. No one was near enough to hear, plus music flowing from the store's overhead speakers was loud enough to cover their conversation. In mid-glance she caught sight of something that startled her. Kevin Shaw had just walked in the front door. She saw him pick up a carry basket like her own, then continue on to another part of the store.

Lia turned back to Crystal, who was waiting. "I've been finding out plenty of bits and pieces but not enough yet to make a difference." One of those bits had just entered the supermarket, one whose long-ago alibi Lia had found to be shaky, but she didn't share that.

Crystal looked disappointed. "I feel bad about Cori. I know nothing will bring her back. But if someone did that to her, if it wasn't just an accident, I want to see that person punished."

Lia agreed. But she'd just seen Kevin enter the produce area, though he seemed to be concentrating on watermelons and hadn't noticed her. Had Pete talked to him about his alibi or the questions that Lia had raised? She didn't know, but she didn't want to get into it here in case Pete had. She hadn't grabbed her fruit yet, but she'd come back for it later, after Kevin moved on.

Lia ended her conversation with Crystal, promising again to keep her updated, and hurried off in search of mayonnaise.

The mayonnaise aisle was crowded, and Lia had to wait as a couple dithered over nonfat and low-fat. Finally they left, and Lia grabbed her own jar. As she added it to her basket, she saw Kevin walk by and glance down her aisle. There were others around her, so chances were he didn't see her. But she started to feel a bit silly. Was she hiding from him? Not really. Just wanting to avoid a potentially uncomfortable encounter there in the middle of a busy supermarket.

Lia headed back to the produce section and picked out three ripe peaches, dropping them into a plastic bag. If she thought about it, she could probably come up with several more items—which was the way of food shopping for her—but she instead went directly to the checkout registers.

The self-checkout kiosk had the shortest line. But Lia used it so rarely that she knew she'd probably fumble over it. She got in the ten-items-or-fewer queue but soon noticed that a couple of people in front of her apparently had trouble counting. She glanced over to other lines but saw piled-high baskets. She stayed where she was.

A delay occurred in her line when the checker needed a price check. That moved the woman directly ahead of Lia to turn and roll her eyes. Lia shrugged and smiled. Finally the line edged forward, and within minutes Lia was loading her own items onto the conveyor belt. As she waited for the woman in front to complete her transaction, Lia noticed that Kevin was standing in the self-checkout area and was next in line. But Lia's checkout was close to the exit. When her turn came, she ran her credit card, picked up her bag, and slipped out of the store.

The evening was surprisingly darker than when Lia had arrived. She'd lost track of time, during both her walk and her shopping. The parking lot was brightly lit, but the sidewalks beyond were dimmer. And much less crowded.

Lia headed for home, seeing fewer and fewer people as she left the center of Crandalsburg and walked toward her quiet neighborhood. She passed one dog walker, an older gentleman with a friendly terrier. The gentleman nodded, and the terrier veered toward her to sniff. But after that, Lia was alone.

She had gone two blocks when she heard the footsteps. They'd appeared out of nowhere but now seemed to be keeping pace with her. When she came to an intersection, she stopped, then glanced back. She saw no one. But had someone slipped behind that tree, or was it a trick of the headlights when a car turned onto her street? Lia walked quicker after crossing the intersection.

And she heard the footsteps once again.

Lia had two more blocks to go. If she picked up her pace any more she'd be running. In sandals. With a bag holding a heavy mayonnaise jar among other things. And whoever was behind her could close the distance between them within seconds. Could she use the mayo jar as a weapon? Maybe for half a second. And then what?

She heard a car approach from behind her and saw its headlights catching up to her. The car slowed. Lia felt her heart rate double. A friend? Or an accomplice of her stalker?

As a million thoughts of action raced through her head, none of which seemed achievable, a voice called out from the lowered car window.

"Mom? Is that you? What are you doing out here? C'mon. Get in!"

Lia heaved a relieved sigh. Hayley.

Lia looked back before she climbed into the car but saw no one behind her. But there *had* been, of that she was convinced. Not a neighbor or a friendly stroller, who, if that were the case, would still be approaching and would offer a friendly "Good evening" before going on.

Instead there was nothing.

Chapter 34

"Mom, I'm driving you to the craft fair," Hayley said as she faced Lia. "And that's that." Standing as she did, feet apart and hands on hips, she resembled Lia's own mother when she informed her that if she didn't do what she was told—*right now*—she was in big trouble. When had her daughter turned into her mother?

"Hayley, there's no need—"

"No need? After what happened last night?"

They'd already thoroughly discussed Lia's scare as she made her way home from the supermarket the night before. Though Kevin Shaw rated top spot as her stalker because of his presence at the store, Lia knew she could have easily missed other suspects among the many shoppers inside or out in the parking lot. The footsteps could also have been totally innocent, though she hadn't convinced herself of that.

"What happened last night," Lia argued, "was in semi-darkness. I'll be coming and going to the craft fair on a bright, sunny day."

"But you won't be coming and going alone because I'm driving you."

Lia saw the mix of determination and concern on Hayley's face, which told her this was something Hayley needed to do. "Let me get my things," she said, giving in, and started up the stairs.

As they rode, Hayley lectured Lia about staying in crowded areas at all times, as if that were hard to do at the craft fair. In return, Lia begged Hayley to be watchful of her own safety.

"And Daphne's," Hayley added. "But yes, I promise. We'll keep an eye on each other."

Hayley helped Lia carry her boxes of knit items to her booth, greeted several vendors who were also arriving, then gave Lia a longer-than-usual hug. On her way out, Lia saw Hayley pause near the entranceway to talk with Maggie and guessed she was asking the quilter to keep an eye on Lia. That was confirmed when Maggie came over immediately after.

"What's this about you being in danger?" she demanded. Maggie had a voice that carried, and Lia quickly drew her out of the line of passing vendors and into her booth.

"I don't know that for sure," Lia said in a softer voice she hoped Maggie would match. She described the situation, which had truly frightened her at the time but which she now tried to minimize.

But Maggie wasn't about to be fooled. "Lia Geiger, don't you give me that. It was a threat, pure and simple, and you'd better be taking it seriously."

Lia sighed. "I am. But I don't intend to let it paralyze me. I allowed Hayley to drive me today, but that can't continue.

The only way to put an end to it is to find out who is doing this. Did Hayley tell you about Daphne?"

"Daphne?" Maggie glanced around. "Who's that?"

"Our cat." Lia gave Maggie the short version of Daphne's experience, though it was enough to bring up a look of dismay.

"Lia . . ."

Lia braced herself for a string of warnings and advice, but Bill Landry called out, "Five minutes, people!"

Maggie, who still held a quilt she needed to hang, said, "I'll have to get back to you. But behave yourself, Lia Geiger!"

Lia grinned and got busy with readying her own booth, knowing she'd have Maggie's watchful eye on her for the rest of the day. After a bit, Lia noticed Olivia looking at her worriedly from the next booth. The expression wasn't unusual for her typically anxious friend, but Lia suspected she'd overheard some of the exchange.

"Everything okay?" Olivia asked.

Lia mover closer to the divider between them. "It's fine. It's just . . ." Lia paused. She hadn't shared her questions about Cori's death with Olivia. The younger woman tended to worry about the least of things, and Lia tried not to add to that. "Well," she said, "I've been talking to a lot of people about Cori since her death. It seems I might have, um, annoyed someone in the process."

"Oh!" Olivia said, relaxing. "I'm sure if you tell this person you meant well, it will fix things."

"It's possible," Lia said. She picked up a red shawl Jen Beasley had knitted and refolded it. "I'll just need to find the right moment." *And the right person.*

Olivia nodded. "It'll come," she said, satisfied. "Did you know Belinda has a new vendor to take over Cori's booth?"

"No, I didn't!" Lia turned to her left and noticed for the first time that the flower vases were gone from Cori's front counter. All that remained was the sign explaining her absence. Soon that would be gone, too. "Who is it?"

"I don't know. Maybe Belinda will make an announcement." A shopper paused at Olivia's counter, and she excused herself to attend to business.

Lia stepped closer to the vacant booth. The emptiness of it was sad, but it almost felt worse to think of Cori being replaced. As she gazed, thinking about that, a voice interrupted. "Her things are starting to show up on the Internet." Lia turned to see a woman who looked vaguely familiar, someone Lia must have seen at the craft fair before. Not one of her own customers—she was pretty good at remembering them. But Lia might have waited on her when she'd helped Cori on that super-busy day.

"On the Internet?" Lia asked.

"Yes," the middle-aged woman said, shifting her large purse to the opposite shoulder. "Sites that sell crafty things, you know. eBay, too."

"Are you sure they're Cori's?" Lia asked.

"Pretty sure." The woman grinned. "They have her name on them."

"Oh!"

"But the prices were higher," the woman said. "I guess that's what happens when the artist passes away. I'm glad I bought what I did when she was here." She grimaced. "Sad, though."

Lia nodded, and as the shopper moved on, her thoughts flew back to her visit at Paxworth. Judith had said "Robin" at one time, then later, "shouldn't sell." Was this what she was referring to? It appeared so, since who else would have access to Cori's many crocheted pieces? And there were many. What Lia had seen spread out on Cori's worktable was the tip of the iceberg. There had been boxes under and behind the table overflowing with crochet work.

It made sense, she supposed, to sell off most of it. But surely not all. Surely Robin would hold on to those that meant the most to her and to her mother. Judith, it would seem, didn't agree with selling any. Or was it a particular piece that she'd wanted held back? As Lia's mind ran over the crocheted pieces she'd seen at the house, it stopped at the Jack and Jill diorama. Not your usual cheery crochet art. What would Robin do with that?

Despite the warmth of the craft fair barn, Lia rubbed at her arms, feeling a sudden chill.

L ater that day, Lia managed to catch Belinda.
"I hear there'll be a new vendor joining us," she said.

"Hah! News travels fast," Belinda said.

"I'm crushed that I'm apparently the last to know," Lia said with a grin.

"Blame that on Florrie Goodwin," Belinda said, nodding toward Florrie's husband, Zach, whose booth was across the way. "She stopped by yesterday afternoon, just as Will was leaving after signing the contract, and I introduced them."

"What is his craft?" Lia hoped it wouldn't be crochet art, though she wouldn't blame Belinda for going with a craft that had drawn so many followers during Cori's short time with them.

"Leathercraft," Belinda said. "He makes beautiful stuff. But I warned him to have a good range, from small and affordable to his higher-end things."

"Leathercraft," Lia repeated, pleased. "That should be a

good addition." She then remembered Nicole's hope that she could take Cori's booth when it became available. She passed that on to Belinda.

"Sure, I think we can do that. Will can take Nicole's booth. No problem." Belinda left, and Lia was approached by a shopper interested in the knit kitchen pieces spread out on Lia's counter. The woman dithered awhile, but Lia eventually rang up a nice set of knit dishcloths and pot holders for her.

As that shopper left, another, who'd been browsing over Olivia's handmade soaps, stepped over to take her place. Lia was sifting through her floor boxes for replacement items for her counter and said without glancing up, "I'll be with you in a minute." When she eventually straightened, she recognized Bethanne King standing at her booth.

Swallowing a gulp, Lia immediately thought, *Does she know who I am?* The sign over the booth said *Ninth Street Knits*, not *Lia Geiger*. And it seemed unlikely Bethanne would recognize Lia from that episode in the mall. She seemed interested in a knit purse Maureen had done. So if Lia simply—

"Did you make this?" Bethanne asked, holding up the purse.

"I didn't. We, Ninth Street Knits, are a group of knitters. This purse was made by another member."

Bethanne set the purse down. "So, what did you make?" she asked glancing around the booth. The question sounded challenging, as though Lia needed to justify her claim to be a knitter. Though unpleasant, the tone didn't particularly surprise Lia after having listened to Bethanne harangue her own daughter over simple things.

Lia reached for the afghan she'd done, an ambitious, multicolored piece over which she'd worked her fingers nearly to the bone. But it had received many admiring comments. She set it before Bethanne, who lifted a corner disdainfully.

"Another granny afghan," she said with a sniff. "Don't you make anything up-to-date?" She pushed the piece aside, scrunching the kitchen items, and pointed toward the sweaters hanging behind Lia. "How about those? Did you knit any of them?"

Lia took a deep breath, knowing how Tiffany must feel and wondering how she'd managed to put up with that on a daily basis. "Those don't happen to be my work, though I recently finished a cardigan that was a special order. I made it from—" She stopped herself from adding what yarn she'd used.

Bethanne, however, shot her a *gotcha* look.

"What were you going to say?" she asked sharply. "That you made it from alpaca yarn?" She leaned forward. "Do you think I don't know about your connection to the Weber farm?" she asked, her voice now dripping acid. "You call yourself a knitter, but it seems you spend most of your time interfering in other people's business."

"Is that what you came here to say?" Lia asked. She picked up the afghan but held her ground, facing the woman squarely.

"You should be more careful about who you cross, *Ms. Geiger*," Bethanne said, fairly spitting out the name. "It's a bad mistake to pick someone with as much influence in this town as I have. That is, if you care about this little venture of yours here."

"Is that a threat, Ms. King?" Lia asked calmly. "Because I've heard worse, and I just wanted to be sure."

"I'm sure you have heard worse, given what you do. But I don't make threats. I don't need to. There are natural consequences to actions, Ms. Geiger. I merely thought you should be reminded of that. Far-reaching consequences." She swept a cool gaze around the craft fair barn. "I suppose your daughter could get a little work here if she needed to. Making paper flowers, perhaps? That is, if there still is a craft fair. Customers can be so fickle, can't they?"

With that, Bethanne turned and left, pausing just long enough at booths along the way to give Lia plenty of time to watch her—and to think about what she'd said.

Not a threat, she'd claimed, but Lia knew otherwise. She didn't know how much influence Bethanne King really held over Crandalsburg, but it didn't take much to start enough damaging rumors against a business that depended greatly on word of mouth. Then there was Hayley's job at the Weber farm, a job that she loved. How secure was that against someone like Bethanne?

Lia watched as Bethanne left the craft barn without a backward glance. *Cool as a cucumber*, Lia thought, and a woman who didn't like to be crossed. She'd threatened action against Hayley and against the craft fair. Bad enough, but of what else was she capable in order to get her way?

Chapter 35

Lia debated about mentioning Bethanne's visit to Hayley but decided she should know. On their drive home that evening, Lia repeated Bethanne's words, which were locked in her memory.

"Oh, that woman!" Hayley cried. "I wish I'd been there."

The car picked up speed as Hayley's foot pressed down on the gas pedal, until Lia cleared her throat and pointed to the rapidly approaching speed limit sign. Hayley eased up, but her fingers tapped briskly against her steering wheel.

"I'm glad you weren't there," Lia said. "It was all I could do to keep from losing my cool. She's quite a piece of work. Might she be an actual threat to your job, Hayley?"

"I don't know." Hayley stared at the road ahead. "I can't see her sabotaging the fundraiser in order to blame me. That'd be cutting off her own nose. But things out of my control could go wrong, and she could try to put the blame on me."

Hayley glanced sharply at Lia. "Then again, if she's our murderer, she could do much worse than get me fired."

"Yes, and it's worried me because of how accessible you are to her."

"Me! What about you? She showed up at your booth!" Hayley needed to ease up on the gas pedal again.

"Let's think about this," Lia said. "First of all, could Bethanne be our cat-napper?"

"Sure! Daphne's the easiest cat in the world to grab. She wouldn't give Bethanne a stitch of trouble." Hayley considered that a little longer. "And she lives alone. In a house, not a condo, from what I heard. Easy in, easy out, with no one the wiser that you've carried in a strange cat."

"But how would she know about Muriel Burgess's yard?"

"Just by driving around, I suppose. It's a corner lot, so the backyard is easy to see and to get to."

"But why drop Daphne there at all?" Lia asked. "She could leave her anywhere, a place where we'd never find her. Or worse." Lia shuddered.

"I don't know. I agree that part's a puzzle," Hayley said. "Though I suppose it's possible she might have a soft spot for animals. Unlike what's obviously not there for humans."

"Then what about my stalker?" Lia asked. "That doesn't sound like something she'd do, does it? How she acted today, confronting me face-to-face, is more her style."

"You forget, Mom, that if Bethanne killed both Jessica and Cori, she had to be stealthy about it. She'll do in-your-face to warn someone off, and it's probably her favorite mode. But people like her can be just as sneaky as anyone when they need to be." Hayley looked over to Lia. "I think she's someone you need to watch out for—big-time."

"And you," Lia reminded her. But she still had questions

regarding Bethanne—which didn't mean she wouldn't be
on her guard.

Hayley had invited Brady over for dinner that evening.
Lia suspected it was to stay close at hand, though she
had no objection to that whatsoever. Brady deserved a big
thank-you for his calming response and help when Daphne
went missing. Plus, Hayley had fixed a great meal, which
Lia needed only to sit down to after her long craft fair day.

Brady was greeted as usual with Daphne's demonstra-
tions of undying love as she wove between his ankles with
glass-rattling purrs and rolled at his feet.

"Daphne!" Hayley cried in mock horror. "You're never
that happy to see *me*!"

"It's because she doesn't see Brady as much," Lia said.

Brady reached down and ruffled Daphne's fur. "Glad
you're okay, girl. You gave us a scare the other night."

"There's more to tell you," Hayley said. "But let's eat
first. Mom, want to hold on to Daphne? I need Brady to cut
up the chicken for me."

"Sure." Lia scooped up the cat to free Brady, feeling
quite pampered as Hayley and Brady did the last-minute
preps and put dinner on the table. Hayley had roasted the
chicken in Lia's slow cooker, which allowed her to leave the
house worry-free to pick up Lia at the craft fair.

"But I browned it a few minutes in the oven afterward, to
get a crispy skin," Hayley said as she pulled up her chair,
proud of her accomplishment. A store-bought potato salad,
dinner rolls, and a tossed salad rounded out the meal, topped
with wine contributed by Brady.

"This is such a treat," Lia said, passing dishes and still
amazed by her daughter's ongoing display of culinary skills.

"I thought about making the potato salad myself," Hayley said as she scooped some onto her plate. "For about a minute, until I remembered the one you picked up once, Mom. I thought it was just as good as, if not better than, any I could do." She grinned. "And a lot less work."

"I agree," Lia said. "I mean about its being good and work saving."

They got down to eating, mingled with small talk. When offers of second and even third helpings were declined, Brady picked up his wineglass and leaned back in his chair.

"So, what's happened that you wanted to tell me?"

Hayley told him about Lia's scare as she walked home from the supermarket.

Lia, feeling Hayley had overdramatized it, said, "All I can really confirm is that I heard footsteps behind me."

"But you said they kept pace, Mom," Hayley said, adding to Brady, "And whoever it was jumped out of sight whenever she turned around."

Brady frowned. "You never saw this person?"

"I didn't, and yes, I was frightened, mostly because I was alone on a darkened street. But then Hayley happened along."

"Thank goodness!" Hayley said. "Because who knows what might have happened if I hadn't. And that's not all," Hayley said. She summarized Bethanne King's appearance at the craft fair for Brady.

"Did you feel threatened by her?" he asked Lia.

"To some extent. Maybe more like warned," Lia said. "She clearly didn't like that I'd spoken to her daughter, Tiffany. What happened between them after that I don't know, but it definitely upset Bethanne."

"Enough to show up and try to scare Mom and warn her off," Hayley said. "Just like kidnapping Daphne and then stalking."

"We don't know who did those things," Lia said. She reminded Hayley of Kevin Shaw's presence at the supermarket.
"And Mark Bernard could have been there for all I know."

"I think you should report this, officially, I mean," Brady
said. "Not just to me."

"But what could be done about it?" Lia asked. "I'd just
be wasting everyone's time."

"At least it would be on record," Hayley said. "Right?"

"It would. And I think you should also heed Bethanne
King's warning and stop what you've been doing."

"And let the police handle it?" Lia asked Brady. "Do you
genuinely believe the police will start reinvestigating Jessica's and Cori's deaths?"

Brady cleared his throat but instead of answering
straightened the fork and knife at his place.

"That's what I thought," Lia said.

"Brady," Hayley said, "you can talk to somebody again,
right? Tell them everything that's happened. It could stir
them to reopen the cases. That's all Mom wants, right, Mom?"

"I'll see what I can do," Brady said, which Lia took as
Don't get your hopes up. Which she totally understood.
There was no hard evidence. The police could do nothing
without that.

"And, Mom, I'm driving you to the craft fair again tomorrow," Hayley said. "No argument."

Lia sighed but nodded. She'd go along with it because it
made Hayley feel better. On Monday, though, Hayley would
have to go back to work. She couldn't babysit Lia forever. But
she wouldn't need to. Lia felt deep down that things were
coming to a head and that with or without police help the
questions surrounding Jessica's and Cori's deaths would be
resolved—ideally soon and with no one else getting hurt. But
that, she also understood deep down, was out of her hands.

Chapter 36

With no boxes to help carry into the craft barn Sunday morning, Hayley simply dropped Lia off, but with a final warning added to the string that Lia had already heard on the drive over. Things like *Keep your phone with you at all times, Don't wander off during breaks, Always stay in a crowd,* and so on. If it had been anyone else, Lia might have become exasperated. But she knew Hayley's warnings came from love, and Lia accepted them as such, only gently asking her daughter to try to relax.

"I promise to behave like a sensible adult the entire day," she said. "So please go do something fun and take your mind off of all this."

Hayley looked at her as though she'd been told to take up alligator wrestling that afternoon, so Lia changed tack. "Just focus on your own work. I'm sure you have loose ends to tie up for the fundraiser."

That clicked with Hayley, and she nodded. "Lots of

them. But I'll be doing that from home. Call me anytime if
you need me."

Lia promised, gave her daughter a hug, and hurried off
to join the other vendors in the craft barn. The hum of pre-
opening activity was comforting in its familiarity and
enough to take Lia's mind off anything other than her knitting booth for the time being. Olivia greeted her with a
distracted smile, and even Maggie appeared too preoccu-
pied with her quilts to run over with more advice. Before
long, Bill Landry gave them the heads-up, and the Crandalsburg Craft Fair got underway, its doors opening wide
to welcome the new day's shoppers.

As the day progressed, Lia was pleased to sell a knit
scarf, one of Tracy's baby blankets, and a set of place mats.
One shopper was even excited over the afghan that Bethanne had sneeringly referred to as "granny" and "dated,"
but the woman decided to sleep on the purchase decision
for a bit.

It was late afternoon when Lia had a surprise. She had
just sat down to knit, things having calmed at her booth. As
she gazed about, she caught sight of an unexpected face.
Megan stood at Tricia Newman's booth, browsing through
the handcrafted jewelry.

Seeing her was startling enough that Lia paused her
stitching to watch as the young college student moved
slowly from booth to booth, finally making her way to Olivia's. At that point, Megan spotted Lia. She set down the
package of essential oils she'd picked up and hurried over.

"Lia! I forgot you worked here."

Lia set aside her knitting and joined her at the counter.
"How nice to see you, Megan. Is this your first visit to the
craft fair?"

"Uh-huh. My friend Allison suggested it." Megan gestured vaguely toward the far side of the barn. "She loves crafty things. She's an art major."

Lia nodded. "How have you been?" she asked. Close up, her young friend didn't look all that well to her.

Megan shrugged and managed a weak smile. "Okay, I guess." She glanced around. No one was near enough to hear, but she still lowered her voice and leaned forward. "Marc's been struggling."

"*Marc* has?"

"I know, I know." Megan shook her head. "I wasn't going to see him, but . . ."

Lia braced herself.

"I can't help it, Lia."

"You can't help what exactly?"

"Feeling sorry for him." Megan rubbed at her bare arms, looking miserable. "Don't worry. I'm not seeing him again. We're just talking. But he's going through a tough time."

Lia sucked in a breath. Her impulse was to take Megan by the shoulders and shake her, but support was called for, not scolding. "What is he finding so tough?" she asked, keeping her tone as neutral as possible.

"Our breakup. It's been harder on him than I expected. I feel guilty, like, maybe I did it all wrong."

"Megan . . ." Lia paused. What to say to convince this young woman that the responsibility was all Marc's? Megan had started off so well. But she was facing a master manipulator.

"Megan," Lia began again. "Monday, when I came to the coffee shop to return the bracelet you'd dropped, Marc came in and you introduced us. He stayed at your counter after I sat down. Apparently he wasn't able to talk you into something."

Megan nodded. "Right. He wanted to pick me up at the end of my shift and I said no."

"He didn't like hearing that, did he?" When Megan shook her head, Lia said, "Marc came to my table after that and sat down."

"Yes, I saw that."

"It might have looked to you like a friendly stop on his way out," Lia said, "but it was far from that. He was angry. Not hurt or disappointed. Angry. At me for whatever part I had in your change toward him."

"Oh! But I never told him—"

"He guessed. And he made sure I knew how he felt about it. It wasn't explicit, but Marc made sure I understood he was warning me off. It wasn't pleasant."

Megan frowned worriedly. "I'm sorry. I didn't know."

Lia laid a hand over Megan's. "I just don't think you should believe any sad story of his about hurt feelings. He's a person who can't stand losing control. He's working you to get it back."

Megan nodded slowly. After a long silence she asked, "Did he ever come to your house?"

"My house?" Lia asked, surprised. "No. Why?"

"He asked me where you lived. He brought it up so casually. He said there was a new instructor at the college who was looking for a place to live, that she was single and didn't want anything very big. I remembered Ava told me Hayley was staying with you and that there wasn't much room for all her stuff. She mentioned the neighborhood, and I told Marc. Now, after what you said, I wonder if he asked me for another reason."

Lia thought back to Daphne's disappearance. "Were you with Marc Wednesday afternoon?" she asked.

"Wednesday? No, I was working then. Why?"

"What about Friday evening?" Frightening Lia on her dark walk home seemed very like something Marc would do.

"Yes," Megan said. "I went out with Marc after Beans and Bakes closed."

"What time was that?"

"Ten."

Lia had been walking back from the supermarket around nine. Plenty of time for her stalker to make it to Megan's coffee shop. But was it Marc?

"Megan, can you promise me not to be alone with Marc for now? I know you want to be kind, but would you make any excuse you can to keep away from him?"

Megan searched Lia's face. "He wouldn't ever hurt me, Lia, if that's what you're thinking."

"I don't know exactly what I'm thinking, but I can't take a chance. Just do this for me, would you?"

Megan hesitated, then nodded. "I will."

"Good."

A shopper came up to Lia's booth and started looking through the knit items. At the same time Megan heard her name called, and she turned.

"That's Allison." She waved back to the young woman who was beckoning to her. "I'd better go." She squeezed Lia's hand, then stepped away just as the shopper held up a pair of mittens.

"Do you have these in red?" the woman asked, and Lia got back to work.

Later, as the craft fair was winding down, Lia checked her phone in case Hayley had left a message about picking her up. She found a call waiting for her in voice mail, but it was from Shirley.

"Hi, this is Shirley. Hope you get this. I wondered if

you'd come over tomorrow. Maybe around three? There were things we never got to talk about the last time." She left her number.

Lia called but got Shirley's answering machine. "Three o'clock tomorrow will be fine," Lia said to the machine. "I'll see you then."

Chapter 37

The next day, Lia had just finished her lunch and was thinking about her upcoming visit to Shirley when Maureen called.

"Got a minute?" she asked.

"Sure," Lia said. "Something about your sweater commission?"

"No, it's not that. I heard from a former coworker yesterday," Maureen said. "A woman who'd been at the office when Cori did temp work for us."

That got Lia's attention, and she sat up straighter. "Yes?"

"Patti—that's her name—didn't know what had happened to Cori. After I told her, we got to talking about her. Patti was surprised to know that Cori had moved back to Crandalsburg."

"Why was that?" Daphne was wiggling at Lia's feet, wanting to jump up to her lap, but Lia held her back.

"Because Cori had talked to Patti one time about why

she left Crandalsburg to move to York. She said she needed to be away from her sister."

"Needed?" Lia's brows rose. "Did she explain why?"

"No, that was all Cori said. You knew Cori. She wasn't much of a talker. Frankly, I'm surprised she said that much, although Patti is a really easy person to talk with. I thought you'd want to know."

"Yes, thank you, Maureen. I'm going to meet with someone today who knew both sisters well. Maybe she can explain that."

Lia ended the call and let Daphne jump up. She petted the cat absently, her thoughts on what she'd just heard, and wished she could run over to Shirley's place right then.

Hello there!" Shirley called from her door as Lia climbed out of her car. "Wonderful to see you!" She held the door for Lia, then led the way to her living room, where the silver tea set once again waited, Shirley's rubber-tipped cane tapping softly as she went. "I never put my lovely set away after you were here," she said, "so I made tea for us. But I can get you something cold if you'd rather?"

"I'd love the hot tea," Lia said.

Shirley busied herself pouring it out, then settled back on her sofa holding her own cup. The tea was good, but Lia was glad Shirley's air-conditioning was running efficiently on that warm day. Since her hostess had set up the meeting, Lia figured there was something she wanted to say. She waited to hear it.

Shirley set her cup down carefully on her table. "I went to see Judith yesterday," she said.

"How is she? I was there on Friday," Lia said.

"Friday? Then of course you don't know."

"Know what?" Lia feared the worst after the condition she'd seen Judith in. But Shirley surprised her.

"She's had a turnaround." Shirley beamed. "Yes! They called me from the nursing home yesterday morning because Judith was asking to see me. I was delighted, of course, to drop everything and go! The last few times I'd been, she barely knew me."

"That's how she was when I was there," Lia said. "I'm so glad to hear this. What brought it about?"

Shirley shook her head. "They really couldn't explain it, at least for me to understand. I'm putting it down to pure stubbornness, that Judith just decided she'd had enough." Shirley cackled before adding thoughtfully, "She was in quite a forgiving mood."

"Forgiving of what?" Lia asked.

"Oh, of a lot of things. The cause of her injuries, for one, the accident, I mean. But who knows? That feeling may pass." She picked up her cup for another sip.

"I didn't get your message until yesterday, by the way," Shirley said. "The one you left asking how to reach Robin. That darned blinking thing on my machine doesn't always light up like it should. My granddaughter tells me I should get rid of it and just use my cell phone for everything. She might be right. Anyway, your message said something about the nursing home trying to reach her. They apparently did. Judith said Robin had been there earlier."

Shirley frowned.

After a long silence Lia asked, "Is something wrong?"

Shirley looked up. "Just that one of the aides told me Robin hadn't been to see her mother for some time." She shook her head. "I suppose it could have been because Judith was so out of it for a while there. I know it was hard for me, sometimes, to just sit there when she couldn't talk to me. And Robin has her business to attend to. It's the kind of work that can come and go. When it picks up, you have to jump to it, don't you?"

Lia remembered the woman at the playground event, who had spotted Robin knocking at the door across the street. She'd suggested Robin's work had been in a slump lately, but perhaps that had ended.

"What can you tell me about Robin's relationship with Cori?" Lia asked. "Did they get along?"

"Their relationship?" Shirley asked. "Yes, that's what we never got to last time, wasn't it? Well, there was quite an age difference, you know. Robin was eight when Cori was born. They couldn't really be playmates. And babies take up a lot of a mother's time, of course. I'm sure Robin didn't like that, at that age."

"Did it improve?" Lia asked. "As they got older?"

"I'm afraid not," Shirley said sadly. "Partly, I'd say, because Cori had her problems. She was an anxious child. But I always thought Robin could have . . ." Shirley's voice trailed off, and she looked away.

"Yes?" Lia prompted.

"Robin could have been more sympathetic, to my mind," Shirley said, turning back. "Especially once she got into her teens and could understand better. I'm afraid she let her jealousy take hold. She was often . . . unkind to her sister."

"Verbally or physically?"

"Oh, verbally," Shirley said quickly. "Judith wouldn't have allowed any sort of violence. But words can hurt just as much, can't they?"

Lia thought of Bethanne's hurtful words to her daughter, Tiffany, and thought they had surely left their mark. "Cori left Crandalsburg for a few months," Lia said. "About a year ago, to work in York. I understand it was her first time living on her own."

"It was. It was a huge step," Shirley said. "Judith was supportive, but also concerned. I had mixed feelings about it myself. On the one hand, I was proud of her for taking the leap. But I also thought staying closer to home, at least at first, would have been better."

"Robin told me there was an efficiency apartment in her building she wished Cori had taken."

"Did she?" Shirley looked surprised. "I'm not sure that would have appealed to either of them."

"Because of its nearness?"

"Yes. When I said Cori would have been better off staying closer to home, I meant closer to her mother. A place where Judith could have popped in if Cori needed a little help adjusting. But Judith wouldn't have overdone it, I know."

"And Robin?" Lia asked.

"I can't say, really." Shirley's lined face drooped. "Having the two sisters living in the same building might have pleased Judith. She did tend to deny there was any problem between them, or if there was, that it would somehow work itself out. But to my mind that wasn't going to happen."

She made an effort to be more positive. "But Robin did have a lovely wake for Cori, didn't she?" The forced smile began to falter, and she reached for her teacup to cover that with a sip.

Chapter 38

Lia stopped at Robin's office after leaving Shirley's house. Her talk with Shirley had raised questions she wanted answers to, but she quickly saw the place was closed. Out on another job, she supposed. Lia considered leaving a message but decided to hold off on that. Instead she went home.

As had become her habit since their scare with Daphne, Lia checked on the cat's whereabouts immediately on entering her house. She found Daphne dozing peacefully on Hayley's bed and, satisfied, let her be. There were things Lia wanted to mull over, and her favorite place to do that was in her knitting chair, stitching away on the cardigan Helen had ordered two weeks ago, which was growing nicely. Fortunately, she'd reached a less complicated section, which freed her mind to go where it would. There would be no audiobook playing this time. She had her own mystery to deal with.

Lia had just set down her needles to rest her hands when her phone rang.

"Hi, Mom," Hayley said. "Just wanted to let you know I'm going to grab dinner here at the farm café. I've got a lot to do."

"Okay. Hope you get something good to eat." Lia knew the café handled only lunches for visitors, so cold leftovers would likely be Hayley's choice. But she'd survive. "How late will you be?"

"Don't know," Hayley said. "But I'll text when I'm on my way home, okay?"

"That'll be fine. See you then."

Talk of food made Lia's stomach rumble, and she got up to rummage through her own leftovers. Noises in the kitchen usually brought Daphne to investigate, so it was no surprise when she soon appeared. Lia made sure Daphne's bowls were filled, then fixed a hearty salad for herself from Hayley's slow-cooked chicken and various vegetables, making enough for two in case Hayley came home hungry.

After her dinner, Lia went upstairs to log onto her laptop. Her knitting session had brought up thoughts that she wanted to look into more deeply. That required the Internet and a search engine, and she settled at her desk, placing a fresh mug of coffee at its side. Her searches might take a bit of time and take her on a wild-goose chase but could at least help narrow her scope.

It was after Lia had brought up a second coffee that she leaned toward her screen, frowning. What she'd turned up was more surprising than she'd expected. It led to more questions than she'd started with, questions that required a face-to-face discussion. Robin had been difficult to reach lately, with her office seeming to be always closed. After hours looked like Lia's best chance. She did a quick online search for Robin's home address and checked the time. It was edging close to the limits of a social visit, but Lia ignored that consideration. She had to talk to Robin. If an unexpected knock at her door annoyed the woman, so be it.

Her GPS system failed Lia, sending her in a circle near Robin's apartment complex, which, it also turned out, had more than one building. She had to stop and ask a pedestrian, who pointed out the correct turn, a street whose sign had been shadowed by an overhanging tree branch. Lia finally pulled her car into an available parking spot, some distance away from the front entrance of the correct building.

She was about to get out when she saw a young couple step out of the doorway, followed shortly after by a lone figure that turned in Lia's direction. It was Robin.

Something about her manner kept Lia from calling out to her. She walked quickly, her head down, and looked like a woman with a plan. Whatever that was, Lia picked up vibes that told her Robin didn't want to be stopped. She watched Robin climb into a Kia, and as it backed up and pulled out of the parking area, Lia decided to follow.

As she pulled out of her own parking spot, Lia knew that decision could simply take her to a 7-Eleven and make her feel foolish. But Robin led her, instead, through Crandalsburg and eventually out onto the highway. Traffic grew heavy but not so dense that Lia lost sight of the Kia, and she drove for several miles, feeling confident that Robin was unaware of her.

When they left the highway, following became more difficult, and at one point Lia had dropped back enough that she worried she'd lost Robin altogether on the dark road. But the distinctive boxy shape of Robin's car helped Lia identify it, and as she closed in at a four-way stop, she was able to confirm the license plate number, which she'd memorized back in Crandalsburg.

Before long, Lia knew where they were heading: the nursing facility that cared for Judith Littlefield. Was this an emergency? Lia wondered. It certainly wasn't usual visiting hours. Although Shirley had said Judith had greatly improved, a relapse wasn't out of the question. But again, Robin's look as she left her apartment building signaled something else to Lia. Exactly what, she wasn't sure. But it kept her on the trail, when she could have turned around and gone home. She needed to see this out.

They came to the long, open drive leading to the Paxworth facility, a problem for Lia if Robin had been checking her rearview mirror. But an ambulance with no flashing lights or siren slipped between them, effectively covering Lia until they closed in on the building. The ambulance then turned onto a side driveway as Robin continued straight ahead, Lia slowing but staying on track.

The visitors parking lot was nearly empty, attesting to the after-hours time period, and Robin turned into it. Lia could hardly follow without announcing her presence and after a moment's debate pulled into one of several free reserved parking spots close to the entrance. Expecting Robin to walk past in a minute, Lia wished she had a cap of some sort to pull down. But as she kept watch in her rearview and side mirrors, Lia was startled to see Robin's dark figure instead slip around the side of the building.

Lia quickly jumped out. Was there a second visitors entrance in another part of the building? Doubtful. But where was Robin going?

Lia made it to the corner of the building and caught sight of Robin quick-stepping toward the back along a driveway whose sign had stated DELIVERY VEHICLES ONLY. She disappeared around the far corner, causing Lia to scurry to catch up. When she got there, she saw a large van parked at an open door in the center of the building, MEDICAL LINEN SERVICE written on its side. A uniformed worker came out of the door carrying two large, tied bags, which he tossed into the van. At the same time, a second man rolled a cart, presumably filled with clean linens, into the building. He was soon followed by the first worker with a second cart. The door was left open, and there was no sign of Robin. Had she entered through that door when neither worker was around? Most likely. Robin obviously hadn't wanted to be seen going through the main entrance. Something was very wrong.

Lia hurried over to the open door and peered around it to see a short, empty hallway. Taking a deep breath, she stepped in and scurried to the end of the hallway. Coming to a T, she spotted the two workers from the van several yards to her left, talking with a woman wearing a house-cleaning uniform. There was plenty of laughter, and Lia felt confident enough to slip unnoticed to the right and continue down that hall. Had Robin gone that way? Did it lead to Judith's room? Lia had no idea, but she kept on, passing rooms that looked like offices, their interiors behind win-dowed doors darkened.

She stopped when she came to another T. The halls on both sides were empty. The rooms down the way to her left looked like patient rooms on each side. Was Judith's one of them? When Lia had visited, the nursing assistant, Alice, had led her, chatting most of the way so that Lia hadn't paid close attention to where they were going. They'd also come from the front entrance, not the back. Lia thought hard, trying to picture the room number on Judith's door. She remembered glancing at a few as they'd walked, then at the one where they'd finally stopped. She concentrated until 144 popped into her head. That was it, she was sure! She checked the number of the room closest to her: 120. With luck, if she continued on, she'd come to Judith's, where, she'd become sure, she'd find Robin.

The room numbers climbed upward as Lia walked: 130 . . . 138 . . . 142 . . . then 144. She stopped. The door was closed. Lia pressed her ear to it and heard a muffled voice—too low to know whose it was or what was said. She gripped the doorknob and slowly turned it, then eased the door open enough to hear. It was Robin's voice, definitely, and it rose and faded as she paced.

"It's always been that way, Mother. You know it has. Everything centered around Cori."

Lia listened but heard no response. The sliver of light coming through the crack in the door changed as Robin's shadow moved across it.

"Cori, Cori, Cori!" Robin said. "The *world* centered around Cori, and why? Because she was so pitiful! Yes, pitiful! You couldn't look at her sideways without her breaking into hysterics. Then everyone jumped to coddle her. And pointed fingers to put the blame on me. Well, I got sick of it." There was a pause. "What's that you say, Mother?"

The shadow had stopped. Lia caught a faint squeak, as of someone trying to speak but unable to.

"You'll have to speak up, Mother. Oh, that's right. You can't. It's the sedative taking hold, that's all, Mother. Don't worry. It's just to make it easier. For you, but mostly for me."

The pacing picked up again.

"It would have been a *lot* easier for me if you hadn't gotten better. You were at death's door, you know. At least that's what they told me. And then poof! You're back to life. Just when I got a nice offer on the house. Bad timing. I've got debts, you see. Big ones, with my business going down the tubes. Selling Cori's crappy crochets won't cover it. Not by a long shot.

"Oh, and on top of reviving, you now say you want to drop the accident lawsuit? You're suddenly *so sorry* for the guy whose brakes went bad and hit you? You're sorry for *him*! What about me? Did you think I wanted to go even more broke paying for your maintenance for the next twenty years? I thought you were on your way out. I'd already got rid of Cori."

Another squeak.

"Yes, that's right, Mother. Did you think I wanted to be *her* caregiver the rest of my life? You *had* to bring her back to Crandalsburg. She finally gets out of the house, out of my life! But you had to bring her back, so it's your fault. You think her running a booth two days a week was going to support her? No, she was going to turn right back into the parasite she's always been, and on top of that get half of everything that should by rights come to me.

"And now it will. The house and the nice lawsuit that will bring in a tidy sum because you'll have nothing to say about it anymore."

There was silence, and the movement of the light had stopped. Lia opened the door enough to see Judith's bed, with Robin leaning over it, pressing a pillow over Judith's face.

"No!" Lia jumped into the room.

Robin's head turned, but she kept hold of the pillow.

Lia grabbed at Robin's arm, but Robin swung, surprising Lia and knocking her hard in the face. Lia staggered but pulled at Robin again, managing to loosen her hold on the suffocating pillow. She heard Judith gasp.

"Get out of here," Robin cried, her features distorted into an ugly mask of fury. She grabbed Lia's shoulders and shoved hard, but Lia caught hold of the bed rail and kicked out. She reached for the flower vase on Judith's bed table and smashed it into Robin's head, then snatched at the pillow, running out with it to shout in the hall.

"Help! Help! Somebody! I need help!"

An orderly appeared at the far corner. He leaped into action, catching hold of Robin as she started to run from the room, Lia shouting her explanation of what had gone on. An aide came out of nowhere and dashed into Judith's room to see to her and press call buttons. Alarms rang and security guards arrived, all within minutes, though at the time it seemed like hours to Lia as Robin screamed her innocence and struggled to free herself.

It was horror and pandemonium, but most important, Judith's murder had been prevented. And the puzzle of Cori's death had been answered—pitiably, but at least answered.

For the moment, at least, that would have to do.

Chapter 39

It was close to midnight by the time Lia got home. The York police had been called, and Lia needed to stay and talk with them. When she'd called Hayley, she had urged her not to wait up but knew it was a waste of her breath. At least she managed to keep her daughter from rushing to the Paxworth facility.

"There's nothing you can do," Lia had insisted.

"I can take you home," Hayley protested.

"No, Hayley. I will drive myself home. I'm perfectly able to do that. I only called to let you know why I wasn't home—and that I was fine."

"But—"

"No," Lia repeated and got a reluctant assent from her daughter.

But she wasn't surprised to see Hayley hurry out of the house as soon as she pulled up. And she didn't mind. A little fussing and TLC appealed greatly by then.

Once inside, Hayley set Lia firmly in her knitting chair, brought over a footstool, and had a mug of tea ready for her. "I warmed it as soon as I spotted your car," she said. Lia turned down the offer of food but sipped her tea gratefully before leaning her head back with a deep sigh.

"Mom," Hayley said as she took her seat on the sofa, her tone scolding. "What am I going to do with you?"

"I beg your pardon?" Lia opened her eyes.

"Well, I apparently can't let you out of my sight."

"Said the girl who—"

"I know, I know," Hayley said. "Don't remind me. But that incident was a long time ago. I've learned since then. But you?"

"Not quite the same situation," Lia said, ignoring the fact that the long-ago time period Hayley referred to had been barely four months. "I didn't confront Robin in some isolated place. There was always available help nearby. Though I admit I wasn't expecting what I ran into, at least not at first."

"Well, it was a good thing you were there," Hayley said, her tone softening. "Poor Judith. Alive, but now having to deal with the terrible truth."

After a brief silence Hayley asked for more details than Lia had given over the phone, including the why of it all. Lia shared what she knew about the accident lawsuit she'd discovered during her Internet search.

"It would be a significant windfall, assuming the entire amount was awarded, and Judith apparently was considering dropping it. How seriously, I don't know. Perhaps if Robin had only tried to talk to her." Lia stopped and took a bracing sip of her tea before continuing. "But since Robin admitted that she killed Cori, she obviously chose a more reliable solution to the problem."

"What about Jessica?" Hayley asked. "Did Robin kill her, too?"

"I don't see that to be the case." Lia lifted Daphne to cuddle on her lap, then leaned her face tiredly against Daphne's warm, furry head. "But I just don't know. It's something we might never learn."

The next evening, Brady arrived with the take-out dinners Hayley had ordered. Besides the food, he had updated information on Robin, which he promised to share—after they'd eaten.

Lia was fine with that, though Hayley was less so, and once they got to their coffee, she handed Brady his, saying, "Okay, shoot! What do you know?"

Brady stirred in his cream before answering. "First of all, Robin learned about the linen-service delivery time from a condo neighbor of hers. According to that woman, they had chatted in the building's laundry room when the coincidence of Robin's mother staying at Paxworth and this neighbor's son running the service for them came up."

"So she knew when and how to get in without being seen," Hayley said.

"Right. And," Brady added, "Robin probably had been to the facility often enough to know its routines, things like when staff would be scarce."

"Did she talk about Cori?" Lia asked.

"She did." Brady frowned and shifted in his chair. "We already knew a lot because of what you overheard at the nursing home. Robin had financial troubles. When it looked like her mother wouldn't survive her accident, Robin didn't want to split the lawsuit money and inheritance with Cori.

She also didn't want the burden of looking after her sister. Her solution was to get rid of Cori.

"Robin used Cori's well-known nightmares about Jessica and set it up to look as though Cori took her own life at the same spot that Jessica died. She'd lured Cori up there by saying she had come to believe Cori's story about what she saw but needed her to explain it more thoroughly at the place."

"And afterward," Lia said, "she told anyone who would listen that Cori had long been suicidal."

"Evil woman," Hayley said.

The three of them fell silent, pondering that, Lia also thinking how frighteningly normal someone could appear while hiding terrible thoughts and deeds.

The next morning, after Hayley had gone off to work, Lia's neighbor from across the street came to see her. A busy working mother of a toddler, Kelly Butler had exchanged only a few words and quick waves with Lia before then. So Lia was surprised to find the pretty redhead at her door.

"My husband and I just found out something we thought you should know," Kelly explained. Lia quickly brought her in.

"We have this teen who cuts our grass for us," Kelly said as she perched on the edge of the chair Lia offered her. "Andrew. He's a good kid, always shows up when he says he will and does a good job. But, well, he's fourteen, so . . ."

"Yes?"

"So he didn't say anything to us about what happened, I mean about your cat. Which is why, when your daughter came over, looking for her, we didn't have a clue."

"What did Andrew finally tell you?" Lia asked, moving to the edge of her own seat.

"That day, when your cat went missing, none of us were at home, but Andrew was there to cut our grass. He said he saw—what was her name? The cat?"

"Daphne."

"Right. He saw Daphne out in your yard. He hadn't started the mower yet—he had to fill up the gas—and Daphne looked like she was going to come across the street to him. That worried him, so he went over and picked her up. He knocked at your door, but I guess nobody was home."

"Right. My daughter and I were both out."

"Well, Andrew said he wasn't sure what to do, when this woman pulled up."

"This woman?" Lia repeated.

"That's how he put it. He didn't know who she was. But it must have been Robin Wendt, because he said she had a lot of fabric stuff in the back of her car. I had actually asked her to drop off some samples—we're thinking of redoing . . . well, never mind about that. But I never made the connection until now."

"What did she do?" Lia asked.

"Andrew said she asked him if that was your cat—she mentioned your name—and he said he supposed so, that he just found her out in the yard but nobody was home. She said she was a friend of yours, and she'd take care of it. Andrew, taking her word for it, handed Daphne over. Then he promptly forgot about it and got to work on our grass. It wasn't until all this latest stuff was on the news that he thought about it again."

Kelly shivered. "We never did hire her, thank goodness. But I wanted you to know."

"Thank you, Kelly," Lia said. "That was a part of the puzzle we still had questions about." Lia offered her coffee, but Kelly said she had to run.

Before she did, she picked up Daphne, who had come downstairs to investigate. "I'm so glad she didn't hurt you!" Kelly said. She rubbed Daphne's ears and gave her a few squeezes, which Daphne enjoyed, obviously agreeing with her.

Lia thought that might be her last puzzle piece, that there would always be a blank space next to the question of Jessica's death. But then she heard from the man who had been one of her top suspects. He called Thursday morning and left a message asking if she would meet him for coffee.

After careful thought and knowing they'd be in a public place, Lia returned the call and agreed. When she arrived at Marie's Diner, she saw Kevin Shaw waiting for her at a window booth. He rose to greet her.

"Thank you for coming," he said, retaking his seat as she slipped in across from him. He waited until the waitress had served them both coffee before saying anything more.

"It was so many years ago," he began. "I had hoped I could put it all behind me and forget. But of course, that was impossible."

Shaw looked like a man who hadn't slept much lately, and Lia waited quietly for what he would say.

"I should have known as soon as I heard about Cori's fall that it would all come up again." He stared down at his coffee but didn't touch it, then raised his head. "It was all a terrible accident."

"You mean Jessica, of course," Lia said. "What exactly happened?"

He drew a deep breath. "First of all, I was crazy about Jessica back then, but, well, it wasn't easy. She broke up with me more than once. But then we'd get back together. It got to be pretty awful," he said, "at least for me." He shook his head. "I have a feeling she enjoyed the drama. That it was some kind of game to her."

Kevin rubbed his face and looked out the window for several moments before picking up his story. "That day, she asked me to meet her at the falls. I was excited. I thought it meant we were good. But we weren't. She got me up there only to tell me we were through. That was her idea of fun— to raise someone's hopes only to dash them."

"Did it make you angry?" Lia asked.

He laughed. "Actually, no. Now it does, as I look back. But at the time I was still desperate. I was upset, yes, but I argued about it, at least at first. Then I actually begged." He stopped, then picked up his coffee mug for the first time to drink from it.

After a long silence, Lia asked, "How did Jessica respond?"

Kevin made a derisive snort. "She laughed. She actually laughed. Then she just started talking about her next big role, Juliet, like that was all that mattered. She got more and more excited talking about it, and she jumped up on some of the higher rocks, posing, I guess like Juliet, and reciting lines. And that's when she fell."

"She fell?" Lia asked. "On her own?"

Kevin looked steadily at Lia. "On her own. I swear it. I was several feet away when she slipped and lost her balance, and just . . . fell. It happened so suddenly that I froze. I couldn't believe what I saw. But there was nothing, nothing I could have done to stop it. After some moments I ran to the edge."

"Could you see her?"

"Barely. She was wearing something red, which helped.

But she had gone all the way down—I don't know, sixty or seventy feet?—into the water. I knew she had to be dead. I was in shock. But then this little girl appeared out of nowhere screaming Jessica's name! I turned to stare at her, probably scaring her because she screamed and ran away. I . . . I'm ashamed to say I did, too. Not after her; I just wanted to get out of there. I could barely grasp what had happened, and all I could think was to run."

Kevin took another swallow from his mug. "Afterward, when they'd found Jessica's body and I'd had time to think, I was scared. I thought everyone would somehow know Jessica had come to break up with me and that I had pushed her over. So when police started talking to everybody she knew, I begged my friend for an alibi. And that was the end of it. I thought.

"I didn't know the little girl was Cori or how it had affected her. I don't honestly know what I would have done if I had known. I was barely twenty then and, I'm ashamed to say, thought only of myself."

"You knew Jessica babysat Cori," Lia said, remembering what he'd said at the pizza place. "When Cori had that hysterical episode at your dental office, you must have known who she was."

Kevin nodded. "I did eventually, but not at the time. The whole thing was jarring, but when her mother came to apologize about the scene, she explained that Cori was easily upset and had been frightened by seeing a strange new dentist. It was only recently that I made the connection to the little girl at the falls and what she saw, or thought she saw there."

They were silent for several moments. Lia picked up her coffee but found it had gone cold and set it back down.

"What are you going to do?" she finally asked.

"What I should have done a long time ago," Kevin said. "Tell the truth. I've started with you. Next will be the police. Something I wish I had done from the first. If I had, maybe it would have helped Cori. Maybe she wouldn't have had such a troubled life." He paused. "And maybe she'd still be alive today."

Lia sighed. She didn't know if that would be the case, nor did she know exactly what would happen next. Legal consequences of some sort, she supposed. Possible effects on Kevin's professional and personal life when it all came to light. But she saw courage as well as determination in Kevin Shaw. He would handle it and take whatever came. And he'd be minus a long-held burden.

Chapter 40

The fundraising event for the Crandalsburg Parks Booster Club took place at the alpaca farm Thursday evening, the Ninth Street Knitters' regular meeting night. Not about to miss her daughter's first big event, Lia had invited her knitting friends to join her if they didn't mind postponing the meeting. They all jumped at the idea.

It was a perfect August evening, and to Hayley's delight, her publicity efforts had stirred significant early ticket sales, with more selling at the entrance. Lia strolled among colorful tents and streamers with her friends, lemonade in hand and raising her voice slightly over the music as she answered questions they still had concerning her recent days.

"Lia, you're a hero," Maureen said. Overriding Lia's immediate denial, she insisted, "If you hadn't followed your instincts with such presence of mind, that poor woman would be dead."

"And that terrible daughter might have got away with it all," Diana said.

"But I wouldn't have made it to that point without everyone's help," Lia said, her gaze sweeping the four women fondly.

When they ran out of questions, Tracy asked, "Is the yarn shop open?" The other three turned to Lia with eager faces, and she was pleased to inform them it was and to point the way. She had seen Belinda and Chad arrive and excused herself to catch up with them.

Lia hurried past the face-painting stand, where a little boy was getting his face temporarily transformed into an alpaca's, and caught up with Belinda at the cupcake kiosk, handled by the craft fair's own Carolyn Hanson. Most of the other food or game stands were managed by booster club volunteers.

"There she is!" Carolyn cried, spotting Lia after handing Chad a chocolate cupcake. Belinda and Chad turned.

"Thank you so much for coming!" Lia said to them. "Carolyn, I'm going to return for one of those red-sprinkled ones."

"They're going fast!" Carolyn said. "Hayley's stirred up a great cake-loving crowd." The three stepped away to stroll toward the alpaca pens, where lines of families waited for their close-encounter turns.

Belinda added her praise to Carolyn's. "Hayley's done an impressive job."

Lia beamed. "She's certainly worked hard on it." They paused at the fence to watch two young girls pose for photos with a friendly tan-and-white alpaca under the watchful eye of one of the farm employees.

"Chad has news about Marc Bernard," Belinda said. She licked a bit of frosting from her hand.

Chad nodded as Lia turned to him. "Rumor has it that one of his students has reported their inappropriate relationship. Administration will likely take it very seriously."

Megan, Lia thought, smiling. *She's worked up the courage.* "I'm glad to hear it," she said. "What will happen next?"

Chad shrugged. "Disciplinary action of some sort. If more students come forward, that could lead to firing, at least."

"That's all?" Belinda asked.

"If the student is eighteen or over, which most of ours are, there's no legal action warranted," Chad said.

"What if he'd preyed on more students than Jessica when he taught at the high school?" Belinda asked.

"That," Chad said, "would be a different story."

Belinda nodded. "With someone like Marc, that must have been the case. If so, I hope someone who was underaged at the time will speak up, once this comes out."

"Then he'll deserve jail time," Lia said, feeling proud of Megan for setting things in motion that might finally stop a predator.

They gazed at the alpacas silently for a while until Chad said he'd like to try his hand at the football toss he'd noticed. It had hula hoops strung together, with the center hoop being the top prize winner. Lia walked over with them, and while Chad waited in line for his turn, she spotted Tiffany talking with one of the volunteers at the ice cream stand.

Lia had expected Bethanne to show up as the head of the booster club but hadn't seen her yet. She excused herself to head over and saw that Tiffany held a clipboard. As Lia closed in, she picked up a discussion about volunteer sign-ups and schedules. Tiffany started to move on but stopped when she noticed Lia. She smiled.

"How are things going?" Lia asked.

"Quite well. Everyone's shown up who promised to, and the games and food tents have been doing a brisk business."

"That must have been a lot to organize," Lia said.

"Yes, but that's one thing my mother is really good at." Tiffany chuckled. "Drill sergeants can be highly efficient at keeping people in line." Her smile faded. "I'm sorry about the hassle she caused your daughter. And you, too. I learned about her visit to the craft fair."

Lia made a slight nod, unsure what to say.

"She's not here tonight," Tiffany said. "I'm taking her place. And that's actually a good sign."

"Of what?"

"That my mother recognizes she crossed a line and is uncomfortable about it. Don't expect a direct apology, but I can almost guarantee she'll find ways to make up for it."

"That would be nice," Lia said. "Especially for my daughter's sake."

Tiffany nodded. "I wouldn't be surprised if Mother recommends the alpaca farm for future events. And," she added, "sends friends to your knitting booth. But you won't see her there herself."

"I'll take what I can get," Lia said, smiling. "You seem to understand your mother well."

"She can be challenging," Tiffany admitted. "But there are also positives." She paused. "I know for one thing that she helped find a way for Jessica's family to afford grief counseling for a younger sister when she heard the girl had been struggling for quite a while."

"I wasn't aware of that," Lia said.

"I wasn't, either, until recently. But it wasn't from any kind of guilt. I'm convinced my mother had nothing to do with Jessica's fall."

Lia nodded. "Since we last talked, a witness other than Cori has come forward to swear that the fall was accidental, as it was originally ruled."

"Good to know," Tiffany said. She tapped her pen lightly against the clipboard. "I'd better check on a few more stands."

Tiffany left, and Lia stood alone, mulling over what she'd just learned about Bethanne King. It made her doubly glad that she hadn't mentioned her earlier suspicions about the woman to Pete Sullivan when they'd talked. She hadn't seen him since that day at the falls, though Brady had passed on that Pete had asked how she was doing.

As if conjured by her thoughts, the man himself suddenly appeared in her line of vision, wandering the grounds. Pete greeted several people along the way but never paused more than a second, seeming to be searching the area. His gaze turned her way and caught her watching. He smiled and headed her way.

"Hello, Lia," he said, stopping.

"How nice to see you, Pete," Lia said. "Supporting the Crandalsburg Parks Boosters?"

"It's a good organization. But it sounded like a fun time, too. Believe it or not, I've never been to this farm."

"I guess that's a good sign," Lia said with a smile. "No problems that the police needed to take care of." She thought of asking about Kevin Shaw but decided she'd find out anything she needed to know in good time. This was Pete's night off.

"Have you been to see the alpacas yet?" she asked instead.

"I haven't. Care to show me the way?" Pete asked.

Lia did, and they strolled toward the barn, Pete continuing to be greeted by passersby. Lia found herself feeling the

most relaxed she had for some time. Music floated through
the summer air, children skipped about, laughing, and
when she reached the pen, Hayley's favorite alpaca, Rosie,
came over to nuzzle her hand. As she was introducing Pete
to Rosie, Jen Beasley came up, clutching a large bag of
what surely was alpaca yarn.

"Lia, there you are!" Jen cried. "And Pete! How good to
see you. We're all meeting at the food tent. Why don't you
join us?"

Pete quickly agreed, and he and Lia ended up side by
side at one of several long tables, eating barbecued ribs and
corn on the cob, surrounded by Lia's knitting friends, as
well as Belinda and Chad and several of Lia's neighbors.
Craft fair vendors stopped to say hello, as did friends of
Pete.

It was the best Lia had felt in quite a while, and she silently blessed Belinda for urging her to move to Crandalsburg, and her daughter for eventually joining her there and
for making this evening possible.

Before long, Hayley came by, taking a breather from her
duties. Lia introduced her to Pete, and after they exchanged
a few words, Hayley slipped onto the bench next to Lia. She
beamed at the praise that came her way while also pointing
out what a group effort it was. Then, as the others returned
to their dinners, she leaned closer to Lia.

"You'll be getting your house back before long," she
said, her eyes twinkling.

Lia nearly dropped her corn before setting it down carefully. "What?"

"I found a place. I can move in anytime."

Lia turned toward her. "I didn't know you were even
looking."

"I wasn't, at least not much. No time! But one of the girls

here at the farm told me about it, and I ran over for a quick look."

"A quick look," Lia repeated. Exactly like Hayley, whereas she, Lia, would have ruminated over it, probably made a long list of the pros and cons, and discussed it with everyone she knew before finally deciding. But her daughter's method seemed to work for her.

"I'll miss having you around," Lia said. "But that's great. You need your own place. Has Brady seen it?" Brady, she knew, was on duty that night, much to Hayley's disappointment.

"No. And I haven't told him yet. I think he was hoping . . . well, never mind. We'll work it out. Want to take a look? We could go tomorrow."

"Of course."

Hayley gave her a quick hug and jumped up to get back to work. Lia watched her go, mixed feelings swirling. She was happy for her daughter, had actually looked forward to her moving on and giving Lia her space back. But she'd also grown used to the company. Now there would be another emptiness ahead to deal with. But, she thought, as she glanced around at the table filled with friends, she was getting rather good at it.

"Can I get you something more to drink?" Pete asked as he got up to refill his own empty cup.

Lia looked up at him. She almost declined before changing her mind and catching herself. "Yes," she said, smiling. "I think I'd like that."

ACKNOWLEDGMENTS

An author writes the story, but it takes a skilled team to mold it into a polished, readable book. I'm very grateful to my excellent editor, Sarah Blumenstock, and copy editor Eileen G. Chetti, as well as cover artist Mary Ann Lasher, who topped it off so beautifully. Then there are the many behind-the-scenes people at Berkley Prime Crime who make such a major difference in a book's success.

A huge thank-you as well to my amazing agent, James McGowan.

I'm ever grateful to my long-running critique group: Shaun Taylor Bevins, Becky Hutchison, Debbi Mack, Sherriel Mattingly, Bonnie Settle, Marcia Talley, and Cathy Wiley.

And last—but always first in my eyes—my husband, Terry, whose crafty suggestions helped me stitch together my often discombobulated thoughts into something sensible. *Go raibh maith agat* and *djiekuje*!

Don't miss the next Craft Fair Knitters Mystery

Knits, Knots, and Knives

Coming Fall 2022 from Berkley Prime Crime!

L et's hope for the best."
    Lia turned to her petite next-door neighbor, Sharon Kuhn, aware of the uneasiness that comment came from, and shot her a look of sympathy. As they began their stroll of the Schumacher grounds together, however, Lia couldn't help feeling excited. The long-awaited day of the annual Battle of Crandalsburg reenactment had arrived.

    As a relative newcomer to the town, Lia would be experiencing this event for the first time, and as a vendor with the Crandalsburg Craft Fair, she would be a participant of sorts, not just an onlooker, because of the barn that regularly housed the craft fair.

    The Schumacher barn, owned by the family for generations, was historical, having been used as a hospital during the actual Civil War battle. Each year that scenario was re-created inside, and vendors' booths, including Lia's Ninth

Street Knits, had been moved outdoors a short distance away.

In addition, all the vendors had added Civil War–era items to their usual fare. For Lia and her fellow Ninth Street Knitters, that had meant weeks of knitting woolen socks and scarves from patterns followed by women of that period. Most would be worn that day by many of the reenactors, while some would be available to buy at Lia's booth.

"I feel like I should be wearing a hoopskirt while I'm making these," Maureen had said at their last meeting, with the others agreeing. Lia, herself, had often felt transported back in time as she knitted at home, the cozy pre–Civil War house she'd moved to after her husband Tom's untimely death.

That feeling returned as she and Sharon entered the living history section of the grounds. A woman stirred porridge in a large pot that hung over an open fire. She looked up and smiled at them. No hoopskirt for her. She wore a long plain cotton dress with an apron, a kerchief holding back her hair.

A young man, dressed in suspendered Union-blue pants and a gray shirt, sat outside a tent playing a whistle-like instrument that reminded Lia of the recorder her daughter, Hayley, had learned to play in fourth grade. A second man whittled at a piece of wood nearby. Lia and Sharon paused to listen to the high-pitched notes, and Lia recognized "Tenting on the Old Camp Ground."

"I'm glad the weather is cool enough for those woolen shirts and jackets the men have to wear," she said.

"Yes, lucky for them that the battle occurred in October," Sharon said. "They'll have to do a lot of running in those heavy uniforms."

"And the women have to work in those long dresses over campfires. And in the sun."

"Makes you wonder how they all managed back then, doesn't it?" Sharon asked. "But it's been kept as historically accurate as possible; that is, until Sprouse took over."

Lia nodded. She knew about the shift in leadership of the reenactors that had caused disruption lately. Sharon's husband, Jack, had been involved with the group for years after discovering that an ancestor, Captain Josiah Kuhn, had played an important part in the battle. As group leader, Jack had been a stickler for absolute accuracy, down to the underwear worn by the soldiers and the food they ate during the two-day event. No burgers or Cokes would be seen in the campgrounds, or even wristwatches worn while in uniform.

Arden Sprouse, on the other hand, had dismissed such details as unimportant. With the significant financial contribution he brought to the reenactment himself and from donors he'd rounded up, his opinions ruled, much to Jack's dismay. Jack stayed in the group but had been demoted from captain to an unnamed sergeant, while Sprouse took the role of Captain Anderson, a person whose connection to the battle appeared iffy but whom Sprouse claimed as a newly discovered forebear.

Continuing their stroll, Lia and Sharon came upon Olivia Byrd, a young mother who sold her homemade soaps and essential oils each weekend next to Lia's craft fair booth. For living history, she had volunteered to demonstrate soapmaking as done in the mid-1800s. Dressed in period costume, the sleeves of her calico dress rolled up, Olivia definitely looked the part, especially standing next to a huge black pot hanging over the makings of a campfire.

Her normally anxious expression was glowing for a change. It brightened even more when she saw Lia.

Lia marveled at the difference in historic Olivia. The woman Lia saw each weekend was reserved—sweet but often fretful. Today's Olivia was energized and clearly enjoying herself to the hilt. For the first time, Lia fully understood why Olivia did what she did. Her friend absolutely loved making soap, and that included even the crudest form of it.

"Looks like you're ready to go," Lia said. The event would start admitting spectators within half an hour.

"I can't wait," Olivia said. "Soap wouldn't normally have been made near a battlefield. But I'll be able to demonstrate how it was done back then, from simple wood ashes that every house collected and animal fats. Lye from the ashes and fat, the two basic ingredients. Isn't it amazing? A formula that was stumbled upon who knows how long ago, and we still use it today—with certain refinements, of course."

"Of course." Lia thought of the lovely scents that floated over from Olivia's booth from her own soaps, as well as the various oils she used in place of animal fat.

"You'll be a good teacher," Sharon said, which brought a pleased flush to Olivia's cheeks.

Lia seconded the thought, then noticed a crowd gathering in a field off to the left. "What's going on there?"

"Oh! That must be the bayonet fencing demo," Sharon said. "Come, you have to see this."

They bid good-bye to Olivia and hustled over to the area as Sharon explained what Lia was about to watch. "Our soldiers can't have bayonets on their rifles during the reenactment. It's much too dangerous, even with dull ones. So every year, two volunteers demonstrate how they might have been used during a battle. But they do it very carefully."

Lia and Sharon made it to the roped-off area and joined the crowd gathered around the large circle. In the center were two uniformed reenactors, one in blue, the other in gray. Each held a long rifle with a menacing-looking bayonet at the end. A third man off to the left explained what they were about to do and how it would be done in slow motion for safety's sake.

Lia watched, fascinated, but at the same time disturbed to think that this was once done in real life, person to person, in deadly fashion. Seeing the glint of the steel edges, she also worried about a current accidental injury.

"They practice this for hours," Sharon said softly, perhaps sensing Lia's fears. "It's all carefully choreographed."

Lia nodded. The demonstration was impressive, and when it ended, the crowd showed its appreciation with enthusiastic claps. The two uniformed soldiers acknowledged them, then turned to each other and shook hands.

"That's Jack's rifle," Sharon said, indicating the one held by the gray-uniformed fellow.

Lia knew about Jack's collection of antique guns, some of which were quite valuable. "Good of him to lend it." She glanced around but didn't see him. "I hope it'll be carefully looked after."

"Oh, yes," Sharon assured her. "They'll do one more fencing demo, then hand both rifles over to Jack. The other one belongs to Lucas Webb."

She said it with a sniff, prompting Lia to ask who that was.

"Arden Sprouse's son-in-law. I don't think he's a collector like Jack. He probably bought it just to show off, pretty much like his father-in-law."

Lia thought it best not to stay on the subject and instead said, "I'll need to be at my booth in a few minutes. I'd love to take a peek at the hospital setup first."

Sharon said she'd also like to see it, and they headed toward the barn. As they passed by the living history area again, Lia noticed a woman sitting at a spinning wheel some distance away and asked about her.

"That's Rona Dickens," Sharon said. "She's spinning flax, not wool, in case you wondered. A friend of hers weaves it into linen, which is then made into clothes for some of the reenactors."

As they reached the barn and walked in, Lia barely recognized it. Craft booths had been replaced with lines of cots occupied by life-sized and bandaged mannequins. There was also a surgery of sorts, which consisted of a wooden table covered with several instruments used at the time.

Most were tools for amputations, the most common treatment of the time, doctors having little knowledge of how to treat bullet wounds. Lacking antibiotics, more patients died from infection and disease than on the battlefield. As a former surgical nurse, Lia shuddered at the thought of what the soldiers must have gone through.

"I'm glad we were born when we were," Sharon said, looking over the grim display.

"Amen to that," Lia said. "But thank goodness at least for Florence Nightingale."

"Why? She wasn't here, was she?"

"She was a British nurse who worked during the Crimean War, once they actually allowed her to, that is. It wasn't considered seemly at the time. The first thing she and her nurses did was scrub down the field hospitals, which apparently were filthy. She saw the survival difference in patients who were bathed from those who weren't and argued for better hygiene. This carried over to our Civil War practices and probably saved lots of lives. Soldiers were ordered to bathe regularly, something many weren't in the habit of doing, and it helped keep down the spread of disease, at least to some extent."

"Wow." Sharon shook her head. "You could be running this part of the living history, Lia."

Lia shook her head, smiling. "I've had my fill of surgery," she said. "I'm happy to stick to knitting. Which reminds me, I'd better get over to my booth."

"I'm going to look for Jack," Sharon said. "See how he's doing. I'll catch you later."

They split up, and Lia headed over to the vendors' booths—separated from the living history and battle reenactment area but close enough for spectators to wander over to. The booths were gathered under a large canopy, essential protection from possible rain, but remained open on all sides to the currently lovely fresh air. Jen Beasley, who hosted the weekly Ninth Street Knitters meetings at her home in York, had driven over with her husband, Bob, to help move the group's sweaters, afghans, and shawls to the new setting as well as deliver the mounds of soldiers' socks and scarves. Pretty much everything, therefore, was in order, and all Lia had to do was handle the sales, as she'd done each weekend for the group for the last several months.

Lia greeted her fellow vendors as she walked by but didn't stop to chat, as all were busily readying their booths. Having much less to do, thanks to Jen and Bob, Lia had time to relax and look around at her new surroundings once she made it to her own spot.

"We lucked out with the weather," a voice said, and Lia

turned to her left to see her friend and the craft fair manager, Belinda, approaching.

"Wow, didn't we?" Lia said. "The storms they predicted for last night didn't materialize, thank goodness."

"Would have been a soggy mess in these fields," Belinda said, her gaze taking in the mowed acres surrounding them.

"I know one person who might not have minded," Lia said. "My neighbor, Jack Kuhn. From what I understand, the actual battle was fought in mud. Jack is big on historical accuracy."

"That's fine for him and his soldiers," Belinda said. "Our craft vendors prefer dry, tidy land. I heard about the kerfuffle in the reenactment group. So that was your neighbor?"

Lia nodded. "It was a bit of a power struggle between him and the new guy, Arden Sprouse. Sprouse won out. I don't know anything about Sprouse, but Jack's a great guy and I understand he's put a lot of time and effort into the reenactments."

"He has," Maggie Wood said from her quilt booth, which had been set next to Lia's. "And it's a darned shame how Sprouse treated him. I fault the others, too, who should have stood up for Jack. But Sprouse's money apparently spoke louder than loyalty."

"So who is Arden Sprouse?" Lia asked. "Has he lived in Crandalsburg awhile? If so, why has he just now become so involved?"

"He and his family showed up after he bought the Hubbard Hotel a few months ago," Maggie said. "He has some other businesses, but what those are, exactly, I have no idea." Her lips curled derisively. "I don't mind newcomers joining in. But I don't much care for people who show up in our town and decide to start running things." Maggie's already florid complexion had reddened close to the shade of her long curly hair. The quilter was never one for soft-pedaling her opinions.

"Guys," Nicole warned from her booth to Lia's left. "That's Mrs. Sprouse heading over right now."

Heads turned toward the figure Nicole indicated with a head tilt, Lia's included. She watched as the stout fifty-something woman made her way gradually toward them, dressed in period costume that indicated participation in the day's event. She paused for a few moments at Gilbert Bowen's candle booth, where she chatted briefly, before moving on.

Lia's group turned their attention away from the woman as she approached, except for Lia, who continued to watch. When their eyes met, Mrs. Sprouse smiled an open, dimpled smile. Lia returned it.

"You must be Lia Geiger!" Arden Sprouse's wife said. "I've heard so many good things about your wonderful knits. I'm Heidi Sprouse."

"I'm glad to meet you," Lia said. "Have you met our craft fair manager?" Lia introduced Belinda, who had looked back, and the two took in Heidi's compliments on the fair's offerings.

"I haven't managed to visit before, but I intend to make up for that," she said. Heidi talked enthusiastically about the craft booth items she'd already seen. "Arden would love the metal sculptures, I know."

At Heidi's mention of her husband, Lia felt a twinge of guilt on Jack's behalf, though she wasn't chatting with his nemesis. She supposed Jack would forgive her for being amiable with Arden's wife, who couldn't be blamed for her husband's actions. At least so far.

"I see you're dressed in costume," Lia said. "Are you playing a role in the activities?"

"Oh!" Heidi said, flapping a hand dismissively. "A very minor one." She tucked a stray gray-brown lock back into her cotton bonnet. "I like to look after our young men—you know, just making sure everyone has what they need. My son-in-law is one of them, you know. I guess you could say I play a Civil War mother. Or maybe the mother those poor soldiers would have liked to have close by."

She shook her head. "Of course, someone like that wouldn't have been near the battlefield. More likely helping at the hospital. But I'll be backstage, so to speak. No one to be noticed."

Heidi pulled a cell phone out of her skirt pocket and checked it. "I'd best get back. I just wanted to take a quick peek at your craft fair. But I'll be here again, you can count on that! So nice to meet you!"

Heidi bustled off, swerving toward two more booths on her way out as though unable to resist another look.

Lia leaned toward Maggie, who'd kept back among her quilts but who must have heard most of the conversation.

"What do you think? She seemed nice."

"I suppose," Maggie conceded, though reluctantly. "At least she's not taking over center stage like her husband. But . . . oh, I don't know. I'll wait until I see more."

Lia thought she'd do the same, if only out of loyalty to Jack.

Ready to find
your next great read?

Let us help.

Visit prh.com/nextread